EVIL ON THE SOUTHERN BORDER

AN ELI COLT NOVEL
BOOK 2

WILL MARLER

JOIN MY LEGACY READERS CLUB

Will Marler's Legacy Readers Club members get free books and unique items to accompany the novels.

Members are always the first to hear about Will's new book launches and publications.

At the end of the book there is more information on how you can sign up and receive a free gift.

PART 1

ONE

West Texas Desert—Ten Minutes Before the Raid.

Desert air whipped through the FBI assault vehicle's open roof hatch, carrying sand and slivers of sagebrush. Despite the cool temperature, sweat trickled under Ex-Army Ranger Eli Colt's combat shirt and winter jacket. The starry night calm contrasted with the stress inside the vehicle as the ten-man hostage rescue team checked their gear and weapons.

"Clear path to target," tactical operations in Terlingua crackled through Eli's earpieces. "Drone's thermal imaging identifies multiple heat signatures inside."

Over the squared shoulders of the burly driver and beyond the dusty windshield, mountains loomed like sentries guarding the desert expanse. Eli shifted his weight on the bench seat between two wiry FBI operators with close-cropped hair and steely stares.

Team Leader Marcus Blackwell, a twenty-year veteran of the Bureau, pulled back the slide of his Glock 17 with an ebony hand. "Sniper team, what's your status?" His Georgia drawl blared through the tactical comm.

"Ready," came the response from support snipers Eli knew to be on the hills above the targeted compound.

A swirling haze of dust trailed outside the rear windows, announcing the FBI assault team's presence in the remote desert. Would the traffickers at the compound notice this telltale sign of their approach?

"Target. One mike," tactical operations reported. One minute until the assault.

"Get ready for impact." Blackwell's tone was calm and determined.

Eli's partner, Dakota Sutcliffe, the assertive 25-year-old former FBI agent-in-training, locked arms with Blackwell from the adjacent seat. Dakota's bronze skin, courtesy of countless hours waterskiing the South Louisiana bayous, glistened with perspiration under the desert moonlight. Sun-bleached locks peeked out from beneath his tactical helmet, a foil against his black armor that hugged his taut frame. He winked a glacier blue eye at Eli, betraying the same bravado that served them well since they'd been working together.

The assault vehicle turned. The windshield framed the cinderblock compound. Eli mirrored the arm-locking gesture with the operators to his right and left. The truck closed the distance without slowing, not stopping until it plowed through the compound's front wall.

Amid crushed cinderblock and what remained of a living room, two armed traffickers lay across an overturned couch.

Blackwell rose and tossed a flashbang grenade forward out of the open hatch. "Fire in the hole!" he yelled.

Bang. Whizz. A bright light flashed in whirls of smoke.

"Let's move," Blackwell commanded.

Trailing those to his right, Eli jumped from the rear

doors, the fifth man out. He tilted his M-4 muzzle slightly up, indexing his finger alongside the trigger guard.

The team rushed through the living room into a dimly lit hallway, quickstepping in single file. The lead and second operator entered the first room to the right.

"Clear!" one of them shouted.

The two trailing operators entered the next room, arcing their weapons in a slicing-the-pie motion to cover their field of vision. "Clear."

Eli reached a turn in the hallway and halted, spotting two tangos ahead. One wielded a shotgun.

Pulling a flashbang from his chest rig, Eli flipped the spoon and tossed the grenade down the hall. "Fire in the hole!" he screamed before turning away and covering his eyes.

Bang. Whiz. White light.

He turned the corner. "Hands up!" he shouted.

One man, his gold teeth glinting, dropped to his knees without hesitation. His wild-eyed companion, barely out of his teens, swung the shotgun muzzle toward Eli.

Eli fired. Tap tap. Tap tap. "Tango down."

Dakota bolted past, his carbine aimed at the man with raised hands. "On the ground, now!" Dakota shouted.

"No dispares. No dispares!" the survivor screamed on his way to the ground.

Pressing his knee to the man's spine, Dakota secured the man's hands and feet with flex ties.

Furious gunfire roared on the other side of the compound for several heart-pounding seconds.

At a closed door just past the tangos, Eli grabbed its knob and turned. Locked. "Need a breach!" he roared.

An operator with a Benelli shotgun positioned himself in front of the door, readying for the explosion. He pressed the breach barrel attachment against the knob and fired.

The door swung open with a crash.

Eli tossed in a stun grenade, bracing himself for the impending explosion of light and sound. As the chaos subsided, he leveled his rifle and charged into the room.

Inside, seven wide-eyed girls recoiled to the rear of seven oversized dog crates, the type typically found for large breeds in a pet store.

"Trinity Madison!" Eli tried to shout over the hostages' screams. "Trinity Madison!" It was the girl's name he'd been commissioned to rescue.

Blackwell's voice came through Eli's earpiece. "Four tangos down."

"Copy," Eli replied. "One tango down. One in custody."

Eli pulled open the Velcro patch on his sleeve to reveal a headshot photo of seventeen-year-old Trinity Madison. He compared the image to each girl as he opened their cages. The fifth one yielded success—Trinity Madison, her red hair matted and her freckled face pale and soiled.

Eli pulled down his goggles and wiped his brow.

Dakota stepped in beside him. "Mission accomplished." He scanned the half dozen other girls. "And then some."

"Team leader," Eli said into his voice-activated microphone. "We've secured our girl and six others."

"That's a good copy," Blackwell's voice came back. "TOC. Location secured. Send us the transport."

"Team leader," a voice unfamiliar to Eli interrupted over the comms, "we're at a storage facility about ten meters from the main building. Need bolt cutters to check inside."

Leaving Dakota with Trinity, Eli exited the back door of the building to get some air. A cold, brisk wind bit his face, shocking him into reflection on what he and Dakota had accomplished—again.

It had been four months since they'd established the Redemption Rescue Investigation Agency in Madisonville, Louisiana. It had been soon after rescuing Eli's niece from a cult in the Gulf of Mexico aboard the yacht *Leviathan*. The organization's stated purpose was to combat human trafficking and the sexual exploitation of children. This latest mission had been set into motion just three days prior when Eli, posing as a pimp, had struck a deal for Trinity based on information garnered from the dark web by his brother's widow and Redemption Rescue associate, Julia Colt. With the help of Dakota's FBI connections, they'd tracked down the compound in the West Texas desert.

A towering HRT operator, his night-vision goggles glowing faintly, waited by a padlocked double door in a nearby building. Another, similarly clad in a dark tactical uniform but with bolt cutters slung across his back, rushed to join him.

Eli did his breathing exercises to control his anxiety. He hadn't had a PTSD episode since he'd witnessed Zoe Prevost's autopsy in New Orleans. He thanked the Good Lord daily for his fiancée, Lindsey Crenshaw, a clinical psychologist who'd helped him and Dakota save Eli's niece, Tara, the previous year. "Well, Eli," he said to himself. "Looks like you earned your pay today."

The operator clamped the bolt-cutter blades onto the padlock's metal shank and squeezed the handles together.

A sharp metallic snap and the padlock hit the ground. The operator swung the door open, and a thunderous explosion erupted from within the building. Searing heat hit Eli and lifted him off the gravel.

Everything slowed into a blur of chaos and an endless ringing in his ears.

Then the darkness followed—darkness fierce, darkness absolute, darkness again.

———

DISTORTED CLOUDS outside the assault vehicle's roof hatch came into focus as Eli drifted back to consciousness. His head pounded as if a bass drum were struck out of rhythm inside his skull. The world around him was light and shadow—a disorienting haze of indistinct shapes and uncertain movements that teased the fringes of his awareness.

Dakota's blurry face leaned over Eli.

He winced at the stinging pain from a large lump just above his left temple. "What happened?"

"A building exploded, sending you into a wall pretty hard," Dakota said.

Eli's vision swam for a moment before stabilizing. His memory tried to return. The mission to rescue Trinity. The other girls they'd found.

Dakota helped Eli into a sitting position and handed him a bottle of water.

Taking a long gulp, the cool liquid soothed his dry throat as his mind raced to piece together the situation. "Trinity? The girls?" His voice was strained and thirsty for answers.

"They're fine," Dakota said, his words low and sympathetic. "Just a few scrapes and scratches from broken glass flying around."

Eli managed to sit straighter, a monumental effort, the

pain sharp and biting. "So much for getting some fresh air. I think I'm going to be sick."

Dakota offered Eli his dented helmet as a makeshift bucket, but he pushed it away. "Help me outside."

With Dakota's support, Eli forced himself up despite the throbbing in his head, swaying for a moment before steadying himself against his partner. Together, they made their way out of the vehicle and into the desert air. There, the smell of cordite and burned flesh assaulted Eli's nostrils.

As they stepped outside, Team Leader Marcus Blackwell approached them. "You must be hard to kill," he remarked.

Eli managed a weak smile. "How many casualties?"

Blackwell's expression darkened like black clouds invading a clear day. "Two. Franetti and Taylor. They shouldn't have tried to open that building. That's why we brought the BearCat." He lifted his chin at the armored vehicle.

"Any more kids in the compound?" Eli asked.

Blackwell glanced back at the main building. "Only the seven. We'll process them back in Terlingua. Most are too traumatized to talk. There's your girl from El Paso. The others, from what we can gather, are from its sister city in Chihuahua, Mexico—Juarez."

Another wave of nausea washed over Eli like a rising tide. He closed his eyes hoping to regain his composure.

"We'll be moving out soon," Blackwell said. "Get you back to TOC and then airlift you to Pecos and a hospital."

Eli's breaths came in shallow, measured bursts as he willed the nausea to recede. "Not Pecos. El Paso. That's where this mission ends."

Blackwell seemed to hesitate before continuing, passing a

piece of paper to Dakota. "Speaking of missions, I admire what you're doing. Rescuing these kids from these devils is a noble cause." He extended his hand to Eli. "I've hit my twenty with the FBI and I'm retiring. In fact, this is my last op. So, if you need an old operator in the future to help with missions like this, give me a call. Plus, I know a few guys who'd also be interested."

Eli grasped Blackwell's hand. "I may just do that. Thanks."

———

AFTER THE TRANSPORT bus and the assault vehicle arrived at the mobile command unit in Terlingua, Dakota arranged for lodging and tended to Eli until the helicopter arrived. Despite the exhaustion, despite the lure of sleep, despite the quietude that blanketed the area, Eli found himself bound to wakefulness.

He reached for the phone to call his fiancée Lindsey. He checked his watch wondering if she'd be in her office at Safe Harbor Home for Girls where she treated victims of sex trafficking.

"Hello?" She answered the phone on the first ring. "Eli, is that you?"

A jolt of pain laced through his skull. "Uh...Lindsey?" The world tilted sideways. Why was he in this room, on the phone? Who had called? He or Lindsey?

"Yes, darling, it's me." Lindsey's voice was high-pitched and breathless. "Are you okay?"

The mission. The explosion. His head slamming into that wall. He closed his eyes trying to block out the alarm bell screaming in his ears. "Banged up a little. That's all." Eli ran his sleeve across his nostrils to wipe his runny nose. "Nothing serious."

Lindsey let out a skeptical sigh. "And what about Dakota?"

"You know Dakota. Walked away without a scratch."

"And the girl? Trinity? Did you find her?"

"Yes. And six other girls who were in the compound. We got them all safe and sound."

"That's great, Eli." Worry was still thick in her tone. "Where are the other girls from?"

"Juarez. A border town in Mexico."

TWO

Monday, 4:55 PM, Juarez City

Twenty-three-year-old Karina Castillo stirred, the soft whisper of running water pulling her from a long, lazy nap. She stretched, her olive skin sliding against the silky sheets of her king-sized bed in the Hotel Celebracion suite. Her heavy eyelids blinked away the remnants of sleep. She reached out, expecting to feel Cesar's warmth, but her fingers found only a cool, empty space. "Cesar?" Her husky Juarez accent colored the name. Karina sat up, causing strands of her long, dark hair to drape her bare shoulders.

The mirror across the room caught her reflection—high cheekbones, a straight nose, and the curves that had first caught Cesar's eye. She looked every bit the beautiful Latina woman who turned men's heads in the streets of Juarez.

Clothed in a robe bearing the Hotel Celebracion's emblem, Cesar Lorenzo Garza, billionaire industrialist and hotel proprietor, emerged from the bathroom. "I need to get home. It's my son's birthday and my wife's planned a party."

Karina averted her gaze to hide her irritation. "Mustn't be late for that," she grumbled, her voice tight.

A vivid canvas of terra-cotta, turquoise, and red buildings adorned the cityscape outside the floor-to-ceiling windows. In the distance, the mud-brown Rio Grande River wound its way through the landscape, and the El Paso skyline rose beyond the US border.

Cesar disappeared into the walk-in closet, the size of a sidewalk boutique. "What time does your shift start?" he asked.

"Five." The word carried a sour edge.

"Why don't you take the evening off? The club can run without your managerial skills for one evening. You can go see your mother and your beautiful little sister."

A bitter taste rose from Karina's belly. She didn't like how Cesar referred to her sister Sofia. And why was he giving her the night off?

"You've been working too hard lately," he said. "Relax. Rest. Spend time with your family."

"I may do that." She hadn't seen her mother and sister or even her strange brother much since she'd become Cesar's mistress. "But I hate leaving Raul shorthanded."

"Don't worry about Raul. He hired a new girl to help out temporarily. Now you don't have to be in the club all the time."

Her assistant manager had hired a new girl without conferring with Karina? Didn't she have carte blanche authority to hire and fire in the nightclub? Or maybe this girl was more than temporary help.

Karina had replaced Cesar's last mistress who'd replaced another, and so on. She understood the arrangement but hadn't expected her tenure as Cesar's paramour to end so soon. She gazed again at the mirror. Had she grown older since she'd moved into this suite two years ago?

Karina spent most of her time working when Cesar was home or at one of his manufacturing plants spread throughout Chihuahua. She enjoyed managing the most glamorous club in Juarez atop its most prestigious hotel. Did Cesar appreciate her efforts, or was she just as her mother would say, a "*puta* in fine clothes?" Maybe she should spend more time with her family. She missed her sister and mother and even her brother Emilio. "*Gracias*. I think I will."

"*Excellente*." Cesar emerged from the closet dressed impeccably in a dark blue, tailor-cut Hugo Boss. He bent over to kiss her forehead. "*Hast mañana, mi amor*." And like that, he was gone.

Karina wrapped her body in linen sheets and a down-filled duvet, creating a sumptuous cocoon of softness. She grabbed the remote from the nightstand and clicked on CBS 4, a local El Paso television channel. On the bottom of the screen flashed a chyron—

LOCAL GIRL RESCUED FROM MEXICAN TRAFFICKERS.

A man in a gray suit, tall and meticulously groomed, stood at a podium that displayed the American FBI seal. The name, Special Agent Trey Donahue, appeared in the chyron below him. Men in combat gear, with stern expressions beneath their helmets, stood at attention behind him.

"Ladies and gentlemen," Donahue said. "Today, we're proud to share with you the unwavering dedication and courage of the FBI working hand and glove with private citizens." Donahue turned and glanced at the men behind him. "Early this morning, an FBI hostage rescue team led by Special Agent Marcus Blackwell rescued seven girls in Study Butte near Terlingua, Texas. Among these victims was seventeen-year-old Trinity Madison, an El Paso native who disappeared six weeks ago."

Karina sat up in her bed. Rumors whispered throughout Juarez of six girls who'd gone missing from the city—a frightening subject given Juarez's past. She thought of her little sister, Sofia, who complained to Karina that their mother never let her leave the house alone.

Donahue concluded his statement with, "I'll take a few questions now." Camera clicks clamored, flashes flickered, and a tumult of chaotic voices erupted. The spokesman gestured at someone out of sight behind the camera.

"Who are these private citizens?" a male voice chimed in with rapid fire. "And what condition were these children in when they were found?"

"The girls were understandably shaken," Donahue said. "They're currently undergoing evaluations from therapists within the department. But there are no physical injuries outside of a few scratches. As for the private citizens, Special Agent Blackwell procured valuable information from Redemption Rescue, a private detective firm from Louisiana, who also participated in the rescue."

A different reporter shouted, "Are they here for questions?"

"I'm afraid not."

"Where are the other girls from?" another reported howled. "Are they Americans?"

"We're not ready to reveal information related to these children at this time."

"Are any from Juarez?" The accent was Hispanic. Female.

"I'm not sure."

"Do you have the traffickers in custody?" The same Latina voice. "Are they *Los Diablos*?"

A sour expression washed over the spokesperson's face. "We have yet to identify the traffickers, but they are Mexican. We'll update the press as more information becomes available."

"Liars!" Karina shouted. "You're scared of Diablos. Even the FBI in El Paso fears the cartel."

THREE

Tuesday, 8:55 AM. Las Palmas Del Sol Hospital, El Paso, Texas

Eli sank into the cushioned chair nestled in the ER waiting room. On the mounted television in the corner of the earthy beige walls, a local newscaster recounted the mission in the West Texas desert.

Where was Dakota?

As if to answer Eli's question, Dakota rounded the corner down the hall, Styrofoam cups in hand. "Took me a while but I finally found coffee," he said, raising both containers.

Eli tapped his fingers on the chair's rest, struggling to ground himself in the present. Moments turned into milliseconds. "Okay," Eli said, hiding his confusion.

"The cafeteria." Concern flickered in Dakota's eyes. "You'd sent me for coffee, remember?"

Eli didn't remember. He had been forgetting a lot of simple things since the desert rescue the previous day.

"You okay?" Dakota said. "That blow to the head didn't turn your brain to Swiss cheese, did it?"

Eli rubbed the bandage over his temple. The explosion. Him flying head first into a solid wall. "That's what we're here to find out, right?" He tried to laugh off what that Dakota had suggested could be more fact than fiction.

A nurse in baby blue scrubs with pink and yellow flowers emerged from behind a closed door. "Mr. Colt, Dr. Galbraith will see you now."

Eli glanced at Dakota with a touch of apprehension. "I'll see you later if I can find my way back."

Dakota chuckled, but Eli didn't laugh. He trailed the nurse, each step like wading through quicksand, the hallway stretching out before him like a dark maze without an exit. They turned a corner and then entered a doorway. Inside stood the doctor wearing green scrubs, a white lab coat, and a serious expression. "Please, sit down." Dr. Galbraith waved at the examination table without looking up from a clipboard.

Eli complied, his stomach swimming with anticipation of bad news.

"Say's here, you've had quite a blow to the head." Galbraith set his clipboard on a counter and snapped on plastic gloves. "Let's take a look." He removed the bandage from above Eli's temple and ruffled his fingers through Eli's closely cropped hair. "Yes. That's quite a lump. Hematoma with a contusion. Any discomfort or pain when I press here?"

A sting seared though Eli's scalp. "Owe." Eli jerked his head to the side.

Galbraith returned to his clipboard. "Are you suffering any memory lapses?"

Eli shifted on the table. "Memory lapses?" His gaze drifted away from the probing Galbraith. "Nothing major. Just some hazy moments, you know."

"Hazy, huh?" Galbraith looked up from his clipboard. "Any gaps in your memory that concern you?" His tone was friendly, but his question pointed.

Eli managed a smile. "Not that I can remember."

Galbraith square jaw wrinkled as he smiled. "Funny." His gray eyes shifted back to the clipboard on the counter. "Let's test your strength, shall we?"

He asked Eli to perform a series of simple muscle tests, including squeezing a handgrip and pushing his foot against Galbraith's thigh. Eli's leg wobbled as if it were encased in molasses.

Galbraith tapped Eli's knees and elbows. A faint furrow appeared on the doctor's brow confirming to Eli his reflexes were sluggish.

Galbraith made notes on his clipboard. "Let's stand, shall we, and balance on one foot."

Eli complied.

"Now, touch your nose," Galbraith said.

Eli stumbled.

The exam continued with hearing tests. To Eli's surprise, his hearing seemed unaffected, which was a small comfort amid the mounting concerns about his condition.

Then came a variety of pinpricks and temperature gages and Galbraith's thoughtful expressions.

Finally, the doctor shot a series of questions that Eli guessed gauged memory and cognitive ability. His answers revealed nagging memory lapses and moments of confusion.

Galbraith stepped back from his examination and regarded Eli. "Mr. Colt, there seem to be some cognitive issues and basic motor skill concerns. An MRI will help us determine the full extent of the damage and plan your course of treatment."

Eli's worry deepened. Galbraith's evaluation had

brought his head wound into sharp focus. "I understand. I'll get that done as soon I'm back home in Louisiana."

The physician offered a reassuring smile. "That's a good plan. In the meantime, try not to overexert yourself or engage in any strenuous activities."

ELI SANK into the chair beside Dakota, the doctor's assessment weighing him down. "Doc gave me a clean bill of health," he lied, forcing a reassuring tone. "All I need is a bit of downtime and I'll be back in top form."

Lines etched across Dakota's forehead "You're sure? What about you forgetting things?"

Eli waved him off. "Says it's a temporary thing. I've had worse, trust me."

Dakota's eyes remained on Eli as if searching for any hint of deception. "If you say so."

"Relax, Dakota. I'm fine. When do the Madisons get here?"

Dakota glanced at his watch. "About now."

Eli forced himself up and took a few shaky paces, before righting himself down the polished hallway. With each step, Eli found solace in the fact that he'd kept his health concerns from Dakota, at least for now. Because now was the time to enjoy the fruits of their mission—to witness the joy of Trinity Madison reunited with her parents. But beneath his veneer of optimism, uncertainty lingered. When would he be fit for another mission?

OUTSIDE THE HOSPITAL, beneath a bright Texas sun and boundless blue skies, Eli stood off to the side of the cluster of humanity, as Trinity Madison embraced her mother and father. A semicircle of reporters and cameramen formed around the family, their lenses trained on the emotional reunion. City officials hovered nearby, their faces plastered with wide grins, eager to be caught in the frame of the heartwarming scene.

Eli's chest swelled with a mix of pride and humility as he witnessed the moment he'd worked tirelessly for months to make possible. Even the throbbing in his head, the gaps in his memory, and the uncertainty about his health seemed worth it. He hung back, allowing the family their moment in the spotlight.

Trinity's father, his voice choked with emotion, stepped forward to address the television cameras. He praised Eli, Dakota, and the FBI for their heroism in saving his only child and bringing her captors to justice. As he spoke, Eli noticed a few of the cameramen glancing his way, no doubt identifying those mentioned in the father's speech.

When Trinity's father finished, the reporters and cameras swiveled en masse, their attention zeroing in on Eli and Dakota. Eli felt exposed as the lenses focused on him, the attention falling like a leaden jacket. His chest tightened. He stood rooted to the spot, just a few yards from the hospital entrance, suddenly feeling every inch the reluctant hero thrust into the limelight.

But thirty yards beyond the reporters, beyond the city officials, beyond the Madisons and their joy, stood six Mexican girls separated from the celebration of Trinity's reunion with her parents, in the shadow of a long bus emblazoned with Immigration and Customs Enforcement. Their sunken shoulders and tear-streaked faces forged a contrasting backdrop to the radiant smiles of the celebrating throng.

Questions ate at Eli's mood like relentless mosquitoes in a Louisiana marsh. Why weren't these girls rejoicing like Trinity and her family? Weren't they going home too? A tall lean man wearing a worn coat and worn features stood near the open door to the bus. Marcus Blackwell was next to him and waved for Eli to join them.

Maneuvering through and around city officials and reporters, Eli ambled to Blackwell with Dakota trailing behind him.

Eli pointed to the parade of six girls. "What's with these kids?"

Blackwell shifted his gaze to the first girl stepping on the bus. "They're going to Immigrations to be processed, then home to Juarez."

"When?" Colt asked.

"Tomorrow afternoon," Blackwells said.

"They don't look too happy about it," Dakota chimed.

"No, they don't," Blackwell replied with a hint of concern.

"And why's that?" Eli asked.

Blackwell gestured to the man in the shabby jacket who'd helped the last girl board the bus. "Emilio, I'd like you to meet someone."

Emilio turned. His sun-weathered skin told of countless hours outdoors. Deep-set eyes, dark and soulful, met Eli's gaze beneath lines etched deep into his forehead. There was a quiet strength in this man's demeanor. The threadbare jacket, the well-worn shoes, and the puzzling presence alongside six traumatized girls spoke of some sense of duty.

"Emilio is a preacher from Juarez," Blackwell patted the

man's shoulder. "He can explain why those girls are more sad than happy."

"I didn't see anything happy about them," Dakota said.

"You're right, my friend," Emilio explained. "The danger these girls have encountered is likely not over. Not like it is for the American girl."

"Why?" Eli asked.

"The gang responsible for their abduction holds power in Juarez," Emilio said. "To them, these girls are a threat, living evidence of their crimes."

The words pierced Eli with an icy sting. "What will happen to them?"

Emilio's eyes hardened, betraying a steadfast resolve beneath his calm exterior. "If these girls return without protection, their lives will be in grave danger. Recapture or worse could await them."

The message this preacher preached circled the space like smoke in a burning building. Eli turned to Blackwell. "There must be something you can do. You can't just abandon them like this."

Blackwell's posture wilted. "I wish I could offer a solution, but these girls aren't American citizens. And for another few weeks, I'm still FBI."

Dakota leaned in, his gung-ho nature clashing with Eli's pragmatism. "You can't just walk away from this, Marcus."

"Like I said, my hands are tied. It's a shame, but at this point, there's nothing I can do."

Eli turned to Emilio. "What will you do?"

Emilio breathed in a huge intake of air. "I'll go back with these girls to Juarez tomorrow afternoon. But as far as protecting the girls from Los Diablos, I'm afraid that's close to impossible."

"Los Diablos?" Dakota asked.

"Yes. A ruthless cartel of sicarios and traffickers. They have eyes everywhere. Even in El Paso."

"So, you'll just leave them to this cartel? This Los Diablos?" Eli's disbelief mingled with frustration.

"I'm only one man. Most men in Juarez are scared. But I'll do my best to comfort their *familias*," Emilio breathed in again. "And then I'll do the only thing I can."

"Yeah," said Dakota with a frustrated scowl. "What's that?"

"Pray," Emilio said.

The simple response had Eli recounting a visit to a doctor's office in Mississippi. Doc Leena, a pediatrician from Solace where Eli had worked as a detective, once told Eli that God raised her husband from the dead after she'd fervently prayed. The story was hard to believe, but the woman wasn't.

"Is that all?" Dakota asked.

"I'm afraid so," Blackwell replied.

"Maybe we can help?" Dakota suggested. "How many of these girls will return?"

"All of them," Blackwell said.

Eli glanced at the bus, scanning the of eyes each girl. "Is there any way we can keep these girls in the United States?"

Blackwell shook his head. "I'm afraid not."

FOUR

Maria Perez hurried to restock the candy beneath the bodega's front counter. The M&M wrappers crinkled between the fifteen-year-old's light-brown fingers as time slipped away. She glanced up at the clock behind the register, its relentless tick-tick-ticking, a reminder of her little brother waiting for help with his homework and the danger that loomed after dark on the murderous streets of Juarez—the city of lost girls.

Finished with her last chore, she lifted her petite frame and untied her ponytail, letting her dark hair flow to her faded blue T-shirt. She stepped toward the back office to gather her schoolbooks and inform Señor Campagna she'd be going home.

Clang-clang. The bell over the front door jangled.

"Hola, chica." The gravelly voice of Hector Ramirez froze her with her back to the door. "Where's Señor Campagna."

An icy chill coursed through Maria. Hector was a Los

Diablos captain and little brother of Carlos Ramirez the cartel's leader.

Hector reached a tattoo-decorated arm around her and grabbed a handful of candy bars. "Don't be like that, *niña bonita*." Hector leaned in close, pressing his angular jaw against her shoulder. His alcohol-laced breath warmed her ear. "Maybe you come party with me tonight, eh? Have some real fun."

Maria's stomach lurched. "*No, gracias*," she exhaled.

The bell sounded again. Footfalls followed.

Maria glanced over her shoulder. Two more from the cartel with ink-covered necks entered the store. They wore baggy white shirts and blue bandanas draped across their foreheads. Their hands hung heavy below the pistoles tucked in their jeans.

Los Diablos collected from every business in the neighborhood. It was rumored they also trafficked drugs, weapons, and girls. These crimes had made Carlos Ramirez the most infamous man in Juarez.

Señor Campagna shuffled in from the stock room scratching his wispy white hair. "Maria? Is everything okay?"

Hector grabbed the butt of his pistol tucked in his chinos and strolled to Maria's employer. "*Mi bueno amigo*, where's my money?"

Señor Campagna lowered his eyes to the floor. "I'm sorry, I don't have it all right now. Business has been—"

Hector cracked his pistol against Señor Campagna's forehead.

The old man collapsed.

Ramirez's goons laughed.

"I don't want your pathetic excuses, old man," Hector snarled. He rifled through the cash register, stuffing bills into his pockets. "You owe me. You owe Los Diablos. And we always collect."

With a disdainful kick, Hector toppled Señor Campagna's lifeless form onto the bloodstained floor. He turned to Maria, his twisted grin reflecting a sadistic pleasure in her terror. With a flick of his wrist, he signaled to his crew, who followed him out of the store like a pack of hungry wolves.

Maria struggled to grab a paper towel from the coffee counter, then rushed to press it against the bleeding cut over Mr. Campagna's right eye.

"I'm so sorry," he mumbled, ashamed. "You shouldn't have to deal with this."

Maria helped Mr. Campagna to his feet and supported him as they made their way to the stock room. He winced with each step, one hand pressed to his forehead to staunch the bleeding.

Once in the dingy room, Maria eased the old man down at his desk. She hurried to grab the first aid kit, her mind racing about her walk home.

Mr. Campagna hung his head. "I never wanted you mixed up in all this."

"I-It's not your fault." Maria hurriedly pressed a gauze to the wound. "Someone needs to stand up to those lawless bullies."

Mr. Campagna sighed heavily. "If only it were that easy. Los Diablos is all over Juarez, especially here in Aldama. Nowhere is safe from them anymore." He glanced at Maria, then out to the emptied cash register. "I planned on giving you a few hundred pesos to help your family. I know it's been rough since your father was laid off."

It had been rough. That's why Maria was here working

after dark. It's the only job she could find as a fifteen-year-old. Without the money she earned, her family might starve.

Maria clutched the crucifix on the chain around her neck and kissed it, then helped her old boss stand. "We'll get through this. God always prevails over evil in the end."

"Go home, Maria." Mr. Campagna flashed a brief smile. "It's getting late."

Maria bid Mr. Campagna goodnight and stepped outside. The sun dipped below the horizon. This twilight draped the street in an eerie gloom. The stories she'd heard of young girls vanishing haunted every nook and cranny, making the oncoming darkness more surreal.

She kept her head down and hurried alongside the busy thoroughfare where most of the streetlights still flickered weakly through layers of grime. The air was thick with an acrid scent of exhaust fumes mixed with the smells of sizzling meats from the roadside taco stands. Neon signs buzzed and blinked sporadically, revealing the broken pavement and graffiti-laden walls with a ghostly glow. Shopkeepers shuttered their metal grates, the clatter adding to the cacophony of car horns and distant yells.

The sounds of shuffling footsteps keeping pace with her own emerged behind Maria. An icy dread settled in her gut. She quickened her stride and her stomach twisted. She didn't dare look back, focusing instead on the uneven ground and the dim pools of light under each sporadic streetlamp. The footfalls kept pace, each echo amplifying her terror. Maria's pulse pounded in her ears, drowning out the chaotic symphony of the waking night around her.

A group of women unloaded baskets from a vegetable cart just ahead. Maria started to run to them. But a rough hand clutched her shoulder and pulled her into an alley.

There, she stood face-to-face with the leering eyes of Hector Ramirez.

"What's your hurry, *niña?*" He tightened his grip on Maria's upper arm.

Adrenaline rushed through her. She stomped down hard on his instep.

Hector howled.

She wrenched her arms free and sprinted. Her heart raced in a wild rhythm. But as she neared the women at the vegetable cart, a black sedan screamed to a halt beside her, tires screeching against the asphalt. The two cartel goons with Hector at the bodega jumped out of the vehicle and dragged her to the open trunk.

Maria thrashed and kicked and screamed for help. *"Me deja ir!"* she hollered.

The women at the baskets yelled.

A thunderous crack ripped through the night; the scent of gunpowder followed.

The women retreated.

Calloused hands forced Maria into the trunk and closed her into darkness.

Maria kicked at the trunk lid.

The engine roared.

The car jerked forward.

What had just happened? One second she was walking home to her family. The next, she bounced in the trunk of a speeding car.

She struggled to steady her breathing, desperately searching for a way out. Her hands traced the cramped space, feeling for a latch, a crowbar—anything.

Nothing.

What of her family? Her mother would worry. Her father would look for her at the convenience store. But what if the cartel had targeted her? Would that put her family in danger?

The car swerved. Maria slammed against the trunk wall. What if she kicked out a taillight? Would that get somebody's attention? Bracing herself against the bumps and turns, Maria pulled her knees to her chest and kicked at the faint light with everything.

She kicked again and again, but the light held firm. Exhausted, she collapsed against the smelly trunk carpet.

Time stretched into infinity. Maria swallowed what little moisture remained on her tongue. How long would she be trapped in this tight trunk? How far would they take her?

The car turned onto a rough road. The transition was jarring, and Maria winced with every rut and bump beneath her as the vehicle bounced along.

She searched for hope in her *Hail Marys* and *Our Fathers* and *Glory Be's* and kissed the crucifix that hung from her neck after each prayer. But despite her determined invocations, she couldn't banish the chilling thought that her life would soon come to a brutal end.

The car slowed, then squealed to a halt. Muffled voices blared outside.

Maria held her breath, straining to understand the muted conversation.

Laughter followed.

Dim light flooded the trunk as it slowly opened.

Bendita Madre de Dios. Would Maria ever see her family again?

FIVE

Wednesday, 4:59 AM—El Paso, Texas

Just before sunrise, the persistent doorbell shattered US Attorney Juan Morales' peaceful sleep. Flickering blue lights danced like restless spirits on his bedroom ceiling and walls, prompting his wife Lolita to bury her head beneath her pillow. He grabbed his robe from the bedside chair to check on his children. Eight-year-old Camila, her auburn curls fanned out on her pillow, and five-year-old Miguel, clutching his favorite stuffed dinosaur, slept peacefully in their bedrooms, their gentle breathing undisturbed by the commotion outside.

A loud knock on the door spurned Morales to rush down the curved wooden staircase.

Another knock.

"Hold on, I'm coming," Morales said as his bare feet hit the foyer's cold marble tiles. He tied his robe closed and peeked through the sidelight. Detective Consuelo Lopez, a frequent witness for cases he'd prosecuted, stood waiting on his front porch. Her face was taut with a stern expression, framed by dark hair pulled back into a practical bun. The tailored lines of her charcoal suit betrayed a subtle strain against her slightly overweight frame.

He twisted the bolt lock and opened the door. "Good morning, Detective. What's going on?"

"I'm afraid it's not good, Counselor." She wrinkled her forehead with lines of concern. "It's your neighbor across the street. Daniel Ortega was abducted from his home about an hour ago."

Morales stepped outside and glanced at Ortega's home. Assistant District Attorney Daniel Ortega, an El Paso prosecutor who'd moved into the neighborhood with his wife last spring, had gained recent notoriety for indicting two street thugs for the murder of a local hardware store owner who'd refused to pay their extortion demands. Now, his yard was bathed in a glow of blue and white lights from two police cars parked haphazardly along the curb. The front door of the house hung ajar, a clear sign of forced entry. Uniformed officers bustled in and out, their flashlights cutting through the pre-dawn darkness.

Curious neighbors stood on their porches or peeked between slits in the blinds from inside their homes.

A knot of worry formed in Morales' chest. He offered a silent prayer for the Ortega family and his family. "And his wife, Linda?"

"Visiting her mother in Waco."

Morales rubbed his forehead. "Who called you?"

"Ah..." Lopez referred to her notepad. "Rich Isaac from next door."

Morales looked at Isaac's house. Every window was lit up. "I was sound asleep, Detective. I didn't hear or see a thing."

"I understand, sir." Lopez's voice carried a slight tremor. "But can we talk?"

"Sure. Come inside, I'll put some coffee on."

The morning event brought a darkness to Morales as he loaded the coffee maker with water and grinds. He struggled to absorb that Daniel, in this safe, suburban neighborhood, had been forcefully abducted from his home.

Once the coffee finished brewing, Morales poured Lopez and himself a cup.

"I can't help but fear that this is connected to the Los Diablos case." Lopez's eyes reflected the worry in her voice.

Morales' muscles froze. "Los Diablos? You mean the kids who killed the hardware owner in the barrio near the border?"

"It won't be the first time those thugs have abducted someone in El Paso, only to transport them across the border." Lopez's eyes flitted to the window and the scene across the street. "And it's no secret that they have a network working both sides of the border—Juarez and El Paso."

Morales couldn't escape the unsettled feeling that justice, the cornerstone of his profession, was under siege. If Daniel Ortega's abduction was indeed connected to the Juarez cartel, it revealed a closely concealed danger in El Paso, considered one of the safest cities in the United States.

He exchanged glances with Lopez. A shadow of worry clouded her gaze, hinting at the test Morales was about to face. He'd been assigned to prosecute the lone trafficker who'd survived the FBI raid in Study Butte that had been plastered all over the news. Could this be why Ortega was taken—to send Morales a message?

Could he rise to the challenge as a man of God.

MORALES AMBLED upstairs to be close to his wife and two children, once Lopez returned to the crime scene across the street. He entered his study, where his Bible sat open on his bureau. He knelt beside it.

The words he whispered were pleas for courage, for boldness, for the unwavering strength to fulfill his duty as a federal prosecutor.

"Lord," he began, his voice soft yet resolute, "grant me the courage to stand for justice, to be Your beacon of righteousness in these trying times. Guide my decisions so that they may serve the cause of truth and fairness."

A powerful spirit overwhelmed him. "Father, protect my wife and children—the treasures you gave me. Protect them for they're yours. Let them wake each morning covered by your grace, unburdened by the fear that's common to this area."

The minutes passed as he poured out his concerns. Only the distant conversations of the police outside penetrated the quiet.

Morales rose from his knees and cast a lingering gaze at his Bible.

"Honey," his wife called from their bedroom. "What's going on across the street? Is everything okay?"

"Everything's fine, sweetheart. Pack some bags for you and the children. You're going to stay with your parents in Dallas."

She should like that. It'd been months since she'd seen them.

"Okay. But aren't you coming?"

"No, dear," Morales said with conviction. "I'm staying. There's work I must do in El Paso. Important work." God's work.

Before waking his children, Morales quietly entered

Camila and Miguel's rooms. As he watched their peaceful slumber, a wave of worry overwhelmed him. What if they were taken, like Trinity Madison? The idea hit him like a gallon of frigid water, shocking his system into high alert.

Was his life insurance enough if something were to happen? Would Lolita and the kids be taken care of in the event of his demise? He made a mental note to review his policies as soon as possible.

He gently brushed Camila's curls from her forehead, then adjusted Miguel's dinosaur, tucking it closer to his chest. As he closed their doors, Morales steeled himself for the challenges that lay ahead. He had to protect his family, serve justice, and keep his faith strong.

SIX

Karina stepped out of her red Audi, straightened her camel-colored Chanel blazer, and grabbed the shopping bag from the back seat of the car.

Why am I here? To check on my family? To ease my guilt? Or because I'm scared of what Cesar might do when he tires of me? The questions nagged at her as she surveyed the run-down neighborhood. Ramshackle buildings and worn streets painted a picture of hardship, a place filled with memories—more bitter than sweet.

Her Jimmy Choo heels sank into the dusty, dirt driveway outside her childhood home. As she approached the front door, apprehension quickened her heartbeat. How would her mother act?

The door creaked open, revealing the worn face of her brother Emilio, a reformed drug addict and now a street preacher. He wore a clean white T-shirt, faded jeans, and a threadbare coat that hung loosely over his wiry frame.

"Karina. What a wonderful surprise! When was the last time?"

"Emilio." Her heart swelled with anger and surprise. "What are you doing here?" Her brother who'd found God was now, by all appearances, a distinct opposite to the "*puta*" Karina had become.

"Same as you, I suppose," Emilio said. "I've come to visit Mamá and Sofia."

She pushed past Emilio into the small house, into the remnants of their shared history. Her nose twitched at the familiar scent of corn tortillas and slow-cooked pork.

She halted abruptly. Her gaze locked on the photograph hanging with honor on the living room wall. Papa's kind eyes stared back at her from behind the sparkling glass, his police uniform crisp and proud. Beside it, a freshly polished plaque caught the dim light: "Officer Jorge Castillo—For Valor and Sacrifice."

"Remember when Papa used to lift us both onto his shoulders?" Emilio said in a soft tone.

Karina's trembling fingers traced the frame's edge. "If Los Diablos hadn't—" Her voice caught. She whirled to face her brother, cheeks flushing. "And now you're out there playing holy man? After abandoning Papa's wife and daughters here?" The accusation hung heavy between them, mingling with the echoes of gunshots and her mother's screams from that night when she was twelve—the night her world had shattered.

"Emilio? Who's there?" Her mother's tired voice carried through the small house.

Karina turned on her stilettos. "It's me, Mamá." Her heels thumped against worn linoleum as she entered the kitchen.

Her mother stood at the stove, wiping her hands on a

dishtowel. Her once-lustrous black hair was now gray-streaked and pulled back in a tight knot. Deep lines etched her face like a roadmap of hardship. "Karina," she said as she turned back to her cooking. "This is...unexpected."

In the corner, Sofia perched on a rickety chair, her lanky teenage frame coiled with restless energy. Her fingers tapped an impatient rhythm on her knee, nails bitten to the quick. Karina's chest tightened as she recognized the look in her sister's eyes—a hungry desperation to escape, to be anywhere but here. How many times had Karina worn that same expression, daydreaming of a life beyond these walls? Karina's insides teetered. The streets of Juarez were a ravenous beast, devouring young girls' lives with equal fervor. Karina had clawed her way out, but at what cost? And how long before Sofia would try to do the same?

"I brought presents." Karina opened the shopping bag and pulled out a mocha-colored Italian lambskin coat. "For you." She handed it to Sofia.

Sofia's eyes lit up. She clutched the coat against her chest. "*Gracias. Muchas gracias*, Karina."

"And for Mamá..." Karina produced the latest iPhone, with a recipe app already downloaded. "To call your friends and..." She cleared her throat, hiding her embarrassment. "To call Emilio if you need help."

Her mother offered a forced smile. "Gracias," she said in monotone.

Karina cleared her throat. "Mamá, I... I brought money. To help you and Sofia get by." She pulled out an envelope filled with $500 American and held it out.

Her mother's lips pressed into a thin line. "We don't need your money, Karina. Not when we know where it comes from."

The words stung, but Karina persisted. "Please, Mamá. It's just to help—"

"I said no." Her mother turned back to the stove.

———

LATER THAT NIGHT, Karina sat with Emilio at the kitchen table listening to the news on her mother's radio. "What do you make of those children rescued in Texas."

"I was with them today," Emilio said. "And I'll be going back tomorrow to escort them back to Juarez."

Karina chuckled with bitterness. "Your work is children now?"

"My work is all of God's children and that includes you," Emilio said with affection.

"Isn't that dangerous?" Karina asked, her voice tinged with worry for her brother. "For the girls, I mean."

Emilio hesitated. "Certainly. But the United States is dealing with an immigration problem. These girls are caught up in American politics."

Karina's heart ached. She thought of her childhood, of Sofia, of the risks teenage girls and young women faced in Juarez every day. "How do you go back and forth across the border?"

"I attained a B-visa for my ministry. It allows me to cross the border as I please."

———

AS THE NIGHT WORE ON, tensions rose. Tension between her and her mother. Tension between her and her brother. Tension stemming from the life she had chosen two years ago. Mamá's terse comments each time she'd enter the room, stung, leaving Karina feeling cold and ashamed.

"You have no right to judge me," her voice trembled. "I made my choices, just like Emilio when he left. Maybe my decision was wrong, but I was only trying to survive. It's not safe for a young woman on the streets of Aldama. And with Papa gone, I needed protection."

Her mother's expression remained impassive, showing no sign of softening. "And what about Sofia?"

Yes, what about Sofia? She was at the age when men started to notice. Would she make the same choices as Karina?

It was time to retreat to her suite at the hotel. She'd had enough abuse from her mother for one night. Enough guilt. But the pull of her childhood home resisted. This was her family—the people she loved more than anyone in the world. But the lure of living in luxury had its hold. Could she return to this home when Cesar tired of her?

Emilio and Sofia walked Karina to her car.

A pack of teenage boys with streetwise bravado swaggered down the street, their raucous laughter echoing off crumbling walls. "*Ay, mamacita,*" one called out. Another whistled sharply. Their eyes gleamed with dangerous intent as they nudged each other, voices rising in a cacophony of crude jokes and catcalls.

Karina ignored the foolish display, kissed her sister, and hugged her brother. "I feel I'm leaving more depressed than when I arrived." She pulled the envelope with $500 from her purse and gave it to Emilio. "Please make sure Mamá has food and essentials."

Emilio accepted the money. "May the Lord bless you for this. I'll make sure she has everything she and Sofia need." He passed Karina a slip of paper. "Here's a number to call, if something happens to me. A friend who can help you if I'm gone."

The exuberant chatter from the teenage boys grew louder and closer.

"Help me with what?" Karina said, shifting her eyes to the boys coming from down the street, noticing they were more serious than she'd initially thought.

Sofia clutched Karina's hand. "Los Diablos."

A half-dozen street thugs came into view. "*Hola, Señoritas. Hola, Sofia.*"

"Don't worry." Emilio stepped between his sisters and the teenage boys. "*Son chavos.* Too young to act on their own." He stepped into the street and motioned to the young teenagers. "Go on now. There's nothing for you here."

One of the boys pointed; his expression somewhere between amazement and fear. "*Santo de las Calles.*" His mouth opened into a large O. "*Vamos a salir de aquí.*" The boys ran like they'd seen a strange spirit.

"Saint of the Streets?" Karina snickered. "Is that what they call you?"

"You know Juarez. Everyone gets a crazy nickname eventually." Emilio hugged Karina tighter than before. "Now go on, *mi hermana*. Go with God. And call that number if you need help."

Karina's mind swirled in a dizzying haze as she slid behind the wheel. "Help with what?"

SEVEN

Thursday 6:05 AM—Holiday Inn, El Paso, Texas.

Eli's eyes fluttered open in the dim light of his hotel room. His breaths came in short, jagged intervals. Images from the previous day replayed behind his eyelids—six Juarez girls, young and vulnerable, boarding a bus with fear etched on their faces. The memory stirred the haunting image of Zoe Prevost's body on the New Orleans coroner's autopsy table.

How can I abandon these girls going back to Juarez?

It was the first waking thought that thrummed in Eli's mind. The Mexican street preacher in the worn jacket said protecting these girls in Juarez was next to impossible. And all he could offer them was prayer. But Eli wasn't one to rely solely on faith, despite Lindsey's late-night Bible studies. *I'm a warrior. A fighter. A man who gets things done.* Like the night aboard the *Leviathan*, when he'd saved his niece Tara from certain death.

"Did anyone ever tell you, you scream in your sleep?" Dakota grumbled from the neighboring bed.

Eli swung his legs to the floor and dressed quickly. He

stepped to the window, drew back the curtains, and gazed out at El Paso and the border bridge to Juarez. "Leaving those girls on their own doesn't sit right with me."

Dakota ambled to the coffee station. "Is that your conscience speaking or your scrambled brain?"

Eli chuckled as he turned to face Dakota. "Look, there's something I should tell you."

Dakota filled the coffee pot with water. "I'm all ears."

"Yesterday, I wasn't completely honest." Eli lowered his gaze. "The doc said I need an MRI to determine if I'm suffering from traumatic brain injury."

Dakota stared at the plastic contraption as if that would brew the coffee quicker. "I figured. An MRI is written all over that lump on your head."

Eli hesitated, then blurted what was on his mind. "How do you feel about heading south of the border with those girls?"

"Isn't that the reason we created Redemption Rescue?" Dakota tapped the coffee maker with his index finger. "To save kids?"

Eli fixed on Dakota with a serious look. "Even with the odds so stacked against us?"

Dakota shrugged unconcerned. "We've faced worse odds. Remember Tara? Commodore?"

"From what we saw in Study Butte, this enemy is a bit more significant," Eli pointed out.

Dakota grabbed his phone and waved it. "According to my research on the Internet, the numbers of victims outweigh the risk. Hundreds, if not thousands have been trafficked or killed in Juarez since the nineties. It's a no-brainer." Dakota paused, then added with a smirk, "No pun intended."

Eli couldn't help but grin. "If we do this, we'll need help."

"Blackwell mentioned he's interested in this type of work," Dakota said. "Let's see if he's genuine."

———

AN HOUR LATER, Eli and Dakota sat with Marcus Blackwell and Emilio Castillo in the hotel lobby, discussing plans over breakfast.

"How long to assemble a team?" Dakota asked.

Blackwell's brow lifted. "A week to ten days. Then we'll need to put a plan together and make a few dry runs."

"How many men do you think we'll need?" Eli asked.

Blackwell's gaze turned intense. "A couple of dozen. Maybe more."

Emilio Castillo folded his arms. "You can't protect those girls in Juarez without taking down Los Diablos. And you can't destroy Diablos with a handful of men. They have ten times that number just in Almada. Add in all of Juarez, they have more than 300 soldiers."

"That's young sicarios and gang bangers," Blackwell said with confidence. "We bring a capable team with equipment and we'll let 'em know we're in town."

"And then what?" Emilio argued. "Once you come back to the States, how will you protect the girls then?" Emilio set his jaw firm. "I'm afraid you don't understandDiablos, my friend. They're a product of poverty and corruption. Violent. Persistent. To stop them you must destroy them. Nothing short of that will save those girls. Are you ready to do that?"

Dakota answered with a thumbs up. "Hell, yeah."

Eli took a sip of his coffee. "What do we need to do to destroy this Los Diablos?"

"To kill the snake, you must cut off its head. To destroy Los Diablos, you must kill Carlos Ramirez—*La Serpiente*."

Eli leaned back in his chair. "When do the girls go back to Juarez?"

A worried crease formed on Emilio's forehead. "This afternoon."

"Can we delay?" Eli asked.

Emilio shook his head. "I tried. Border patrol understands our situation and wants to help. But they're overrun with illegals crossing the border. No place to put these girls."

"What about hiding them somewhere until Marcus comes with the cavalry?" Dakota suggested.

Emilio rubbed an early morning shadow. "Maybe. The people of Almada fear Diablos. But if they have hope, I can convince them to help."

Eli shared a glance with Dakota. "Well partner, what do you think? Should we go home? Or should we stay and help these girls?"

"Blackwell will need intel to create a feasible attack plan once he assembles a team," Dakota said. "We may as well go over with the girls, then find this *La Serpiente*."

Eli glanced at Blackwell. "Thoughts?"

"Can't hurt," Blackwell agreed. "I'll need the intel. Emilio?"

"Excuse me, Marcus," Dakota said with a hint of frustration. "Why are we depending on information given to you by..." he paused and glanced at Emilio, "no disrespect, a preacher? Does he have military or law enforcement experience? Is he privy to information you don't have?"

Emilio smiled a warm smile. "I understand your confusion, my friend. And no, I have no military or police experience." His tone turned serious. "But what I do have is information about Diablos and its grip on Juarez. I work in the streets of Almada, one of the most dangerous places on the globe. I grew up there. I live there. And there's something else..."

"Yes," Colt pressed.

"*El Serpiente* killed my father."

A hush fell over the table. Eli's shock matched Dakota's expression.

Emilio continued, "When Diablos learns the girls are with Americans, they'll strike quick, possibly killing you and the girls before you can get them to their families."

"How will Diablos know?" Dakota asked.

"Believe me, my friend," Emilio's soft tone returned. "Corrupt border agents on La Serpiente's payroll will tell him before you cross that bridge."

"I can arrange a drone to monitor Emilio's trip into Juarez," Blackwell said, shifting his attention to Eli and Dakota. "You two can watch them cross before you leave to get a lay of the land, so to speak."

"Okay, then," Eli said. "We'll go across once you've arrived in Almada. We'll gather intel on Diablos and their defenses for Blackwell and his team."

"Specifically," Blackwell interrupted. "I'll need you to assess the strength of any cartel strongholds. Their numbers and disposition, and any pertinent information that will aid us once we come across."

"Any suggestions on where we can stay in Juarez.?" Dakota asked Emilio.

Emilio smiled. "Yes. My sister works at the finest Hotel in Chihuahua."

ELI PACED OUTSIDE his El Paso hotel, its clean lines and bright white façade clashing with the storm brewing inside his mind. The brisk midmorning breeze rustled the American and Texan flags flying high above the hotel's atrium. The automatic doors whooshed open and closed behind him as guests shuffled in and out, their luggage wheels clicking over the walkway.

He strolled between landscaped flower beds with bright-yellow marigolds and purple Texas Sage. He resisted sitting in the teal cushions of the patio chairs as he pulled his phone, which felt heavier than normal, to call Lindsey to break the news he wouldn't be coming home today.

"You're staying?" Lindsey's voice quivered with apprehension.

"Yes. Uh...for a week. Maybe two." Eli's words stumbled out. "The Mexican girls we rescued in the desert—they're being sent back to Juarez. A preacher from that city tells us it's akin to a death sentence."

"But what about your head injury?" Lindsey's worry was clear.

"I don't have time to deal with that now," Eli snapped, his frustration spilling over. "The girls will be crossing the border this afternoon."

Silence stretched between them. Eli cursed himself for his outburst. It was Lindsey who'd talked him through his moments of trauma during his search for his niece Tara. And she continued as his most reliable confidant, even when she disagreed with his decisions.

A soft intake of air conveyed Lindsey's patience. "Look, I understand your dedication to these girls. But I worry about your head wound. I'm a clinical psychologist, not a neurologist, yet I've treated girls who've suffered this injury."

He paused before responding. Should he be totally honest? "I'm forgetting things. Small things. Things that happened moments before."

"Definitely a symptom. Does Dakota know?"

"He's not oblivious. He was there when I hit my head, and he took me to the hospital."

"TBI can be incredibly complex. Memory loss might be only a part of the issue." Lindsey's tone sounded unmistakable concern. "You may face difficulty concentrating, mood swings, and possibly long-term cognitive problems. Going to Juarez with those girls is a big risk."

Eli said nothing as he contemplated the seriousness of her words. Finally, he admitted with a helplessness that surprised him. "I've been feeling some of those symptoms. It's been frustrating, and I'm scared it might affect the mission."

"Okay, darling. I understand." Lindsey's empathy flowed through the line. "But promise me you'll prioritize your health. Don't push yourself too hard. You can't help those girls if you're not well yourself."

"I promise." A shadow of sorrow darkened Eli's tone. "I just wish..."

"What do you wish?" Lindsey prompted gently.

"That there was a place on this earth where the evil that targets children would be crushed into oblivion."

"Maybe there is," Lindsey offered softly.

Eli rubbed against the pain behind his forehead. "And where could that be?"

"Go to Juarez and find out."

EIGHT

Thursday, 9:05 AM—Federal Building, El Paso, Texas

Juan Morales sat at his desk reviewing the file for Marco Domingo, the lone trafficker who'd survived the FBI raid that rescued Trinity Madison and six Mexican girls in Study Butte. Sunlight filtered through the drawn curtains casting a soft light in his office. The familiar scent of polished wood and aged leather floated throughout the room.

As a federal prosecutor within a half mile of Juarez, Morales was no stranger to handling cases that migrated from Mexico. But today's case held a particular weight, one that rested heavily in the El Paso community. His eyes, aided by tortoiseshell glasses perched on his nose, were fixed on the details of the charges he'd filed against Domingo, a member of the notorious Los Diablos cartel. The cartel had wreaked havoc on the El Paso-Juarez border for decades.

Morales flipped through the file, and his eyes lingered on a photo of Trinity Madison taken near a dog cage, her eyes wide with fear, bruises marring her thin arms. His shaky hands set it aside, revealing the victim's testimony punctuated with phrases like "I thought I was going to die" and "They said they'd kill my family."

On to the FBI report to skim his highlighted points, including "forced abduction" and "sexual exploitation."

Morales slammed the file shut, causing a sharp crack to ricochet off the walls. He glanced at his worn Bible at the edge of his desk. He closed his eyes and whispered, "Lord, give me the strength to fight this darkness."

A polite knock echoed from the mahogany door.

Morales slid the file to the side. "Come in."

The silver-haired Eduardo Sanchez, the federal judge assigned to the Domingo case, entered. His shoulders, though slightly stooped with age, still carried a dignified resolve. His piercing dark eyes scanned Morales' office as if he were deliberating an unseen case.

"Good morning, Eduardo," Morales said pointing at a chair across from his desk.

Sanchez sat directly opposite of Morales. "We've got a problem."

"Problem, Your Honor?"

Sanchez's chair creaked as he leaned closer. "This Domingo case may put us both in the crosshairs."

Morales settled back into his leather chair, forming his hands into a steeple. "What do you mean?"

Sanchez pointed at the file. "Look at the defendant's last name."

Morales glanced at the file label. "Domingo?" Morales scratched his head. "What about him?"

"He's Carlos Ramirez's cousin, on his mother's side."

"But Domingo is a common name in these parts," Morales steepled his fingers. "My wife's brother-in-law is a Domingo. A fine man."

"But your brother-in-law is not a member of Los Diablos. Marco is," Sanchez countered. "While we don't have concrete proof they're family, the coincidence is too significant to ignore." Sanchez's shifted his gaze to the window. "Plus, there's something else."

"What?" Morales asked.

"This morning, I received a threatening letter that made it clear that if Marco Domingo stands trial and is found guilty, there'd be severe consequences." Sanchez paused and made eye contact. "I'm not just concerned for my safety mind you, but for yours as well."

"May I see the letter?"

"I turned it over to the marshals, but I'll give you the highlights. In so many words it threatened me, my wife, and my kids."

"Thank you for bringing this to my attention, Judge," Morales said, grateful he'd sent his family to Dallas. He rubbed his chin as he considered the safety of the judge and his family. "Is there a place you can send your family until this business with Domingo is settled?"

"Yes. My wife is at home packing. She and the kids are going to stay with her brother in Roanoke, Virginia. The marshals will escort them there and post a guard outside the home."

"I've sent my wife and kids to stay at her parents."

Sanchez tapped his chin with his forefinger. "Good. I'll order round-the-clock protection at your in-laws' just to be safe. We can't let these *criminales* influence us with their threats."

A wave of calm washed over Morales as Sanchez's words echoed the very essence of justice he'd prayed for that morning. *This is why I became a prosecutor—to stand against evil.* His chest swelled with renewed purpose, knowing he wasn't alone in this fight for what was right.

Sanchez stood and offered his hand, his facial expression somewhere between determination and dread. "You're a man of faith, right Juan?"

"I am."

"Well put it to use and pray we both make it out of this case alive."

———

JUAN MORALES SLID into his corner booth at Café Central, the worn burgundy leather creaking beneath him. Midday sun streamed through arched windows, shining across polished oak floors and brass railings dividing the dining areas. The lunch crowd's chatter melded with the clink of silverware, creating a lively backdrop. A sprawling mural dominated the far wall, its vivid explosions of colors depicting El Paso's pivotal role in the Mexican Revolution—sepia-toned revolutionaries juxtaposed with vibrant modern cityscapes.

Morales's gaze drifted from the artwork to his plate, where he absently prodded a glistening grilled portobello with his fork, its earthy aroma mingling with the scent of freshly baked bread. Despite the sensory distractions, he couldn't stop thinking of his children, Miguel and Camila, and the world they'd grow up in.

A man in his mid-fifties, with a lean frame and hair somewhere between blonde and gray, approached Morales's table with a folded newspaper tucked under his left arm. He wore a charcoal gray suit, a crimson silk tie against a crisp blue shirt, and an air of calculated confidence. From his polished wingtips to his silver tie clasp and cufflinks, every detail of his appearance screamed *lawyer*—the seedy kind.

He reached Morales's table with a broad smile. "Mr. Morales? May I have a word?"

Morales rendered a tight-lipped nod to the empty seat across from him.

The man unbuttoned his jacket, adjusted his cufflinks, and accepted the silent offer.

"What can I do for you, Mister...?" Morales regarded him with a mixture of curiosity and suspicion.

"Somerset." He presented a business card from his jacket pocket. "Preston Somerset. I represent Marco Domingo."

The card had gilded edges, a glossy black finish, overlaid with gold Arial font.

THE LAW OFFICES of Preston T. Somerset
       2252 First Avenue
       San Diego, CA 92101

SOMERSET TOOK a cautious glance around the restaurant before continuing. "I'm aware of your situation in my client's case, and in the interest of justice, I'd like to help."

Morales's neck muscles tightened. "What situation are you referring to, counselor?"

"Gossip has been circulating in the courthouse, and it says the federal judge in this case has been threatened."

How could Somerset be privy to this information if he wasn't part of the crime? "Are you trying to intimidate me, Mr. Somerset?" Morales said as calmly as he could.

Somerset leaned back in his chair with a shrug. "Not at all. I'm merely trying to make you aware of the reality you're dealing with. There's more at stake here than just a court case."

Morales set his eyes on Somerset, allowing the angry fire in his belly to burn. "And what would you *have* me do?"

Somerset's expression turned serious. "I don't know. With me, family comes first. You're in a difficult position, and I sympathize. I'd just like to emphasize something you already know. There's a fine line between justice and protecting your loved ones."

Morales was confident he was grappling with a power that extended far beyond the federal courthouse. According to Somerset, in his carefully constructed threat, the lives of himself and his family hung in the balance.

Somerset stood to leave. "Oh, here's a story that may be of interest." Somerset tossed the newspaper he'd been carrying to the center of the table. "It's hot off *El Diario's* presses. Front page news."

El Diario de Juarez was Juarez's largest newspaper. It's headline read—

"El Paso DA found dead in Juarez."

NINE

Karina rode up the hotel's express elevator alone. After taking the previous night off from work, she wanted to arrive at the club early, well before it opened.

She wore a simple white blouse, ruffled and flirty, with a green skirt and matching jacket that suited her long slender frame. The light floral scent of her perfume pleased her as the elevator climbed.

Her phone buzzed. She tapped her long white nails across the screen to open a text from her brother, Emilio.

"Can you arrange a room for two Americans at your hotel?"

Two Americans? Why would Emilio be helping two gringos? Must have to do with the girls rescued in the Texas desert.

The elevator droned a dull whirling before coming to a complete stop. It opened to reveal the lavish interior of the premier nightclub—walls covered in gold and red velvet, polished cherry wood floors with accented rugs. Afternoon sunlight poured in through a skylight, turning the entire room into a regal purple hue.

The smells of stale alcohol and cigar smoke from the previous night lingered, signaling the air cleaner was either turned off or broken.

Karina scanned the club for Raul to complain. He sat at a corner table wearing one of his many Hawaiian shirts, which today was a loud blend of red and yellow. He spoke through his neatly trimmed handlebar mustache, curled up at the ends.

Cesar lounged next to him sipping expresso from a demitasse.

Behind Cesar stood a stunning young woman no older than twenty. Her long black hair sprawled across bare mocha-colored shoulders. She laughed through ruby-red lips at something Raul had said.

The new girl—Isabella.

Isabella's gaze found Karina. Her laughing ceased and she retreated to the bar.

Cesar's eyes gaped at the girl's curves as they swayed beneath a tight black dress.

Time to meet Isabella.

"I'm Karina Castillo." Karina introduced herself with authority.

The girl struggled to manage a smile. "Sí, Señorita, I'm Isabella. I started last night."

"Where did you work before?"

"At Cesar's...uh...I mean, Mr. Garza's auto-parts plant outside Juarez."

Karina glanced back at Cesar who'd taken a mild interest in the two women's conversation. "So, Mr. Garza hired you?"

With no emotion, Cesar turned back to Raul.

"No, Señorita. He suggested I talk to Raul."

The story sounded familiar. Much like how Karina had started. Except she'd met Cesar while working at a coffee shop near the hotel.

"Did Raul show you how to turn on the air cleaner?"

"No, Señorita. I just welcomed guests as they entered the club."

Eye candy. Like Karina had been before Cesar had invited her up to the suite where she now lived. She knew what would soon follow. She'd be told to vacate the hotel like the girl before her two years ago. Karina would lose everything—the suite, the Audi, the monthly allowance. That should make Mamá happy.

Isabella glanced over Karina's shoulder. Fear flooded the girl's eyes.

Karina turned to see Carlos Ramirez—La Serpiente—the ruthless leader of Los Diablos, standing by the elevator. He wore a crimson suit with a snow-white silk tee-shirt that glowed against his olive skin. A serpent-like head was inked on his neck, its majestic plume spread across his throat. Flanked at Ramirez's side were two young sicarios, their eyes hidden behind aviator sunglasses. Almost every visible inch of their skin below their jawbone bore a tattoo.

She'd known Carlos Ramirez from the streets of Almada. The man who had her father killed.

Isabella's breathing became labored.

"It's okay," Karina said. "They won't hurt you. Go to the kitchen and wait for me."

Ramirez glanced briefly at Karina. His eyes showed recognition. Then he ambled with streetwise swagger across the room to Cesar and Raul.

The two men stood to shake Ramirez's hand. La Serpiente sat, leaving his entourage standing. The conversation that followed was friendly, though terse. It seemed Ramirez had some sort of business proposition for Cesar, who nodded in agreement from time to time.

Finally, Ramirez stood with a smug, pleased-with-himself grin. He glanced at Karina, nodded, and then strutted out of the club.

Perhaps leaving Cesar before he cut ties would be wise. She stepped to Cesar's table. "*Buenos tardes.*"

"Uh, mi amor." Cesar stood and kissed both of Karina's cheeks. "How is your Mamá and hermanita?"

"Fine, thank you." She waved a hand under her nose. "You know it stinks in here?"

Cesar laughed. "See what happens when you take a night off. The place falls apart."

"That's my fault, *Patron.*" Raul bowed his head in submission. "I didn't show the new girl how to turn on the air purifier."

"I'll show her now," Karina said. "And if I may ask for another night to visit my family? My mother is not feeling well."

Cesar glanced at Raul.

Raul shrugged, feigning indifference.

"Yes. Go on. Take care of your family. It'll be slow tonight and Isabella seems to be learning the job quickly."

Did Cesar come back last night after his son's party and help Isabella with some intimate training?

"I may spend the night and be back in the morning."

"Fine, fine," Raul said, way too agreeable.

Karina went to the kitchen, showed Isabelle how to operate the air cleaner, and then pulled out her phone to text Emilio.

"What time will the Americans arrive?"

TEN

Friday, 9:00 AM—United States Courthouse, Western District of Texas, El Paso

On the morning of Marco Domingo's arraignment, Juan Morales took his place behind the podium near Judge Sanchez's bench. The courtroom was a mixture of the formal and informal—lawyers in sharply tailored suits mingled with court spectators clad in casual attire. Journalists scribbled furiously on their notepads, their pens scratching against paper like tiny blades. All were gathered for the first appearance of Marco Domingo, trafficker of young girls. The air was electric—a living, breathing space full of intense anticipation. The familiar tight knot in Morales's stomach that visited him when he'd prosecuted his first case returned.

Marco Domingo shuffled into the courtroom wearing an orange jumpsuit against his tanned skin. Shackles clanged against the wooden floor with his every step. Despite the restraints, he held his head high as his dark defiant eyes examined the room. His smile displayed gold teeth and a casual arrogance that seemed out of place for a man in his position. He nodded to his lawyer, the slim, sharp-suited man with a predatory smile whom Morales recognized from the Central Café—Preston Somerset.

As Judge Sanchez emerged from his chambers and took his seat behind the bench, a hush fell over the courtroom.

"United States versus Marco Domingo." The bailiff's booming voice cut through the whispers. "The honorable Judge Eduardo Sanchez presides."

The chatter fell silent as the bailiff read the charges. "Mr. Domingo is charged with seven counts of violating 18 US Code 1581, human and child trafficking, and seven counts of violating 18 U.S. Code 120, kidnapping in the first degree."

"Mr. Domingo." Judge Sanchez studied the brief containing the charges Morales e-filed the day before. "Do you understand the nature of what you stand accused of?"

With unwavering eyes, Marco Domingo offered an imperceptible nod.

Judge Sanchez looked up from the brief with a professional stare. "Please say, 'Yes, Judge' or 'Yes, Your Honor' for the court reporter."

"Si, Juez." Domingo's accent was thick Mexican.

"Very well," Sanchez continued, "Let the record show that the defendant acknowledges the charges. How do you plea, Mr. Domingo?"

"Not guilty, Juez." His answer could barely be heard.

"The defendant enters a plea of not guilty." Sanchez squared his shoulders and shuffled his papers. "Now, let's proceed with the matter of bail." He glanced at Morales. A silent signal.

Morales cleared his throat. "Your Honor, the government believes that Mr. Domingo poses a significant flight risk and a danger to the community, especially considering the nature of the charges. We're near the Mexican border, and the authorities in Juarez inform us he has a violent past. Plus, he's a foreign national with no substantial ties to this country."

"Any word from the defense?" Sanchez said, shifting his attention to Somerset.

"Preston Somerset for the defense, your honor." A broad smile spread across the defense attorney's face, showing the same poise he'd displayed at Café Central. "My client vehemently denies these charges. But he's willing to surrender his passport, wear electronic monitoring, and post a reasonable bail."

Sanchez considered Somerset with a thoughtful gaze. "So where exactly does your client plan to stay in El Paso? Does he have a place of residence here?"

"No, your honor. But he does have family and friends in El Paso who'll gladly provide accommodation."

Sanchez glared at Domingo. "Mr. Domingo, do you have any connections to this community that would guarantee your presence in court?"

Domingo shrugged indifference. "S*i*."

"Explain, if you will, sir," Sanchez said, his glare intensifying.

"No," Domingo replied flatly, his expression devoid of emotion.

Sanchez shook his head and turned to Morales. "Mr. Morales, does the government have any evidence to suggest that the defendant poses a danger to the community or is likely to flee?"

"Your Honor, the charges involve heinous crimes against vulnerable children who live on both sides of the border. He is also a known affiliate of the Los Diablos cartel and is the cousin of its leader, Carlos Domingo. We believe

Mr. Domingo's release would jeopardize the safety of potential victims and his presence at the trial, and he should be remanded with no bail."

Sanchez knitted his brow feigning contemplation as if he'd played this game before. No way would he allow this man bail to escape across the border and flee justice. Right? The judge peered at Somerset over the rim of his glasses. "Considering the gravity of the charges and the potential risk to the community, this court is inclined to split the baby concerning bail. Five million dollars, cash or bond. Attorneys for the government and defense will meet in my chambers tomorrow morning to discuss a trial date."

The boom of Sanchez's gavel echoed through the courtroom. Federal marshals ushered Domingo away through a side door. Sanchez appeared confident in his decision.

Somerset peered at Morales with a disturbing smile.

The first phase of the United States versus Marco Domingo had concluded but Morales was all too aware of the vast resources of Los Diablos. He knew from media accounts and private conversations the money they took in from their illegal enterprises was substantial. Five million was a steep bail for a non-murder charge. But would it be enough?

ELEVEN

Friday, 4:05 PM—FBI Observation Facility, Near Mexican Border

Eli and Dakota had arrived at the FBI compound to meet with Blackwell and monitor Emilio escorting the six Mexican girls home. The scent of freshly brewed coffee mingled with the hum of electronics as Special Agent Blackwell led them to a large monitor at the back of the room. A man wearing an FBI hoodie sat at a smaller monitor maneuvering a joystick as if he were playing a video game. Then the large monitor flickered to life—a live grainy feed that captured an aerial view of the Bridge of the Americas. Eli's gaze fixed on a white van with the black lettering ICE, that slowly progressed across the border bridge.

"That's our target," Blackwell said to the man in the hoodie. "Zoom in a little, Scotty."

The van grew larger. The sudden movement caused Eli's vision to blur.

"We've got the van wired for sound," Blackwell said.

And a GPS tracking chip was sewn into the clothing we gave each girl before they left."

"Do they know?" Eli asked.

Blackwell shook his head. "No."

"What about the preacher?" Dakota asked.

"Nothing on him, I'm afraid."

Eli nodded that he understood as he absorbed the information. A tic twitched the corner of his eye. He squinted at the snowy screen. His temples pulsed with a dull ache as the ICE van entered Juarez and maneuvered through its winding streets.

Frustration coiled in Eli's chest as he strained to follow the blurred shapes on the screen. The van stopped outside an unremarkable building. His held his breath as he fought to make out the figures emerging from the vehicle. He leaned in closer.

Uniformed men appeared on the fuzzy feed to escort Emilio and the six girls to a waiting police transport vehicle. Eli exhaled.

He found a chair and sat to rub the blur from his eyes. The mission was progressing as planned.

"Phase one complete," Blackwell said. "Now on to phase two."

"Where's the safe house?" Dakota asked.

"An abandoned hotel Emilio arranged outside of Juarez," Blackwell said.

Eli's shifted his focus back to the screen. Two police pickups, each with machine guns mounted on its rear—one in front, one in back—escorted the transportation vehicle that carried Emilio and the six girls through the serpentine streets of Juarez. Eli's breath caught in his throat as the convoy navigated the crowded thoroughfares, their movements against the backdrop of the heavily populated city.

Something caught Eli's attention. A flicker of a scene he'd seen too often in Afghanistan. He stood abruptly and moved to the monitor. "Excuse me," he said to the agent who Blackwell called Scotty. "Could you have the drone focus on that area?"

The drone veered back sharply, and the video feed jerked. Eli's stomach lurched. At Blackwell's command, the camera zoomed, revealing three bodies—two men, one woman—dangling from an overpass, ropes tight around their necks.

"A common scene across the border," Blackwell murmured, his voice tinged with horror. "Los Diablos' handiwork. Let's get back on the convoy."

The camera shifted again and then whipped around, racing to catch up to the convoy. Suddenly, men with blue bandanas and raised guns—RPG and Kalashnikov AK-47s —appeared on a rooftop.

Eli inhaled sharply, his voice tense. "Tangos up top, They're—"

Gunfire cut him off. The trail vehicle's gunner pivoted, aiming at the enemy.

"What the—" Blackwell started, his words lost in the chaos.

Dakota faced him, his urgency clear. "We have to act!"

But it was too late. Gunfire peppered the trailing vehicle. Its windshield exploded. The gunner toppled over, hit multiple times, his body slamming to the pavement.

Eli clenched his fist.

Sutcliffe and Blackwell scrambled around him.

Blackwell bit his lip, eyes darting between the screen and his technician's monitor. "Stay with us, Scotty. Let's see how this unfolds. Is GPS active?"

"Affirmative," Scotty said, his voice shaky.

The gunner from the point vehicle jumped to the street wielding a pistol up and down.

The transport driver jumped from behind his wheel, hands high in surrender. The gunner fired point blank into the driver's chest without warning, dropping him to the ground. With no hesitation, the gunner slid behind the wheel of the transport vehicle. The lead truck lurched forward. The commandeered transport with Emilio and the girls followed, leaving the driver's lifeless body behind.

Eli's hands shook. Sweat flooded his forehead. His pounding temples brought on a migraine.

"I've got 'em," Scotty said with excited bravado. "I can follow them wherever they—"

The overhead screen went snowy, then black.

Blackwell's shoulders slumped. His brow fell into a deep frown.

Dakota widened his eyes as his cheeks grew pale. "What just happened? Why'd we lose visual?"

The lines around Scotty's eyes deepened. "They've taken out the drone." His voice deep in defeat.

"How?" Dakota demanded.

"Sniper rifle or ground-to-air missile," Blackwell said somberly.

"A cartel can do that?" Dakota asked with amazement.

"A well-funded cartel," Blackwell said.

Eli's stomach churned as he stared at the blank screen. "How could this happen?" he whispered.

"What?" Dakota's tone matched Eli's confusion.

"How could a two-pronged ambush happen in broad daylight?" Eli said louder as the scene replayed in his head. "They'd blocked the transport vehicle and neutralized the trail vehicle. And killed that poor driver as he tried to surrender."

"Bring up the GPS map." Blackwell's voice cut like a sharp blade.

Scotty's fingers danced on the keyboard. The once-active live feed was replaced by a digital map—a web of thin strips crisscrossing the screen like a complex spiderweb. Streets and highways formed an intricate network, with major arteries highlighted in bolder lines against a pale background.

Eli kept his eyes glued to the monitor. His grip tightened on the chair's armrest. Six blue dots represented six lives. The six Mexican girls.

"I need those coordinates, Scotty," Blackwell demanded.

Scotty tapped on his keyboard again.

Coordinates denoting longitude and latitude followed the six dots on the screen. They progressed outside the city's boundaries and into a remote area.

"They're moving east into the desert," Scotty said with excitement.

Eli grappled with a newfound dilemma. Had the ambush and capture changed their mission? Would they go to Juarez to find Carlos Ramirez and gather intel to destroy his cartel?

Maybe they could save these girls. Maybe they couldn't. But Diablos must pay for what they'd done.

"Let's gear up, Dakota." Eli's voice rang with resolve. "Time to get ourselves across the border."

TWELVE

Friday, 5:30 PM—Bridge of the Americas (US / Mexican Border)

Eli sat rigid in the passenger seat of the rented Explorer. Outside, the setting sun immersed the Rio Grande in a calm, shimmering glow. The whine of tires on asphalt as they approached the border did nothing to drown out the storm of doubts raging in his mind or penetrate the dread that coiled in his gut like a venomous snake, ready to strike at any moment. He tried to focus on the mission, on gathering intel on Carlos Ramirez and Diablos, but his mind couldn't shake what the drone feed displayed earlier on the large monitor at the FBI compound.

Dakota whistled *Hall of the Mountain King* behind the wheel as he eased the Explorer next to the border station. Colt passed his passport to Dakota, who handed their documents to a stocky border official clad in a crisp green uniform with gold patches. The Mexican's round face twitched, deep-set eyes scrutinizing their papers beneath a damp sweaty brow.

The man's leer lingered on their documents, betraying a

hint of suspicion. Then his attention drifted to the rear of the vehicle. With deliberate steps, he approached the back fender. Cupping his hands around his eyes, he leaned in, his stance tense and guarded, as he scanned inside.

Eli's neck muscles tensed. Beneath their luggage in the spare tire well, he'd concealed the weapons and tactical equipment. He braced himself for his and Dakota's potential arrest.

Just as their mission seemed to unravel before it began, the officer lifted his gaze, directed a smile at Dakota, and nodded. "Welcome to Mexico. Enjoy your stay," he said kindly and waved them through.

Dakota eased the vehicle forward and let out a long breath. "I thought we were done for."

Eli managed a weak smile. "Rough sailing leads to a sweet landing is what my Ranger CO would say."

"You think it's just my nerves or was that guy suspicious?"

"Let's get to the hotel," Eli said, ignoring the question. "We need to check in and talk with Emilio's sister."

As they cleared the border checkpoint, Sutcliffe guided the Explorer off the Bridge of the Americas and onto the streets of Juarez. Dust swirled in their wake, coating the oppressive landscape in a hazy film. At every corner, Colt's mind replayed the drone footage—Emilio and the girls being taken, their escort officers gunned down in cold blood.

Downtown emerged in a blur of activity. The hustle and bustle filled busy streets and cobblestone alleys. Pedestrians darted across the streets, vendors hawked their wares from makeshift stalls, and cars honked impatiently as Dakota navigated the chaotic thoroughfares.

Eli's palms grew clammy as he rehearsed the conversation ahead with Emilio's sister. Dakota parked in the Hotel

Celebracion's courtyard. They stepped from the Explorer past the hotel doorman and a bellman rushed to take the rucksack Eli had retrieved from the Explorer's spare tire well. "I'll need to keep this with me, gracias," Eli said in a low tone, then handed the man five American dollars.

"Any sign of Emilio's sister?" Dakota said as they entered the lobby.

"How would I know who she is?"

They approached the front desk, where a clerk greeted them in Spanish.

"Sorry?" Eli said to the young woman, indicating he didn't speak the language.

"Excuse me, sir." She bowed apologetically. "May I check you in?"

Eli pulled out his wallet. "Yes, please." He handed the woman his passport and an American Express card. The name tag on her crisp uniform read "Lucia." She was petite with striking green eyes and a heart-shaped face framed by dark hair she wore in a short pixie cut.

Lucia read the passport and ran her fingers across a keyboard. "There's a message for you, Señor Colt. Ms. Castillo asked she be called when you arrive." Lucia picked up the receiver and punched three digits on the phone. "*Disculpe, Señorita Castillo. Tu fiesta ha llegado.*"

The clerk listened intently for a few seconds. "*Sí, Señorita.*" She hung up the phone. "She asked you to wait for her in the lobby. She won't be but a minute."

Eli nodded and shared a glance with Dakota.

Moments later, a striking woman appeared, presumably Karina Castillo. She wore a pastel blue suit with a subtle sheen that draped elegantly over her slender frame. A white silk blouse peeked out from beneath the suit jacket. Her black stiletto heels clicked softly on the marble floor with each confident step.

Her face was a study in refined beauty—high cheek-bones accentuated by brown almond-shaped eyes. Her skin was an olive tone, smooth and unblemished. Full lips, painted a muted red, curved into a polite smile. Her thick, dark hair swept over her shoulders. Gold earrings comple-mented a modest gold chain at her throat.

Dakota nudged Eli with his elbow. "Mother of pearl. Would you look at that?"

"Gentlemen. I'm Karina Castillo, welcome to Hotel Celebracion." Her accent was thick, but her English was flawless.

"Ms. Castillo. I'm Eli Colt," he extended his hand. "This is my partner, Dakota Sutcliffe."

She offered a pleasant smile. "Dakota? Isn't that a state in America?"

"Two of them actually," Dakota's words almost faltered into a nervous stutter. "There's a north and a south."

Eli cleared his throat. "Is there a place we can talk in private, Ms. Castillo?"

"Yes. Please, follow me." With a confident stride, she led Eli and Dakota to the lobby bar. She requested a private table with quiet authority.

"Thank you for arranging our accommodations at such a beautiful hotel." The restless energy of sharing her broth-er's capture prickled along Eli's nerve ending. "But I'm afraid I bring bad news."

Karina's eyes narrowed into a probing stare. "Oh."

"I have information about Emilio," Eli said, choosing his words carefully. "He and the girls he brought back to Juarez were taken this afternoon."

A flicker of confusion crossed Karina's face but not surprise. "Taken? How could you know?"

Eli took a deep breath, then lifted his eyes skyward. "We had a drone monitoring their movements. We watched the whole thing go down."

Karina's eyes turned hard and flashed anger. "You gringos always get involved with our problems in Mexico. Now my brother is in the hands of maniacs."

Eli's ears grew warm. "Calm down. We didn't ask your brother to escort those girls across the border. That was his idea. I'm here because he convinced me and Dakota, that we should come over here and destroy Carlos Ramirez."

Silence followed.

Eli held his breath.

Then, like the first crack in a dam spraying water, the hard lines on her forehead softened slightly. "What do you want from me?"

THIRTEEN

Friday, 6:16 PM—United States Courthouse, Western District of Texas, El Paso

Morales sank into a leather chair in Judge Sanchez's chambers, just a few steps from the room where Marco Domingo would be tried for his crimes.

Judge Sanchez sat behind his imposing desk, meticulously studying his case calendar spread out before him with a determined expression. His brow creased in concentration, a pen poised in his hand.

Adorned in a navy-blue pinstripe Armani, pressed white shirt with starched collar, and a red power tie knotted in the Windsor style, defense attorney Preston Somerset lounged in a plush armchair, one leg crossed over the other, his attention seemingly elsewhere. His calendar sat on his lap, closed as if forgotten, planting a seed of apprehension within Morales.

Why was Somerset so detached, as if the trial date held no significance? Was it mere indifference, or did he know something Morales and Sanchez didn't? Despite the task of finding a suitable date that would accommodate every lawyer in the room's schedule, Somerset sat unperturbed, with an easy confidence that didn't match the purpose of the meeting.

The room exuded an unmistakable aura of legal authority—its rich mahogany furnishings—its ornate decorations—its tall bookshelves filled to the brim with law books bearing decades of judicial precedent.

As night is to day, Judge Sanchez pored over his calendar in shirtsleeves and loosely knotted tie, igniting a fire of determination for Morales to walk out of this room with a court date scheduled within a month. He longed to bring his wife and kids back from Dallas. He missed waking to his wife's soft snoring and the morning chaos of fixing Miguel and Camila's breakfast before Lolita rushed them off to school. He would've been taking Miguel to Little League this evening, if not for having to burn night oil preparing for this case.

He took a deep breath, steeling himself for a confrontation. "Mr. Somerset." Morales' voice cut through the sound of Sanchez shuffling papers. "You seem unconcerned about the trial date. Do you know something we don't?"

Somerset's mouth spread into a wide grin. "I assure you, Mr. Morales, I'll be happy with whatever date you and the judge decide," he replied smoothly, his tone devoid of emotion. But there was something hidden in Somerset's demeanor, a flicker beneath his carefree façade.

Whatever secrets Somerset harbored, Morales would have no success revealing them, so he let the matter slide.

"I've got the fifteenth of next month open," said Sanchez, oblivious to Somerset's lack of interest.

Morales turned his calendar to the specified date.

"That works for me, Judge," Somerset said with an

impassive expression. His book remained on his lap, unopened.

But the date didn't work for Morales. "Sorry, your honor. I have a cybercrime hearing in Judge Nguyen's court."

"Fine. What about the twenty-second?"

"All clear," Somerset said as he glanced at the park outside the judge's window.

Sanchez looked up from his calendar. "How about you, Juan?"

"Sorry again. An identity theft case in Judge Johnson's court."

"Okay, then," Sanchez said with no small amount of frustration. "Try giving me a date."

"The twenty-ninth. I'm clear the following week as well."

Somerset brushed an invisible piece of lint from his lapel. "That works for me too."

Sanchez glared at Somerset for a brief second, then dropped his focus to his calendar. "The twenty-ninth it is. If you have any pretrial motions, get them to me by the twenty-second." Sanchez peeked at his watch. "If you'll excuse me, gentlemen, I have to prepare for court."

A subtle chime from Judge Sanchez's phone sifted through the room. Sanchez grasped the receiver. "Yes." His expression shifted like a turbulent sky—his eyes widened as the gravity of whatever was told to him sunk in.

A sinking feeling hit Morales. "Judge?" His voice was edged with urgency as he stood without thinking.

Sanchez waved off Morales and remained focused on the call. "When?" The judge's face reddened. He shook his head. "I've got some bad news, gentlemen," he said as he hung up the phone.

"What is it?" Morales demanded.

Sanchez's eyes grew heavy. "It appears our defendant, Marco Domingo, has disappeared."

Dread roiled in Morales' gut. "How is that possible?" His inflection rose with each word.

Sanchez's lips formed a taut line. "According to the marshalls, they found the ankle monitor they'd placed on him on a stray dog in the barrio where he was staying with his cousin."

"We must find him before he disappears into Mexico," Morales blurted, his tone urgent.

Somerset stood to leave.

Sanchez motioned Somerset back into his chair. "Stay put, Mr. Somerset. We're not done yet."

"Somerset." Morales' tone brimmed over with mistrust. "I can't help but wonder if you had a hand in orchestrating your client's disappearance."

Somerset's cool demeanor remained unchanged. "I can assure you, I had no involvement in this."

The heat of suspicion burned hot within Morales. "You've been acting quite aloof all morning; as if you knew something we didn't."

Somerset's eyes narrowed with a flicker of annoyance. "I'm sorry. Is it your practice to accuse people based on their demeanor? I may have to move my practice to El Paso. I'd clean up."

Sanchez stood. His face burned redder than a desert sunset. "Mr. Somerset." His sharp tone drew all attention to him. "If I find you knew that your client would skip bail, I'll issue a warrant for your arrest and provide you with free accommodations across the street in the county jail."

Somerset's face didn't falter. "I have nothing to hide.

Now, if you'll excuse me..." He peeked at his watch. "There's a flight to San Diego in an hour."

Judge Sanchez turned his attention to Morales. "I want you on top of this, Juan. Find Domingo," he shifted his focus back to Somerset. "And arrest anyone who helped him escape."

"Understood, Your Honor," Morales said meekly, sure that the manhunt would end unresolved at the Mexican border.

FOURTEEN

Friday, 8:26 PM—Somewhere in the Chihuahuan Desert

Maria woke to a blur of confusion. Her thoughts were hazy fragments, her limbs were heavy, unwilling to respond to her mental commands. As she struggled to make sense of her surroundings, shadows and blurred figures rippled around her, gradually coalescing into focus.

Thin metallic bars materialized inches from her face. Nearby, a girl sat huddled in a cage, her knees drawn close to her chest.

Attempting to stretch, Maria encountered the confines of her own cage. A dozen others, each containing a frightened girl, filled the room. A few girls slept restlessly. Some cried quietly. Others gazed blankly at nothing inside the room.

Desperation clawed inside Maria's chest at the reality of her situation. She curled her fingers through the unyielding wire. Fear welled up inside her.

Just as she thought her nightmare couldn't get worse, a door sprung open, with a sprawling beam of light. A boy, not more than seventeen, entered the room. Greasy black hair hung in lank strands over his forehead, and a patchy beard struggled to grow on his rigid jaw. His gaze slithered from cage to cage, like a starving stray cat sizing up a cornered mouse. Finally, his eyes locked onto a girl who looked even younger than Maria, maybe fourteen at most.

The boy approached her.

The young girl, with wide, terrified eyes set in a face still round from childhood, shrank away with trembling hands over her mouth. As the boy got closer to her, she pressed herself further into the corner, her shoulders hunching as if she were trying to disappear.

He grabbed her ankles, pulled her from the cage, and forced her to the open door. Raucous laughter from outside the room followed.

And screams—loud screams from the girl.

Maria's gut twisted. A sour taste crept up from her throat.

The room fell into a stunned silence. The girl's muffled weeping and the men's laughter persisted outside the room.

Muted whispers arose among the remaining girls. Another guard walked in. He was bigger, older, and more menacing than the first. His eyes gleamed with malice as he neared Maria's cage.

He unlatched the door, clutched Maria's arm, and hauled her out.

She stumbled as he dragged her down a long hallway filled with shadows and laughter and the whimpering sobs of the young girl. He halted at a closed door at the end of a hallway and opened it with an old-fashioned key. With a forceful shove, he pushed Maria inside, slamming the door behind her.

The room was small, with a mattress pressed into a

corner. Sunlight with floating dust particles filtered through a small window.

Desperation gripped Maria's entire body.

The door swung open. Hector Ramirez entered. Beside him stood a figure recognized by all in Almada—Emilio Castillo, the Saint of the Streets, the man who'd once saved her mother's life.

Hector's cold eyes honed onto her as if he were shopping and she was something to buy. With a predatory swagger, he approached her. His hands ran through her hair, then trailed down her shoulders and arms. "I brought you and your roommates a hero. Someone to stop all this crying and sniveling. He'll keep you company before we can move you to your new homes."

"Please, let me go back to my papa and mami. Please." Maria's voice trembled.

Hector laughed. "No, no, no, little chica. You'll be leaving with a nice gringo. He'll be here in a few days."

A tidal wave of terror crashed against Maria's fears. "Please, let me go. I won't say anything. I swear."

Hector's lips curled into a cold smirk. His eyes narrowed into menacing slits. "Talk to her, Preacher." He gripped Maria's chin with calloused fingers, turning her face to meet his. "Calm her with those words you preach on the streets." Hector's smile dissolved into a chilling glare. "And explain to her and the others, that if they don't behave, things will get worse."

And with the same suddenness as when he entered the room, Hector Ramirez left through the door.

The tension eased as the door clicked shut.

Maria exhaled a trembling breath. Her gaze darted between Emilio and Hector. Something wasn't right. Where she expected to see terror in Emilio's eyes, there was only calm resolve. His shoulders remained relaxed; his stance steady.

Emilio Castillo's eyes crinkled at the corners with a tender smile. The lines around his mouth softened into compassionate curves. In the street preacher's presence, Maria found a glimmer of comfort in the darkness of this horrible new world.

Maria closed her eyes for a moment, allowing herself to relax, grateful for the temporary reprieve from her suffocating fear.

But why had Hector left her alone in a room with Emilio Castillo? And why was the Saint of the Streets in this compound? Questions she feared to uncover, swirled in her mind.

"I know you, Señor. You're Emilio Castillo. You prayed for my mother when she had breast cancer."

Emilio Castillo's eyes filled with empathy. "Yes, I remember. How is your mother now?"

"Healed. You healed her."

"No, no, Maria. Jesus took a beating before His crucifixion so your mother could be well."

Confusion clouded Maria's mind. What was this good man doing with Diablos? Before she could voice her thoughts, Emilio spoke as if he knew her questions.

"I was taken with six girls. Your captors believe I can keep you and the others calm until you leave."

As Maria's thoughts whirled in uncertainty, she remembered. "You're with the girls who were rescued in Texas?"

"Si." Emilio placed a finger to his lips and leaned in closer. "We must hold on." His eyes darted to the door. "The Americans are coming, and they'll be here soon."

A speck of hope blossomed within her like a cactus

flowering in the desert. Could her distant dream of going home be on the brink of reality?

Yet, beneath her optimism, fear remained. Were the Americans really coming? How would they find her? How would they find Emilio? How would they find the other girls in this place?

But at least she had this newfound hope to combat her uncertainty. Could it be possible that her salvation from Diablos was standing with her in this room?

PART 2

FIFTEEN

Friday, 8:31 PM—Hotel Celebracion Hotel, Juarez City

Karina's fingers dug into her palms as the Americans recounted her brother's abduction across the table in the lobby bar. Her throat tightened with each word, and she blinked rapidly, fighting the sting in her eyes. Emilio's face flashed in her mind—the creases around his kind eyes, the stubble on his chin, his old coat hanging loose on his too-thin frame.

She could almost feel his warm hand on her shoulder as he'd stood between her and those Diablo thugs outside their childhood home. Karina's stomach churned. She pressed a hand to her mouth, willing away the bile that threatened to rise. Carlos Ramirez. Diablos. The cartel had her brother.

She pictured Emilio pleading with the Americans to keep those girls in El Paso with passion and determination. But these gringos—they hadn't listened. And now...

Heat crept up Karina's neck, warming her cheeks. She flared her nostrils as she glared at the Americans, gringos who thought they could fix everything.

Who do you think you are? she wanted to scream. But the words caught in her throat, trapped behind a lump of fear and fury that made it hard to breathe.

"Karina, we understand that this is a difficult time for you." Eli's voice was annoyingly gentle.

Karina slammed her palm against the table, the bang resounding in the quiet bar. "Why are you here? To save my brother? The girls? Your government had the chance in El Paso," she said with a bitter tang. "Do have any idea what it's like for a female to live in this city? To live in constant fear of being taken as you walk down the street?"

Eli and Dakota exchanged uncomfortable glances.

Karina's chest heaved with every breath. "You Americans come to Mexico with your big promises, but what do you know about us, huh?" Her voice rose an octave with each syllable. "You think you can swoop in to be heroes and save the day. Why don't you go back to America and take care of your own troubles, like arresting men who like their girls young."

Dakota slid his chair closer. "We're aware of what girls go through when they're trafficked, Karina. We've done this kind of work before."

"You may have done this kind of work before, but not against Diablos," Karina said in angry English. "And not against Carlos Ramirez—La Serpiente. This won't be easy. The cartel has eyes and ears everywhere."

"We'll do whatever it takes to bring them down." Dakota's intense blue eyes locked onto Karina's.

Eli ran a hand through his hair. "Any word from Blackwell about those tracking chips?"

Dakota shook his head. "Nothing. Either the cartel found and destroyed them, or they're in an area with no signal. Blackwell said they lost all traces shortly after the vehicle entered the desert."

"Great," Eli muttered with frustration. "I was hoping those would give us a lead."

Karina's head swam as she tried to make sense of their conversation. "Tracking chips?"

"We had GPS trackers in the girls' clothes," Eli explained. "But it seems Diablos is more tech-savvy than we anticipated."

Dakota set his jaw in quiet determination. "We need to find another way to locate Emilio and those girls."

Unlike the fake bravado she often saw in men, there was a steadiness to this man Dakota Sutcliffe, a calm resolve that stirred something within her.

He leaned forward slightly, his broad shoulders relaxed despite the tension at the table. "But we'll need your help," he added, his voice low and earnest.

Karina tapped her nervous fingers against the polished table. She couldn't be thinking about calm resolve or quiet strength or bold bravado. The lives of her brother and six girls hung in the balance. The urgency of this situation required action that she couldn't do alone.

Her gaze shifted between Eli and Dakota. How could she trust these men, these outsiders who seemed so disconnected from her people's struggles? They were gringos; ignorant of the harsh realities of life in Juarez. She straightened in her chair. "Fine. Say I believe you're serious about this, what exactly do you need from me?"

Dakota leaned forward, his elbows on the table. "Information. Contacts. Anything that could lead us to Los Diablos' operations."

"And in return?" Karina's voice was sharp—challenging.

Eli met her eyes. "We'll do everything in our power to find Emilio and those girls."

Karina pressed her palms against the table. "That's not enough. I need guarantees."

Eli shook his head. "We can't promise—"

"Then this conversation is over." She started to rise.

"Wait," Dakota said, his hand outstretched but not touching her. "What do you want?"

Karina paused, then slowly sat back down. "Protection. For my family. And when this is over, you get us out of Juarez. To America across the border."

Dakota beamed a toothy smile. "Sure thing. Shouldn't be too difficult. Right, Eli?"

What was it with this gringo Dakota Sutcliffe? Karina took in a deep breath to steady her skepticism. Could she trust these men? If not—why were they here? What could they gain from taking on Carlos Ramirez in Mexico?

Eli. This man was serious. Dakota. He hadn't taken his eyes off her since she'd entered the lobby. But they both exuded confidence and courage. Traits they would need to help her rescue Emilio and protect her mother and Sofia. "So, what's your plan?"

Eli traced the edge of the table with his finger as if he were searching for what to say next. He glanced at Karina and then took a deep breath. "Our primary objective is to find Carlos Ramirez and, to quote your brother, 'cut off the head of the snake.'"

Karina's shoulders sunk with the hope she'd almost placed in these men. "But what about Emilio and the girls? Surely you can't ignore what happened to them."

"It's what your brother wanted," Eli said. "He convinced us to focus on finding Carlos Ramirez and destroy him. He argued it was the only way to protect these and other girls in Juarez."

Karina, steeped with disappointment, thought of Sofia. She could see Emilio insist that the gringos destroy La Serpiente if not for any other reason, but their sister's sake. But that was before he and the girls were kidnapped. "I'm not sure I agree."

Dakota straightened in his chair. "Regardless of our objective, to find Ramirez we must find where Los Diablos operates, right? Surely Emilio's being held somewhere that will lead us to this...what did you call him, the serpent?"

"Probably," Karina conceded. "So, if you find where they're holding Emilio before you find Carlos Ramirez, you'll rescue him? Correct?"

Eli's expression grew intense. "Although rescuing Emilio and those girls is not our stated mission, we can't ignore the immediate danger they're in."

Dakota nodded. "Emilio's capture was not expected, but we've dealt with fluid situations like this before. Finding them is now part of the puzzle, a new priority."

"But," Colt added, "we can't lose sight of the bigger picture. Rescuing your brother and those girls is crucial, but it won't stop Diablos from operating its trafficking enterprise here or in the United States. Gathering intel on Ramirez is just as vital as finding your brother. The mission is not complete until we have enough to bring the cartel down. Understand?"

Karina narrowed her eyes. "So, you'll do both?"

"We have to," Dakota said beaming a smile. "Save the hostages and bring down the cartel. Then we'll have a party."

Eli glanced at his watch. "Time is critical. It's been three hours since Emilio and the girls were kidnapped. If we're going to pick up this trail while it's still warm, we need to hit the streets now. Any ideas on where we should start?"

"Aldama," Karina said as she searched her purse for the number Emilio had given her the last time she'd seen him. "It's where the girls live. It's where I grew up."

SIXTEEN

Friday, 9:35 PM—Juarez City

As Karina pulled her Audi out of Hotel Celebracion's valet area, she glanced in her rearview mirror. The Americans were following in a Ford SUV, probably built with parts manufactured at Cesar's plant just outside of town. Her meeting with Eli and Dakota in the lobby bar had been both reassuring and nerve-wracking. She'd agreed to help them gather intel on Carlos Ramirez in exchange for bringing her and her family to America once they'd rescued Emilio and the six girls. After that, she'd called the number Emilio had given her the last time she'd seen him.

She gripped the steering wheel of her Audi as she navigated the twilight streets of Juarez, its tinted windows offering a false sense of security. The setting sun painted the sky in rich purples and fiery reds, belying the churning anxiety that reeled inside her stomach.

The Audi's shiny exterior drew curious glances as they entered Almada's narrow streets. Karina's skin rippled with each lingering look. Every shadow held potential danger, a reminder of the fear that gripped every woman and girl in this neighborhood.

The pale streetlights cast a gold hue outside of Iglesia Casa De Dios, the destination given to her by the person she'd called before leaving the hotel. The church stood withdrawn with its simple cross and time-worn steps across the street from the mega-grocery, S-Mart.

Karina eased her foot on the brake and searched the grounds for the man who'd directed her to the church. She navigated through a narrow passage in a short cinder block wall and checked her rearview mirror. The man insisted they met alone, therefore, Eli and Dakota remained parked outside the wall on the street.

Gravel crunched beneath the Audi's tires, the sound unnervingly loud in the quiet lot.

Movement caught her eye—a shadow detached itself from the building. Karina's heart raced as she made out the figure of a man waving her over. She pulled into the shadows and unlocked the doors.

The passenger door opened, and a middle-aged man with graying temples and worried eyes slid inside. Karina noted his simple collar and the deep lines etched around his mouth.

"I'm sorry for the secrecy," he said in a hushed tone. "I can't risk being seen talking to you. Diablos soldiers were watching my church earlier today."

Karina nodded to convey she understood. "Thank you for meeting me. I'm Emilio's sister, Karina."

The man's eyes darted around the parking lot before settling on Karina. "I'm Pastor Alejandro. You wish to know where you can find your brother?"

"*Si.*" A torrent of urgency surged through her. "The

cartel has him, no? And the six girls the Americans rescued in Texas."

The pastor's eyes saddened. "Poor Emilio. Always quick to put his life on the line for others."

Karina swallowed hard, pushing down the guilt of questioning her brother's ministry. "I have friends in Juarez who are here to find El Serpiente and destroy Diablos once and for all."

The pastor hesitated for a moment before answering. "A noble mission. But I'm afraid close to impossible."

"Can you help us?"

His eyes blinked with uncertainty, but he nodded nonetheless. "There's someone who might be able to assist you." He scanned the parking lot again, then leaned in closer. "An American journalist has been relentlessly investigating Diablos for the past two years—documenting their operations, their victims, everything. Her sources run deep—from corrupt officials to cartel defectors, even frightened family members of Diablo soldiers." His voice dropped even lower. "She's pieced together intel that would make the National Intelligence Center envious—safe houses, money trails, names of high-ranking members. If anyone can help you find your brother and those girls, it's her." He pulled a notepad from his back pocket. "She also hosts a podcast, exposing the cartel's crimes and the plight of missing girls. But her work has made her a target."

Karina's excitement with this new information was tempered with shame. She'd never heard of this podcast or this woman—too detached from the problems of her people as she enjoyed the fruits of her sin.

The pastor passed the notepad to Karina. "Write down your number. I'll give it to her and ask her to call."

Karina scribbled her number and passed the pad back. "She can call me any time, day or night."

"If she calls, be careful, señorita," the pastor warned, his eyes grave. "You'll be treading near the gates of hell." With a final nod, Pastor Alejandro slipped out of the car and trotted to his church.

Karina searched her rearview mirror. Had she discovered the first step to finding Emilio?

SEVENTEEN

Friday, 11:46 PM—Castillo Residence, Aldama, Juarez

Eli, Dakota, and Karina sat around a scarred wooden table in the compact kitchen of the Castillo home. The enticing aromas of marinated meats, roasted chilies, and tortillas cooking on a griddle permeated the air. Family photos, a sizable crucifix, and a picture of the Virgin of Guadalupe adorned the aged walls.

They'd arrived soon after Karina's meeting with the church pastor, who had promised to connect them with a podcaster who might have information about Emilio's kidnapping.

Eli stirred his coffee under the soft glow of an exposed bulb. "So the pastor gave no indication of when this podcaster would call?"

Karina's fingers tapped anxiously against the worn tabletop. "None. Like I told you. He didn't guarantee she would call."

Karina's mother, a petite woman with gray-streaked hair and worry lines etched deeply into her face, moved slowly and deliberately as she filled Dakota's coffee cup for the third time. "*Mi pobre Emilio. Por favor, bendita virgen, protégelo de estos hombres horribles.*"

Dakota's gaze darted between Karina and her mother.

Karina clasped her mother's hand and smiled. "She said a prayer to the blessed virgin. To protect Emilio from those horrible men."

Karina's phone buzzed across the chipped tabletop.

Dakota's brow lifted in anticipation.

She answered with apparent pent-up tension, "Hola?" After a brief conversation in Spanish, she terminated the call with an exasperated sigh. "It was my assistant from work. He was double-checking about my night off."

Eli lifted his cup for a refill, hoping it would ease the letdown.

With a resigned shrug, Karina set her phone back on the table but kept her gaze on it, as if willing it to ring again.

Eli found himself staring at the phone too as it lay silent. He cleared his throat to break his disappointment. "It's still early yet. She might call tonight. She might call tomorrow. You never know with these things."

A tense line formed along Karina's jaw. "I'm going crazy just sitting here. What do we do if she never calls?"

Dakota shifted in his seat. "Well, there's nothing we can do tonight but wait and bite our nails. Tomorrow's another day. If necessary, Dakota and I will hit the street where Emilio and the girls were captured. See if anyone saw anything that will freshen the trail."

"You can't go there," Karina protested, her voice filled with panic. "Didn't you hear me? Diablos is everywhere."

Dakota leaned over his cup. "And contacting the police is out of the question?"

"The average pay of an El Paso police officer is almost $5000 per month," Karina said. "Here in Juarez, the police barely make $1500. How do you think they survive?"

"Corrupt?" Eli said.

"Mostly," Karina said with a quick nod. "And much of the money comes from the cartel."

The phone danced again. Karina snatched it quickly. "Hola." She listened briefly before her face flushed red. "Isabella?" Karina's voice crackled with anger as she spoke rapid-fire Spanish into the phone.

Sensing Karina's anxiety, Eli's own adrenaline surged.

Karina's eyes flamed, and Dakota glanced at Eli. Should they be worried?

Karina's pitch rose higher and higher as a torrent of Spanish tumbled out of her mouth until she finally ended the call.

Dakota reached across the table to touch Karina's arm. "You okay? What was that about?"

Karina's eyes rolled with an exaggerated sigh as she waved a dismissive hand. "A new employee," she explained, her voice still tinged with anger. "She was calling to ask how to operate the air cleaning machine."

"And that got you upset?" Eli asked.

Karina stood and paced the kitchen floor. "Because she asked where I was." Her tone was sharp. "And that's none of her business."

The phone buzzed once more, its screen illuminated, "Unknown caller."

"Karina!" Eli's voice burst out.

Karina rushed to the table and grabbed the phone with trembling fingers. "Hola?"

A nervous voice broke through the phone in Spanish.

"*Si,*" Karina responded to the caller.

More nervous chatter ensued.

"*Sí, sí. Dónde estás?*" Karina spoke rapidly, then pressed her brow tight as she listened. "*Estaré allí en media hora. Voy a traer a dos hombres conmigo para protegerte,*" Karina said before terminating the call. "We need to go. It was the podcaster. Her name is Anna and Los Diablos is on the way to her building."

EIGHTEEN

Saturday, 12:36 AM—Aldama, Juarez City

Eli crouched low behind the Explorer's steering wheel, eyes fixed across the pothole-riddled street. Dakota sat alert in the passenger seat, his fingers drumming a silent tempo on his knee. Karina occupied the backseat, her perfume failing to mask the smell of burning trash wafting through the evening air.

"That's the place," Eli murmured, nodding toward the graffiti-covered walls. "Your contact said the third floor, right?" he asked, glancing at Karina through the rearview mirror.

"Third floor," Karina said, focused on her phone. "Here it is, a recent podcast from Anna Shroud."

"Welcome back, listeners." Anna's voice filled the vehicle. "Today, we have a special guest joining us—a survivor of an agonizing issue that affects every female in Juarez. I'm talking about human trafficking run by the infamous street gang Los Diablos. This harrowing enterprise has killed hundreds if not thousands of teenage girls and young women since the 1990s and it doesn't appear to be slowing down. I'm Anna Shroud and welcome to *Whispers in the Dark*."

Dakota turned to face Karina. "That's who lives here. Anna Shroud."

"It's not her real name," Karina said. "But yes, and according to my mother, this is her podcast."

The program continued. "Our guest has asked us not to use her name, and for her safety, we've agreed. Thank you for being here."

"Thank you for having me." A woman's Mexican accent quivered in English. "It's not easy reliving those moments, but if sharing my story can save one girl from what I've suffered, it'll be worth it."

"Let's start from the beginning," Anna Shroud said. "Can you walk us through what happened the night you were kidnapped?"

"Sure. It was an ordinary evening. I'd finished my shift at the auto-parts plant and was walking home from the bus stop. That's when three men grabbed me two blocks from home. They blindfolded me and threw me into the trunk of a car."

"The auto-parts store?" The soft gasp came from Karina in the back seat. "Cesar?"

"After riding in that trunk for about an hour," the victim continued. "The car stopped, the trunk opened, and someone jabbed a needle in my arm. When I woke up, I was in a room with ten other girls, all of us caged like dogs in a kennel."

"Oh my," Anna Shroud said. "Who were these other girls."

"All were Latina; most from Mexico. But they had a girl from El Salvador, one from Nicaragua, and two from Honduras."

"And what happened to them?"

There was silence for a few beats before the girl answered. "I don't know. Four of them were taken away during the week I was held captive. Two more girls came when I was there. When I escaped, I had to leave the other girls behind."

"I understand," Anna Shroud said. "Perhaps if you tell us how you escaped, our listeners will realize why you had to leave the others behind."

"To be honest, it was a miracle. One night, one of my captors forgot to lock my cage. After he fell asleep after drinking much beer, I managed to pick the lock of my chains with a loose nail from the floorboards. Then I unlock the door to the room with the keys he left hanging on the wall. Then it was just a matter of slipping away into the desert while the men in the compound were asleep."

"That must have been terrifying," Anna Shroud said. "Where did you go after escaping?"

"I ran as fast as I could, not knowing where I was or where I was going. I stumbled upon a small church in a remote village. The pastor and his wife took me in and gave me shelter. They showed me so much love."

"What happened next?"

"They knew a man from Juarez who helped me get across the border. There, I met a couple who took me to a Christian church in Houston."

"How did you rebuild your life after such a traumatic experience?"

"It hasn't been easy, but with the support of that church that is actively fighting human trafficking, I got the help I needed. Now, I work with other girls, who've been trafficked like me."

"Your strength and resilience are truly remarkable. Thank you for sharing your story with us."

"Thank you for giving me the opportunity to speak out. I pray your listeners will fight to make a difference and bring an end to this evil trade."

"Thank you again," said Anna. "Join us tomorrow when I'll be talking to a former Diablo sicarios who escaped to the United States. I'm Anna Shroud signing off. You've been listening to *Whispers in the Dark*."

A long silence followed the broadcast as Eli absorbed what he'd just heard. Dakota shook his head in disgust. In the rearview mirror, Karina's face paled.

Eli scanned the dark streets. "Looks quiet. You see anything?"

"Nope." Dakota checked his firearm. "Let's go in?"

Light spilled in through the Explorer's rear window, headlights from an approaching car.

"Get down," Eli said.

All three ducked.

The low rumble of the car's engine approached, then its brakes squeaked alongside the Explorer.

Eli pulled his Glock from the small of his back and held his breath.

An eternity passed before the soft whirl of the engine signaled the gradual crawl of the car moving forward.

Eli peeked over the dashboard. The sedan stopped, its doors opened, and three figures climbed out—their bright white shirts stood out against the darkness.

"Diablos," Karina said, her words low and on edge.

Eli's gaze met her eyes in the mirror. "How do they know this Anna Shroud is here?"

"Diablos has eyes everywhere," Karina said. "A neighbor perhaps. Could be a grocer or a waiter or anyone who suspects a white lady in a neighborhood where she doesn't belong." Karina paused for a moment. "These men are here to silence this broadcast. The cartel doesn't tolerate anyone, especially a gringo who reveals their crimes to the whole world."

Dakota squirmed in his seat like a restless dog on a tether. "They seem to know where they're going,"

"Believe me," Karina said. "They do. People say they have better technology than the Mexican Federales."

The image of RPGs and Kalashnikovs aimed at Emilio and the girls flashed in Eli's mind. "They probably got their hands on IP geolocation equipment."

"Or network monitoring tools," Dakota said. "A lot of that stuff was lost in the Central American conflicts."

"You stay here," Eli said to Karina. "Dakota, on me."

Eli ghosted across the street, Dakota a whisper behind him. They melted into an alcove as the trio reached the entrance. Footsteps faded inside. Pulse thrumming, Eli and Dakota slipped in, weapons ready. One step closer to Emilio, the girls, and the Diablos' lair.

Clattering echoes led them up. A latch clicked above—fourth floor. Hinges whined, then a dull thud. They crept higher, Eli easing the stairwell door open a sliver. Three shadows converged on an apartment, low voices blending with the building's restless sighs.

Dakota's hand tightened on Eli's shoulder, signaling readiness as they stayed concealed in the stairway. The Diablos' low murmurs blended with the air conditioning's erratic rattle.

Eli's mind raced. He locked eyes with Dakota, body tense, senses heightened. He couldn't let them enter Anna Shroud's apartment. He tapped Dakota's elbow. "Let's go."

Eli launched himself into the narrow confines of the hallway, Glock first. "Nobody move."

Two thugs scattered, revealing their leader—olive-skinned, white-haired, a serpent's smile curling his lips. His fingers caressed a gold-plated .45 nestled in his waistband. Inked flesh rippled as his young soldiers drew steel with lethal intent.

Eli and Dakota fired.

The sound of exploding rounds mingled with shouts and cries of alarm.

Eli's bullet found the thigh of one Diablo. The man crumpled, then floundered like a fish on dry land, his weapon clattering from his grasp.

The white-haired leader and his minions retreated down the hallway. They fired wayward rounds that thudded harmlessly into the worn walls.

Eli closed the distance to the doorway, his weapon trained on the injured man's torso, whose eyes darted from Eli to his friends who were abandoning him.

Eli kicked out, sending the man's weapon skittering out of reach across the floor.

"Stay down," Eli growled in a low voice. "Don't make me shoot you again."

The wounded man's whimpers filled the hallway; his eyes were wide and unblinking, locked as if expecting his doom.

Dakota slammed his palm on the door. "Anna. Karina sent us. We're here to get you out."

"Hurry up and get inside," Eli ordered Dakota. "We're vulnerable out here."

"Anna," Dakota said. "Don't be afraid, we're coming inside." He stepped back, dipped his shoulder, and rammed the door open.

Eli snatched the wounded Diablos' weapon and hauled him inside.

The apartment was a cluster of high-tech equipment amid shabby surroundings. In the living room, a heavy microphone suspended on an adjustable arm, attached to a metal desk cluttered with various notes and documents. Surrounding the microphone was an assortment of audio mixers and a MacBook laptop. Multiple wires swathed in a chaotic web connecting everything together.

Two large headphones rested on the desk, one placed carefully, the other nearly falling off the side. The walls were used as a pinboard, adorned with clippings, scribbles, and photographs relating to Diablos.

"Anna, where are you," Dakota called out. "We're with Karina Castillo. You're safe now."

Eli zipped tied the wounded man's wrists and ankles and followed Dakota's voice to the bedroom.

"In here," Dakota called out.

Propped up on a bed against pillows, Anna Shroud's gaunt face contorted into a canvas of raw distress. Her pale skin grew paler. Her chest heaved beneath a yellow blouse, each breath threatening to tear the fabric. Wild, hazel eyes dominated by dilated pupils, darted around the room. Strands of blond hair clung to her sweat-dampened forehead.

Eli had been where this woman was now during his own panicking episodes from his PTSD. "Look at me, Anna," Eli said, trying to channel the same reassurance Lindsey had passed on to him. "You're strong. You've got this. You're just having a panic attack. I know, I've been there." He peeked over his shoulder. Dakota leaned over the Diablos Eli had shot, wrapping the man's belt around his upper thigh.

"You need to move, Anna," Eli said, lifting her up by the shoulders. "Now!"

Eli, Dakota, and Anna Shroud exited the apartment, leaving the wounded Diablo where he lay in the living room. As they reached the Explorer, relief seemed to settle into Anna's demeanor.

Two of those men you followed inside left the building like it was on fire," Karina said as she put her arm across Anna Shroud's shoulder. "They sped away a few minutes ago."

"Punch a bully in the face, and that's what happens." Dakota chuckled.

Eli fired up the engine. "Let's get out of here before they come back with more bullies."

———

THREE HOURS LATER, Eli stood in the soft glow of lamplight next to the expansive window of his and Dakota's suite at Hotel Celebracion. Dakota sat rigid on the edge of the sofa. Next to him, Karina leaned back with crossed legs.

Brooke Adams—known to *Whispers in the Dark* listeners as Anna Shroud—sat poised on a high-backed chair, her blonde hair pulled back into a neat ponytail, her hazel eyes calm and measured, unlike the wide-eyed terror she'd displayed back at the Aldama apartment.

Eli turned from the window to face her. "Brooke, any idea where we can find where Carlos Ramirez hangs his hat?"

"Maybe," Brooke replied. "I recently interviewed a source, an ex-Diablo soldier who escaped into America. He knew of several cartel locations in Aldama and Juarez. That's why I'm here—to get photos of these buildings and maybe interview a disgruntled soldier or two. Pastor Alejandro was helping me with that."

Eli slowed his breathing to rein in his excitement. "You have addresses?"

Brooke nodded, reaching into her bag. She flipped through a small notepad, paused, then tore out a page and handed it to Eli. "This is the address of their operation center. It's kind of hidden in plain sight. But I watched from a distance for twelve hours and saw the comings and goings of many high-ranking Diablos."

Eli studied the paper, then pocketed it. "Dakota? Anything you want to ask?"

Dakota shook his head. "I think we've covered the basics."

Brooke's gaze softened. "There's also a compound in the Chihuahuan Desert that the cartel uses as a holding facility for their trafficking operations."

Karina nearly bounced off the couch. "Maybe that's where they took Emilio and the girls." Her words tumbled out in a flurry. "Can you show us where it is, please?"

"I can pin it if you like," Brooke offered, pulling out her phone. "But you need to be careful. I've been out there too. Ramirez has that place guarded like a fortress."

Eli glanced at Dakota. "That will be helpful when our team crosses the border."

Dakota nodded.

Brook stood. "Can you get me to the American Consulate? I'm afraid I've worn out my welcome in Juarez."

"Sure. Dakota and Karina can stake out the operations center." Eli lifted his assault pack and slung it over his shoulder. "I'll drop you off on my way to the desert."

NINETEEN

Monday, 6:40 PM—Two Blocks from Diablos Operations Center, Aldama, Juarez City

Karina's nostrils twitched at the pungent scent of traffic fumes and stale body odor. Dakota dozed, his head lolling against the driver's window, his arms tucked close to his chest.

Pedestrians scurried past the SUV. Two blocks away, the muted brown Diablos' operation center blended seamlessly into its surroundings, its darkened windows mirroring the neighboring structures' vibrant reds, golden yellows, and rich greens.

She took another peek at the sleeping Dakota. She'd found him brash and overly confident when she'd first met him. His unfettered attention in the hotel lobby had been annoying as Karina had dealt with the news of her brother's capture. But after spending more time with him, she appreciated his bravery, his commitment to finding her brother, and his undeniable good looks.

His eyes fluttered open. He breathed in and shifted his

eyes in every direction. "How long have I been sleeping?" His voice was gruff and husky.

"Two hours," Karina said, raising binoculars to her eyes. "Nobody has come or gone since you've been sleeping."

Dakota glanced at the clock on the dashboard. "We're been here over thirty-six hours." He sat up and stretched his arms. "You want to catch some sleep?"

Karina shook her head. "You let me sleep almost six hours last night."

"Hard to believe someone could sleep that long in this cramped vehicle," Dakota said, glancing around the Explorer's interior. "You must feel like you're slumming compared to that Audi you drive."

Karina shrugged. "Not really. I didn't own a car until a year ago."

"Really?" Dakota stretched his arms behind his head and yawned again. "That car fits you like a glove."

"I wouldn't have it without Cesar."

Dakota held out his hand for the binoculars. "How long have you two been dating?"

"Dating?" she scoffed, surrendering the field glasses. "I'm not dating Cesar, Señor Sutcliffe." Karina's words almost faltered. "I'm his mistress."

Dakota's face flushed as if she'd embarrassed him. "Call me Dakota, please."

"I'm not a good woman, Dakota," Karina said. "I know it. My mother knows it. Now you know it."

He said nothing for several seconds before finally breaking his silence. "From what I've learned, you're a brave and beautiful woman." He paused again as if he was gathering courage. "You're the most beautiful woman I've ever seen and the bravest I've ever known."

Karina's stomach fluttered. A warmth blossomed from

her belly to her chest. Yes, she knew men found her attractive. That's why Cesar chose her. But brave?

"I'm not sure my mother would agree," Karina regretfully admitted. "She thinks I'm a whore for the life I live."

A grin spread across Dakota's face as he continued surveying the office building.

The warmth that blanketed Karina grew hotter with rage. "You think that's funny?"

"No, not at all," Dakota said and chuckled. "I was just thinking of some of the things my father called me for the choices I've made."

"Like what?" Karina clenched her fists to calm herself.

Dakota's features fell into subdued remorse. "Irresponsible. Underachiever. A disappointment. A failure."

Karina narrowed her eyes into curious slits. "Why? What did you do?"

"I didn't live up to his expectations." Dakota peeked over the binoculars and squinted. "I was in the FBI. My dad wanted it, but I hated it. This work with Eli feels right."

Karina's anger softened. "And now you're a private investigator who works to free trafficked children?"

"Life has a way of putting you on the right path, I guess. This job kind of evolved from when Eli and I rescued his niece in the Gulf of Mexico."

"So, you did get to act out your love for the navy?"

"Coast Guard, actually," Dakota said. "But that experience led me to a higher calling."

"Saving girls from traffickers?" Karina asked with sincere admiration.

A chuckle slipped out of his lips. "Can't you see the irony?"

"As a woman who grew up in Juarez," Karina said with direct seriousness. "No. I can't."

"What do you mean?" he said, setting the binoculars in his lap.

"Young girls and women have been disappearing from these streets since before I was born." Karina's voice quivered with a sad edge. "Dozens were found buried in the Chihuahuan Desert about thirty years ago. But it hasn't stopped. That's why I'm with Cesar—for protection."

Dakota's gaze met Karina. "I'm sorry, but respectfully, that's not you." There was a gentleness to his tone.

"Isn't it?" Karina challenged, keeping her expression firm.

Dakota returned to the binoculars to spy at the office building. "Look, I used to be in the FBI like my dear ole' dad wanted. I wore a suit and went to an office and sat in seminars to learn how to solve white-collar crimes. I hated it because I was doing something I wasn't made to do."

"What do you mean?" Karina said.

"I mean your destiny may be different than the life you're living right now." He lowered the binoculars and gave Karina a side-eyed glance. "All you need is something good to happen."

"Like you had when you started working with Eli Colt."

Dakota nodded and raised the binoculars again. "Something tells me your life will improve when you and your family live in America."

Goosebumps prickled Karina's skin. A smile rose to her cheekbones. "Where do you live in the United States?"

"Madisonville, Louisiana. It's a little town outside of New Orleans."

"You like it?"

"Absolutely." Dakota's face lit up. "It's loaded with lakes and channels where I can live out one of my passions. Waterskiing."

"I've never waterskied."

"You're in luck. I'm a licensed instructor." Dakota's beaming expression turned serious. "Hold on. Somebody's just arrived." Dakota passed the binoculars to Karina. "See if you recognize anyone."

The binoculars shook slightly in her fingers as she adjusted the focus.

The familiar black Mercedes slid into view. Karina's breath hitched. Cesar Garza emerged, Armani-clad and regal, his chauffeur stood at attention—a silent shadow.

Her spine locked. Binoculars bit into her palms. Cesar. Here. Now. Real life cruelty made flesh.

Betrayal crashed over her, a dizzying tide. Why was her billionaire lover skulking through Aldama's gutters, cozying up to cartel scum?

For a heartbeat, denial beckoned—a siren's false comfort. But her eyes refused to lie, drinking in the truth about the man who shared her bed.

She let the binoculars fall to her lap. America sounded pretty good about now.

"You, okay?" Dakota said.

She passed the binoculars back to him. "The man in the suit, that's Cesar Garza."

Dakota pressed the lenses to his eyes. "Your uh...uh—"

"Lover? Yes."

"Man's a sharp dresser, I'll give him that," Dakota said as if Cesar's presence was insignificant. "Hold on, there's two men coming out of the office. And I recognize one of them." Dakota reached for his phone and handed Karina the binoculars.

But Karina didn't need the binoculars. "Me too," she said with lurid frustration. "The one with the white hair is Hector Ramirez, Carlos's younger brother. The one shaking hands with Cesar is Marco Domingo. He was in my class when I graduated from high school."

Dakota reached to the back seat and pulled a camera with a telescopic lens from his bag. "We arrested that Domingo character in the West Texas desert." He steadied the lens just over the steering wheel, adjusted the focus, and clicked off several shots.

Hector led Cesar inside the office. Domingo strolled to a white Range Rover across the street.

"This camera is blue-toothed so, the photos transfer straight to my phone," Dakota explained. "I'll send them to our contact at the FBI." A faint crease formed over Dakota's brow. "Maybe he can explain why Domingo is not in jail."

"What should we do now?" Karina said. "Stay here or follow Marco?"

Dakota pressed the ignition and shifted the Explorer into drive. "I've caught Domingo once and I'm not too happy he's free. Let's see where he takes us."

TWENTY

Monday, 6:50 PM—Somewhere in the Chihuahuan Desert

Maria cowered in the corner of her cage, enduring the foul smell of her waste bucket. Around her, a dozen other girls were similarly suffering, each face haunted by their suffocating trappings. To her left, a girl with tangled blonde hair rocked back and forth, muttering to herself. Across the room, two dark-haired sisters stared at each other, their eyes wide with fear.

It'd been three days since Emilio Castillo had filled Maria with hope and assured her that the Americans would arrive soon to save them. But how soon was soon? How long would she be confined to a cage with only rancid beans to eat and a plastic bucket to relieve herself?

Burdened by a lengthy chain tethered to the concrete floor, Emilio Castillo humbly collected each girl's bucket to empty into a large metal bin. As he opened the gate to Maria's cage, he offered her a wink and an inspiration. "Be strong, Maria. Jesus loves you."

Compassion flooded her as she smiled back at the man. It was his prayers that prompted God to heal her mother's breast cancer. So, why was God allowing this faithful servant to suffer at the hands of these demonic thugs?

With the last bucket emptied, the Saint of the Streets dragged the bin to the door and knocked on it softly. The door opened, the bin was pulled away, and Emilio Castillo stepped to his chair where he would pray or offer them words of encouragement.

"Ladies," he called out gently, his gaze sweeping over every girl. "I would like to share a message from God's Word with you."

Maria sat straighter, resting her elbows on her knees.

Emilio cleared his throat. "Jesus said in the book of Matthew, 'Do not be afraid of those who kill the body but cannot kill the soul. Rather, be afraid of the One who can destroy both soul and body in hell.'"

Maria loved Emilio's messages, savoring every syllable she'd heard since they'd arrived at the compound. It was as if, for the moments he spoke, she was transported away from her captivity to a place where love wrapped around her, offering her peace amid her captivity.

"Now, listen to me, ladies," Emilio continued. "I know you're totally consumed with the horrors of being held prisoner and are worried about what will happen next. But Jesus reminds us in this passage that only He can determine your eternal destiny."

Emilio paused for a moment, then nodded. "King David left us with this Psalm. He sang, 'God is our refuge and strength, an ever-present help in trouble. Therefore, we will not fear, though the earth give way and the mountains fall into the heart of the sea, though its waters roar and foam and the mountains quake with their surging.'"

Emilio stood tall. "David is telling us that even when the world around us seems to be crumbling, we can find hope in the fact that God, not Diablos, is in control of all things."

Emilio lifted his hands to his shoulders. "It will be Jesus who determines your eternal fate. Your hope should not rest in the strength of others, but in God alone, who promises to be with us, even when this world treats us harshly."

He clasped his hands behind his back and paced between the cages. His heavy chain followed, clattering against the concrete floor. "Listen to the writings of the Apostle Paul. 'Though we may suffer these momentary troubles, this experience is helping us to achieve God's eternal glory that far outweighs this suffering.' This means we can find hope by keeping our focus on Jesus and the promise of something better when we see Him in heaven."

Maria realized at that moment that Jesus would be with her whatever lay ahead. And suddenly, she wasn't afraid anymore.

With a deafening crash, the door burst open and slammed against the wall with a violence that shook the room. An older man with grizzled black hair, a heavy brow, and cold black eyes stormed into the room. He closed in on Emilio and forcibly bound his wrists with thick rope.

A sudden knot got snagged in Maria's throat.

Emilio's face remained stoic as if he'd expected this sudden turn of events.

Horror gripped Maria's heart. Emilio, her only hope in this darkness, was being torn away with a cruelty that hit her like a gut punch. Maria's eyes locked onto Emilio's for a silent farewell. The man yanked him harshly into the shadows beyond the threshold. The door slammed shut with a bang.

The room closed in around her, magnifying the sounds of whimpers and sobs. What would Maria do now without

Emilio here to encourage her and the others? He'd been her rock, her strength, her inspiration against the evil that lived in this building. Without him, she'd be left to navigate her captivity alone.

An eternity stretched with each passing minute. A heavy silence enveloped the room. Emilio's sudden departure left a gaping void that suffocated Maria's smoldering hope.

Would she and the others ever see Emilio again? What would happen to them now? She closed her eyes, trying to remember Emilio's words about finding strength in God. "Please," she whispered under her breath. "Please let the Americans come soon."

TWENTY-ONE

Monday, 7:16 PM—200 yards outside the Diablos desert compound

The sun dipped below the horizon, casting a deep purple across the night desert sky. The stars were vividly bright, the moon so large it tempted Eli, hunkered down behind a rocky outcrop, to reach out and touch it.

The silence was oppressive, broken only by the distant howls of coyotes and the rustle of tumbleweeds. The barren landscape stretched to the horizon. Its only interruption was the compound that spread like a desert fortress two hundred yards away. Floodlights on its corners illuminated the building, revealing a dozen armed men with rifles glinting in the harsh light.

Eli rubbed the rough wound on his scalp. That and his headache reminded him of the explosion that had sent him head first into a wall in Study Butte. He pushed aside that painful memory, focusing instead on the compound.

The desert's solitude helped ease his discomfort—that and his fond thoughts of his fiancée, Lindsey. Oh, how he wished she were with him now—her gentle touch, calming presence, and loving heart—helping him navigate through the darkest corners of his mind.

She'd been his lifeline in the aftermath of Freddy Badeau's attack in the small fishing village in Louisiana. Her skill as a clinical psychologist was a gift that Eli had grown to depend on.

Lindsey's unshakable faith mystified Eli. Their late-night conversations about God's mercy and grace stirred his curiosity, but also his doubts. Where was God's mercy in a world filled with suffering? How could he reconcile God's justice with the evil that killed Aziz, seduced Tara, and now held Emilio and six girls captive?

Buffeted by the harsh realities of his violent world, Eli's faith flickered like a flame in the breeze. He longed for Lindsey's unwavering belief, her comfort, her conviction. But as the desert wind whispered and stars shimmered over-head, Eli realized he needed to find his own path to under-standing God's plan.

A faint stirring inside him, like a whisper in the stillness of the night, begged to question—Was God reaching out to him? Offering him help in this moment of need?

The creak of hinges echoed through the vast desert. A man roughly pushed another out of the compound's front door. Eli pressed his binoculars against his eyelids.

Emilio, hands bound behind his back, stumbled into the desert dust. His captor's pistol shone in the moonlight.

Here's a tightened version with more tension and compelling prose:

Eli's muscles coiled, fingers digging into the binoculars. The armed man jerked his weapon toward the vast desert, shoving Emilio forward. This was no casual stroll—it was a death march.

Scanning the terrain, Eli pinpointed his ambush spot

fifty yards out. Twenty agonizing seconds to cross the rocky, sparse landscape. He melted behind a cactus cluster, heart thundering.

The assassin forced Emilio to his knees. Raised his pistol. Finger slid into the *trigger* guard.

Time slowed. Eli's hand ghosted past his Glock, gripping the M9's hilt instead. He exploded into motion, a lethal blur of steel and determination.

The assassin whirled, eyes wide with shock. Eli's blade found flesh. His free hand clamped over the man's mouth, silencing the death rattle.

The man crumbled under Eli's weight. They fell together, their faces mere inches apart. In that fleeting moment, suspended between life and death, the light in the sicarios's eyes faded to darkness.

Emilio thrashed against the rope that bound him, causing too much commotion.

Grabbing the killer's weapon, Eli rushed to cut Emilio free.

"Quiet," Eli hissed. "We need to move, now." His eyes darted between Emilio and the compound, straining to detect any approaching tango.

A call rang out from the compound. *"Jorge, date prisa. El partido de fútbol está empezando."*

Eli's veins throbbed. He rushed Emilio toward his previous location, snatching his bag in one fluid motion. He aimed the man's pistol left and fired. The sharp crack split the desert air across the empty landscape.

A MUTED BOOM from a gunshot shattered the silence inside the compound. Maria's mind went numb. Tears blurred her vision. Her body tensed as if awaiting a heavy blow.

Was Emilio dead? No, God, please, no.

ELI'S FINGERS dug into Emilio's shoulder, shoving him to Karina's Audi. The car's metal glinted under the full moon. "Get in the car, Emilio. Hurry!" Eli hissed, his command razor-sharp and desperate. But beneath the urgency, a war raged in his gut. With every step to safety, six innocent girls remained in the compound.

LIKE A SNAKE, the dread of Emilio's execution wreathed around Maria's heart, sinking its teeth into her last vestige of hope. Unspoken but understood, the truth hung heavy—the older man had murdered Emilio with a bullet.

The air crackled with chaos from outside the room—muffled shouts and frantic footsteps clattered and grew louder. Was the man who killed Emilio coming to kill them?

The door burst open with a thunderous bang. Three armed guards stood at the threshold with murderous glares.

The men fanned out with their weapons ready. A lone figure emerged from behind them. Maria's pulse thundered in her temples. Her body convulsed as she recognized the man who'd just entered the room—Carlos Ramirez—*La Serpiente*.

Despite the fear that threatened to consume her, Maria's resolve hardened like steel as she recalled Emilio's words. "Though Diablos may take your body, they can never claim your soul." She repeated the phrase to herself to gain courage.

She straightened her shoulders, determined to honor Emilio's memory and cling to the hope he'd instilled in her —the promise of Jesus' persistent presence.

TWENTY-TWO

Monday, 8:23 PM—Juarez City

The traffic buzzed outside Karina's window—car horns honking, pedestrians screaming, tires pounding potholes. Dakota weaved in and out of traffic to keep up with the Range Rover Marco Domingo was recklessly maneuvering through the streets of Juarez.

Domingo cut off a cargo truck, sending it swerving into the next lane. "He's turning right up ahead," Karina said, her voice ripe with tension.

Despite Domingo's careless driving, Dakota navigated through the morass of cars and motorcycles to keep the Range Rover in visible proximity. Karina gripped the door handle for support as Dakota changed lanes to pass a slow-moving delivery truck and made the turn.

For thirty minutes, Dakota trailed Domingo, skillfully weaving the Explorer through traffic. When Domingo veered off the main road, Dakota held back, allowing several cars to pass before following. The Range Rover kicked up dust as it raced down a narrow side street, then disappeared behind a city bus. Rounding another corner, Dakota slowed, scanning the street. Domingo was gone.

"I think we lost him," Dakota muttered in frustration.

Karina leaned forward, straining her vision to catch a cloud of dust settling under the yellow glow of a street light. "There!" She pointed. "He must have turned off there."

Dakota nodded and the Explorer's engine roared to life. To the right at the next corner, the Range Rover's taillights raced about 300 yards ahead. "Good catch. I thought we'd never find him."

"This street leads out of town," Karina said. "He's headed to the desert."

As the urban glow faded behind them, the terrain devolved into a desolate expanse, cloaked in a darkness that was only broken by the bright beam of the Explorer's head-lights. Dakota shut the light down.

"What are you doing?"

Without the cover of traffic, our lights will give us away." He shot her a side-eye wink. "Don't worry, I can navigate at night. Coast Guard training."

The vast emptiness swallowed them. The Range Rover's taillights blazed like fiery embers beckoning them into the depths of unseen danger.

"Any idea where Domingo is going?" Dakota asked.

"I'm scared to think about it. This desert was used as a mass grave for dozens of women three decades ago."

The miles they traveled into the wilderness filled Karina with a mounting fear that Domingo was leading them into a trap.

Dakota's phone buzzed with sudden urgency. He glanced at the screen, his expression unreadable against the faint light.

ELI NAVIGATED the dark desert road confident the cartel hadn't followed. It'd been a close call saving Emilio from the clutches of the cartel. The Audi's headlights cut through the inky darkness, illuminating a narrow strip of cracked asphalt.

"How are the girls holding up? Were all of the six still with you?" Eli said, the words tumbling out through a knot in his throat.

"There were more," Emilio said. "Twelve to be exact."

A hollow ache hit Eli's core. Twelve girls. Twelve lives hanging in the balance.

He blinked hard. His adrenaline spike was fading. Now he fought the exhaustion from dozens of hours without sleep.

"We need to call your sister. She's worried sick." He grabbed his phone from the console and dialed Dakota.

"Eli?" Dakota's voice was calm and confident. "Where are you?"

"About six clicks outside of Aldama. I have Emilio with me and we'll be in town in a few minutes."

Dakota paused to mumble something unintelligible, undoubtedly telling Karina that her brother was okay. A brief burst of excitement from her followed.

"Karina would like to speak to her brother," Dakota said.

"In a minute. Are you guys still watching the Diablo office?"

"Nope. We're in pursuit of Marco Domingo, somewhere in the desert."

"The guy we arrested in Study Butte?"

"The one and the same," Dakota said.

"Where exactly?"

"About a half hour outside of Juarez."

Eli considered his options. Those girls; locked away and terrified. How could he rest knowing he'd failed to save them? Hooking up with Dakota meant strength in numbers. "When you get a chance, pin me your location. We might as well meet up now."

"Sounds like a plan. Here's Karina."

Emilio tried to calm his sister by telling her he was safe and unharmed.

Would a rendezvous be wise, or should he take this victory and wait another day to fight? But those girls left behind...

He had to do something.

Eli downshifted the Audi's transmission as he accelerated the sedan up the desert incline. The vehicle jostled. The suspension groaned. The tires struggled to gain purchase, pelting rocks and gravel against the vehicle's undercarriage.

"I like your sister's car," Eli said to Emilio. "But right now I'd prefer a four-wheel-drive."

With a final push of the gas pedal, Eli guided the sedan over a hump where Karina and Dakota waited. Karina and Dakota stood in the shadows at the top of the hill, scanning the area below.

Karina kicked up dust as she rushed to Emilio at the car's passenger side, wrapping her arms around her brother before he could exit the vehicle. "I thought I'd lost you," she whispered.

"*Estoy bien*," Emilio said with a soft giggle. "*Estoy bien*."

Eli joined Dakota near the Explorer, parked near the top of the escalating hill.

"Looks like you struck pay dirt," Dakota whispered, lifting his chin in Emilio's direction.

"Yeah. But there's a dozen girls we left behind," Eli said, careful to keep his voice low to avoid detection. He set his binoculars to night vision and peered at the valley below. Three greenish silhouettes glowing human forms stood between an SUV and an old truck. "What do we have here?"

"Domingo for one," Dakota said. "The other two pulled up soon after I got here."

Something was familiar about the two figures who talked with Domingo. "I can't put my finger on it," Eli said. "But I think I've seen one of those men before."

"From the compound?" Dakota asked.

"No, it's not that. It's something about how the one on the right stands. His posture, his body language. It just seems so familiar."

"I think the head injury you suffered in Study Butte has your brain playing tricks on you," Dakota said. "What are the chances we run into someone you've crossed paths with before? Why don't you go get some rest while I keep an eye on these guys."

Checking his watch, Eli realized he hadn't had more than a couple of hours of uninterrupted sleep for going on eighty-four hours. "Good advice. Wake me if anything happens," he said as he climbed into the back seat of the Explorer.

TWENTY-THREE

Monday, 9:00 AM—United States Courthouse, Western District of Texas, El Paso

Juan Morales navigated through a bustling throng of court staff and defense attorneys across the bustling atrium of the federal courthouse. He spotted Sarah Cohen, the forty-something court administrator, in an off-white pantsuit, her face buried in a file as she, too, maneuvered through the stream of humanity. Her no-nonsense demeanor highlighted a dedication to her work, which included access to the court's financial records. Morales rushed to her, determined to learn what he could about the five million dollars posted for Marco Domingo's bail.

"Morning, Sarah, How's Dennis and Lisa?" Morales asked, referring to Sarah's husband and daughter.

Sarah halted her steps, raising intelligent green eyes from the file she held. "Hey, Juan, they're fine. How's Lolita and the kids?"

"With her parents in Dallas." Morales placed his hand on Sarah's shoulder and walked with her. "Look, I was hoping you could help me with something."

"Sure, give me a call this afternoon." She tapped the file in her hand. "Right now, I'm in the weeds with court filings."

"What I need is time-sensitive. Can you give me a few minutes in your office?"

Sarah raised a suspicious eyebrow. "Concerning what?"

Morales leaned in slightly, keeping his voice low. "I need to know where the bail for Marco Domingo came from. Can you pull up that information for me?"

Sarah hesitated, her eyes darting around the busy courthouse. "I'm not sure that's Kosher, Juan," she replied, her tone cautious. "Don't you need a warrant?"

A sinking sensation hit Morales at the mention of a warrant. He didn't have time to jump bureaucratic hurdles. "The law's a little fuzzy on that. However, Mr. Domingo is a Mexican national who skipped bail. I think he's waived any rights of privacy."

Sarah glanced nervously at her surroundings, her voice lowering to a whisper. "Juan, I could lose my job if I do this without proper authorization. I can't risk it."

Morales leaned closer. "Sarah, please," his tone pleading, "Lives are at stake here. I need your help."

Sarah chewed on her bottom lip. After a moment of tense silence, she relented with a sigh. "Alright but keep this off the record."

Morales shot Sara a grateful nod. "Your name will never come up, I promise."

Sarah gave Morales a wave of the hand. "Follow me."

Five minutes later, Morales sat across from Sarah. Her fingers tapped against her keyboard in rapid bursts, pausing every few seconds as she studied the screen. "I found it. The money was drawn from El Paso Savings and Loans. The name on the account is Oceanic Holdings."

"With that name, it can't be local?"

She turned the monitor for Morales to see. "It's based in Grand Cayman. Most of the company's information is...let's say...obscured."

"Can you print that out for me?"

"Didn't we talk about our conversation being off the record?"

Morales's mental gears turned with newfound clarity. "Yes, we did." He scribbled down the name of the company and everything he could about its filing. "What do you make of these names on the company records?"

Sarah shook her head. "Not much. It's probably a shell company, given that it was formed in the Caymans. These officers are probably placeholders without real involvement or control of the company's funds. You'll have difficulty finding out who actually does."

After expressing his gratitude to Sarah, Morales rushed from her office and set out for FBI headquarters. There, he intended to confer with the special agent responsible for Domingo's arrest, hopeful that the bureau's insights into the enigmatic Oceanic Holdings would reveal those who aided in Domingo's escape from prosecution.

TUESDAY, *9:17 AM—Chihuahuan Desert—Hilltop Overlooking the Rio Grande River*

In the back of her Audi, Karina's eyes blinked open from a dreamless sleep, the seat's leather clinging to her damp clammy skin. Emilio leaned back in the front passenger seat—alive, safe, a miracle after Diablos had captured him. Outside the windshield, the hulking form of the Explorer where Dakota and Eli had spent the night was about twenty yards uphill.

Karina breathed in the desert air. "Emilio," she said in a low moan.

He turned, his eyes soft with affection. "You're finally awake. You must have been exhausted."

The sun had long since risen, its relentless glare piercing through the tinted windows, the night's chill now replaced by the rising morning heat. She rubbed the sleep from her eyes and sat up, the previous night's elation of her brother's rescue slowly waning. "Why'd did you do it, Emilio? Why did you take such a risk?"

Emilio glared out into the valley but said nothing.

She leaned over the seat, her fingers digging into the leather. "After what happened to Papa? Why would you tempt Diablos?"

Emilio continued his silence.

A cold fist clenched Karina's heart as the past clawed its way to the surface—eleven years ago—the year everything changed. Papa stood proudly in his police uniform, his jaw set in determination, his voice low and stern, as he argued with Mamá about standing up to the cartel. "A man must stand for something, *mi amor*, or he'll fall for anything."

Silver or lead. That's what Diablos offered on a bulletin they nailed to the police station's doors.

Then there was Mamá's wails. The smells of gunpowder and blood—phantom remnants of that horrible day when she'd stood outside their home over her father's dead body. He had been one of six officers gunned down for refusing *La Serpiente's* bribes.

The years passed and Emilio disappeared into a haze of drugs and violence. Then, she threw herself into Cesar's arms. And Mamá... Mamá became a ghost, drifting through their days, her eyes always searching for threats in every shadow.

Karina's throat burned. She swallowed hard, forcing herself back to the present. How could Emilio risk putting them through that hell again?

"I'm sorry, *Hermana*," he said. "I never meant to put you through that."

"Then why?" Karina pressed, frustration creeping into her tone. "Have you thought about what it would do to Mamá and Sofia if something happened to you..." she clutched his hand and squeezed. "What it would do to me?"

Emilio's shoulders tensed. His gaze dropped to his lap. "Karina, I— "

"No." Her words came faster. "You can't keep doing this, Emilio. La Serpiente won't hesitate to kill you. And then what? Who will take care of our family?"

Emilio's gaze drifted to the distant horizon. "Do you remember how I was after Papa died, Karina?" His voice cracked, and each syllable seemed to cost him.

Karina nodded. How could she forget?

"I was lost," Emilio continued, his fingers rubbing the crook of his arm where faded track marks existed. "The drugs, the violence... I was destroying myself and everyone around me."

"But look at you now. You got clean." Karina gripped the headrest, the sudden movement drawing Emilio's attention. "You turned your life around."

Emilio's eyes blazed with an intensity that made her lean back. "Because God cared enough to help me. To show me there was another way..." His words trailed off, the last syllable barely a breath. "These children, Karina... They're trapped in a hell I understand all too well. I can't turn my back on them."

The raw hurt in Karina threatened to unravel her. "I understand that, Emilio. I do. But is it worth risking everything?" Her words came out in a rush. "Ramirez... Diablos... They're not going to stop. They'll kill you if you persist like Papa did."

Emilio reached out and grasped her hand. "I have to believe that what I'm doing matters, *Hermana*. That God has a purpose for me in this."

Frustration bubbled up as Karina pulled her hand away. "And what about us? What about Mamá and Sofia?" Her last word splintered. "What happens to us if you die playing the hero?"

A void opened up between them. Guilt, determination, and something else she couldn't quite name seemed to war across Emilio's face. "I can't stop, Karina. Not when I know I can make a difference." His eyes pleaded. "But I promise you, I'll be careful. I won't leave you alone."

Should she believe him? She wanted to. But as she looked out at the unforgiving landscape, she couldn't shake the feeling that her brother was on a collision course with death.

The fire continued to burn behind Emilio's eyes. "God didn't save me from drugs so I could sit idly by while others suffer," he said, his words steadily increasing in volume. "He gave me a second chance for a reason—a purpose."

Karina's fingers twisted the hem of her wrinkled shirt. "But what if— "

"No more 'what ifs,'" Emilio said. "Faith isn't just about believing, *Hermana*. It's about doing."

"And you really think God will protect us?" The words slipped out, quiet as a secret confession.

Emilio's hand found hers, his grip firm but gentle. "I believe He'll give us the strength to face whatever comes," he said, each word deliberate. "But we can't just sit back and wait."

Karina's chest tightened with a mix of fear—admiration, maybe? She was really seeing him for the first time since he'd conquered drugs. Gone was the hollow-eyed addict, replaced by a passionate man.

"I can't promise I won't worry," she said in a half-laugh, half-sob way.

Emilio exhaled slowly. "I wouldn't expect anything less."

Karina squeezed his hand, feeling the calluses that spoke of his hard life. "Just... promise me you'll be careful," she said.

"Always." A spark of joy lifted the corners of his mouth. "Now, are *you* ready to make a difference?"

Ready? Ready to leave her present life for one of purpose? "Lead the way, *Hermano*," she said, surprised by the strength in her own voice.

They stepped out of the car. For the first time in years, Karina felt a glimmer of hope piercing through the darkness that had surrounded her family for so long.

TWENTY-FOUR

Tuesday, 9:56 AM—Chihuahuan Desert—Hilltop Overlooking the Rio Grande River

Eli's muscles screamed as he unfolded himself out of the Explorer's cramped backseat. The midmorning sun seared into his retinas. He shielded his eyes and fumbled for his sunglasses. Dakota was hunched low by the hood, training his binoculars on the valley below.

"Anything?" Eli's voice came out as a rasp. He cleared his throat and spit out gritty saliva.

Dakota shook his head, remaining focused on the scene below. "Just our friend Domingo, pacing by his Range Rover and checking his watch every ten seconds."

Eli scanned the area. The pickup was missing. "What happened to the two other guys?"

"Left in a huff about a half hour ago," Dakota replied, his voice tight. "Headed west in a beat-up Dodge pickup."

An arctic shudder coursed through Eli as he crouched next to Dakota, peering down at the murky green Rio Grande snaking through the barren landscape.

Footfalls fell in behind them. Karina with Emilio close

behind. Her eyes were red-rimmed, her hair disheveled, her clothes sweat-stained and wrinkled. She opened her mouth to speak, but Eli held up a hand and then locked his focus on movement in the valley. "There," he whispered, pointing.

A battered yellow bus with a plume of brown dust trailing rounded a hill to their west. It lurched to a stop near Domingo, who pointed at his watch, and then waved angry arms at the driver.

"Oh God," Karina whispered.

Children spilled out, herded by men with rifles strapped to their backs. The kids stumbled toward the river-bank, where small boats bobbed in the quick current. A rope stretched across the river to the north bank and America.

Karina's lungs shuttered. "We have to do something," she said with a desperate tone.

The corners of Dakota's lips fell. "Too many coyotes and too well-armed. And who knows what they'd do to the kids."

A coyote pushed a child into a boat. El's vision tunneled onto the boy's terror-stricken face. Afghanistan flashed— another child to be used for adult pleasure?

"Where are they taking them?" Karina's voice stammered.

"Sweatshops. Factories," Emilio said in a low hush. "Perhaps worse—brothels."

Eli's gut coiled. He scurried to the back of the Explorer. *Kids. Traffickers.* He reached for his phone and punched in Blackwell's number.

10:21 AM—FBI *Field Office, El Paso, Texas*

Morales sat across from Special Agent Marcus Blackwell in his office. "Thanks for seeing me on such short notice."

In a white shirt rolled up to his elbows, and a red paisley tie hanging loose around an unbuttoned collar, Blackwell offered a not-a-problem shrug and shake of the head. The walls of his office were adorned with commendations and photos. His off-the-rack blue blazer hung on a hook behind the open door. "Always happy to help a federal prosecutor," he said in a deep-south accent. "Same team and all."

Morales breathed in heavily, unsure if Blackwell would have the same scruples as Sarah. "I was hoping you could help me with a problem I've encountered in prosecuting the man your team arrested in Study Butte."

Blackwell nodded for Morales to continue.

"As I'm sure you've heard, Señor Domingo has disappeared after posting five million dollars for bail." Morales's voice revealed a touch of his frustration. "I've been investigating the source of this large sum, and I've hit a wall where I think you and the bureau can help."

"What wall?" Blackwell asked.

"Oceanic Holdings. It's a company based in Grand Cayman."

Blackwell's expression remained impassive as he grabbed a pen from his desk and scribbled on a notepad.

"I've been informed there's a good chance it's a shell company." Morales watched for any reaction from the special agent.

Blackwell showed nothing. "That island is known for three things—boutiques, beaches, and discreet banks," he said. "And those banks are secure, solvent, and a haven for businesses to hide their money from Uncle Sam."

Morales leaned in. "Can you use the bureau's resources to dig deeper and learn who's behind Oceanic Holdings?"

Blackwell stared at Morales without interruption. Seconds seemed like hours. A nearby copier whirred. Coworkers, passing by the offices, chattered. Finally, Blackwell dropped his pen and offered a strained smile. "Look, I understand your problem." He pressed his lips tight together, and the crow's feet around his eyes deepened. "But I have protocols to follow. I can't investigate a company without proper authorization. Besides, I'm retiring in a few weeks, and this brother ain't about to lose his pension."

Ten years of interrogating witnesses gave Morales a sixth sense to detect people who resisted divulging the truth. But why was the man who'd arrested Marco Domingo hiding information from the prosecutor?

"Agent Blackwell, with all due respect, time is of the essence." Morales edged his tone with urgency. "I'm prepared to issue you with a subpoena if need be. But I'd much rather work with you amicably to find Domingo and bring him to justice."

Blackwell exhaled an exasperated sigh. "Alright, counselor. I'll see what I can do. But I can't make any promises."

"I'm sorry Agent Blackwell, that's not good enough. I need this information and I need it today."

Blackwell's shoulders tensed as he considered Morales for another few seconds. Then, he stood and stepped to the open door. He peered out into the hallway as if thinking about his response.

Morales' stress doubled with every second of silence. But just as his hope for a quick resolution started to waver, Blackwell shut the door.

He sat back at his desk, opened a drawer, removed a

manilla folder, and held it chest-high. "What I'm about to share with you stays in this office. Understood?"

Morales nodded.

He slid the folder across the desk. "I know of two American civilians who've crossed into Juarez to learn what they can about the Diablos cartel. More specifically, its leader Carlos Ramirez." Blackwell leaned back in his chair as if some heavy weight pressing on him had been lifted. "These photos hit my email last night. The two men to the left are Hector Ramirez and your perp, Marco Domingo."

"Who's Hector Ramirez?" Morales said.

"The younger brother of Carlos Ramirez, head honcho of the Diablos cartel."

"Who's this in the Italian suit shaking hands with Domingo?" Morales asked.

Blackwell's brow lifted. "That sir is Cesar Lorenzo Garza."

"The Mexican billionaire?" Morales's mind struggled to keep up with the new information.

Blackwell's expression hardened. "Based on Garza's involvement with the Diablos cartel, I'd bet my pension he's the one behind your Oceanic Holdings."

Morales recounted the bank of record from where the funds had been drawn—El Paso Savings and Loan.

A phone buzzed from Blackwell's coat pocket. He raised his brow as he studied its screen. "Speak of the devil," he said. Blackwell listened intently for fifteen seconds before responding. "Got it. On my way now." He stood and glanced at Morales. "Your boy Domingo is up to no good. You coming?"

TWENTY-FIVE

Tuesday, 11:15 AM—Chihuahuan Desert—North Bank of Rio Grande River

Juan Morales stood on American soil, perspiring in the scorching heat. His dress shoes sunk slightly into the soft, sandy embankment. He shielded his eyes from the glare off the Rio Grande hoping to catch a glimpse of Marco Domingo on the Mexican side of the border.

The river's greenish waters churned below. The faint sounds of Latin voices from the southern bank mingled with the rush of the river current. The air was thick with desert dust. Morales could smell his own sweat and of the border agents around him.

"There," Blackwell said, pointing. "That's where my spies say Domingo's operation will cross."

Morales nodded. Why had Blackwell brought him here? Was it to see the crime he'd been tasked to prosecute unfold in real-time?

Suddenly, overcrowded boats emerged on the river. Children, their ragged clothes clinging to damp bodies, pulled desperately on a slack rope. A young boy's eyes darted between the rushing water and shore, while a teenage girl cradled a crying toddler, both staring with unseeing eyes ahead.

A coldness filled the pit of Morales's stomach, forcing words from his lungs. "My God. Those children..." Now he understood—being here was different from reading a sterile report.

As the boats neared the American shore, pandemonium erupted. Border Patrol agents on ATVs and horses swarmed the area. The smugglers panicked, some attempting to turn back, others abandoning their human cargo in the water.

Morales's hands clenched as he observed the terrified children—their eyes wide with panic, their cries filled with dread. Some leaped from the boats the moment they reached the shore. Others stayed motionless, paralyzed with fear.

A small girl, no more than ten, fell from her boat and was swept away by the current. Her petite frame vanished beneath the rushing water. Without thinking, Morales lunged forward. Blackwell restrained him with an arm across his chest. "Let the professionals handle it. They're trained for this type of work."

A horse mounted by a border agent pounded past Morales kicking up dust and debris, charging into the water with a determination that bordered on recklessness. Morales held his breath. The mounted agent closed the distance between him and where the girl was last seen.

Morales was helpless. His legal training useless, but not the power of prayer. "Please, Lord Jesus, empower this brave agent in his quest to save this girl."

And then, as if God answered without hesitation, in a blur of motion, the horse and rider surged downstream. The agent plunged into the churning water, vanishing for heart-stopping seconds. He erupted from the rapids, the girl clinging to his back like a mountain climber on a sheer cliff. Morales's breath escaped in a rush, a prayer of thanks for this miracle.

Relief vanished as quickly as it came. These children sought safety, yet predators like Domingo exploited their vulnerability. "God," Morales whispered, "let Domingo be caught today."

Morales's frustration simmered as he paced the riverbank, with border agents, children, and captured coyotes. He searched the faces of every adult apprehended, unable to find Marco Domingo among them.

"Any sign of your man?" Blackwell asked, his voice rife with anticipation.

"Nope," Morales said in a low tone. "Probably didn't want to risk crossing the border. Besides. These coyotes are Hondurans, not Mexicans. And so are the kids."

Before Blackwell could respond, the border agent commander called out in a grim tone. "Agent Blackwell, we've found something."

Morales followed Blackwell and the commander to an area fifty yards from the crossing point. The stench of rotting flesh was faint but still prevalent.

"What the hell..." Blackwell muttered as he looked down at a clump of earth before him.

But the clump was not earth. A partially buried body lay exposed under the harsh desert sun, its features twisted in a grotesque distortion of humanity. Bile rose to Morales's throat. "Is that a child?"

"I need to call this in," Blackwell said with a weighty undertone.

"Oh Dear Lord," Morales prayed out loud. "No telling how many children have been killed crossing this river."

The border patrol commander crouched over the body. "Corpses are littered throughout the border area. One is found almost every day by my agents or ranchers nearby."

Morales turned away, his gaze falling on the immigrant children huddled together nearby. The girl who'd narrowly escaped the river's fury clung tightly to the man who'd rescued her. Sadness welled up within Morales as he scanned each innocent face.

Blackwell joined Morales by his side. "I wish the politicians in Washington could be here right now. This country's broken immigration system is just as guilty as these traffickers."

Blackwell gestured at the chaos, frustration etched on his face. Morales took in the scene—border agents, frightened children, smugly confident coyotes.

If only the halls of power in Washington DC could see this.

"These kids are surely caught up in the crossfire of our political divide," Morales said. "But what would be their future if they remained where they came from?"

Morales felt torn. As an American, he saw the harm to his country. As a Christian Latino, his heart ached for these children caught in partisan gridlock. "They're casualties of a broken system," he said, his voice thick. "Easy prey for exploiters."

Morales had come to catch Domingo, but he saw the horrors of his crimes instead. The kids rescued in Study Butte were Mexican. These children were from Honduras. He had to work with others to dismantle the entire system that allowed such atrocities to persist. And he knew exactly where to start—Cesar Lorenzo Garza.

TWENTY-SIX

Tuesday, 7:15 PM—Three Blocks from Los Diablos Operation Center—Aldama, Juarez City

Several hours after Eli had alerted Blackwell about Domingo's river crossing, he peered over the steering wheel of the parked Explorer at the Diablos operation center three blocks ahead. Dakota reclined beside him in the early evening twilight, as relaxed as if he were poolside on a chaise lounge.

Eli glanced at his watch, then back at the building. "I have a mind to just storm this place. So far, Diablos is less than impressive."

Dakota stretched lazily in his seat. "The mission, my friend, is to observe and report. We're spies, not an assault force, remember?"

"When did you become so patient?" Eli said. "You're typically the one who's out the door with guns blazing."

"Don't know what you're talking about, Eli," Dakota yawned. "Relax, why don't you? Sit back."

"Right," Eli muttered. "But after what we saw at the river—"

"I know, I know. Those kids..." Dakota's voice hardened. "But if we go in like Wyatt Earp and Doc Holiday, we might take down a few low-level thugs and let the big fish slip away."

Eli's grip tightened on the steering wheel. "Carlos Ramirez. *La Serpiente*."

"Exactly," Dakota nodded. "We stay put long enough, he'll surface. Trust me."

"We could bring down the whole operation if we do a snatch and grab—haul his backside across the river." Eli chuckled and said, "We could use one of those boats we saw this morning."

Dakota grinned. "Now you're getting it. Besides, I'd rather not get shot at tonight if we can avoid it."

"Well look who's suddenly become restrained."

"Someone's gotta be," Dakota shrugged. "Now if you keep your eyes peeled on that building, I'll catch a few Zs."

The quiet of the night was suddenly broken as an Escalade pulled up to the front of the building. Eli's senses sharpened. Two men exited the building—the man with the white hair who'd attempted to break into the podcaster Brooke Adams' apartment, and another, who Eli confirmed by a photo on his phone.

Carlos Ramirez—their primary target.

Dakota visibly stiffened. His focus zeroed in on *La Serpiente*. "Big brother is here."

Eli cranked the engine and reached for the gear shift. But before he could shift into drive, a blinding glare filled the Explorer as headlights bore down on them from behind. A figure materialized at the driver's window. A pistol pointed at Eli glistened. A figure donned in a white shirt and blue bandana stood behind it.

Eli cursed inwardly. His momentary lapse in focus

could cost them their lives. In a fluid motion, he shifted into gear and slammed his right foot on the accelerator. The engine roared. The tires squealed. The vehicle burst forward like a projectile from an artillery weapon, leaving the headlights and the armed figure behind in a puff of dust.

Eli checked his side mirror. The headlights followed, high beams piercing the darkness as the Explorer darted past Carlos Ramirez and the Escalade.

"I'm open to ideas, Dakota," Eli said as he struggled to map out an escape route through the unfamiliar city.

Dakota's gaze was fixed on the Explorer's navigation system displayed on the dashboard screen. "Hang a left up ahead," he instructed, his voice steady despite the mayhem they'd found themselves in.

Eli veered the Explorer sharply, missing a parked service truck near the corner by inches. Another directive from Dakota had Eli make another turn. His uncertainty deepened—a nagging suspicion they were being funneled into an intricate trap set by those hot on their tail.

Dakota shouted another command. Eli's knuckles whitened on the wheel as he executed another turn. He couldn't shake that his chances of seeing Lindsey again were dwindling with each second.

"I have no idea where we're headed," Eli's voice clamored with agitation.

Dakota's brow crinkled as he leaned over the navigation display. "Head straight for two blocks, then take a sharp right," he said with surprising calm.

Eli surged the Explorer forward, hurtling it through the narrow streets. But the pursuing vehicle stayed close behind with its taunting headlights.

Eli braced himself for the turn ahead. He whipped the

wheel right, sending the Explorer tight into the corner. His body leaned toward Sutcliffe. His seatbelt pressed against his hip and ribcage.

"Keep going straight," Sutcliffe urged. "We're almost there."

"Almost where?"

Eli accelerated. They crested a hill. An unexpected barricade for street repair appeared in their high beams, blocking their path forward.

Dakota sucked in a sharp intake of air. "Oops."

"Hold on—" Eli skidded the Explorer to a stop just short of wooden planks and metal fencing.

Sutcliffe's gaze flickered between the barricade and their pursuers closing in from behind. "What now?" he asked.

Eli's mind searched for options. He found nothing but to stand and fight. But then he saw a dark shadow between the silhouette of two buildings—an alley. He grabbed his rucksack from the backseat and opened the door. "Follow me."

Eli and Dakota quickstepped through the alleyway, the rucksack of armament thumping against Eli's back. But the distant clatter of two men running resounded behind them.

Uncertain of what awaited them at the alley's end, and wary of falling into a trap set by Diablos, Eli stopped to huddle with Sutcliffe inside an alcove amid the stench of a nearby dumpster.

"I guess we fight?" Dakota said, his eyes burning like a warrior in the heat of battle.

The footsteps drew nearer.

"No other option," Eli said, clutching the M4 inside his rucksack. He raised his weapon to eliminate the two threats.

An engine revved and tires hummed behind them.

Eli and Dakota turned as one.

A pickup truck with a mounted machine gun sped toward them. Its weapon gleamed as its barrel swiveled in a slow arc to bare down on them.

TWENTY-SEVEN

Tuesday, 8:04 PM—Castillo Residence—Aldama, Juarez City

Karina ran a nervous finger around the rim of the porcelain coffee cup. Emilio sat across from her mother's worn kitchen table, staring peacefully at the ceiling. The aromas of picadillo and fried poblano peppers filled the room as Mamá stood at the stove preparing chile rellenos, Emilio's favorite meal.

The diminishing light of early evening crept through the curtains, painting silvery patterns across the worn linoleum floor. Everyone remained silent. Karina and Emilio had decided it was best not to tell Mamita about Emilio's recent abduction, knowing it would only add to her worries.

Karina stole a glance at her brother who stared back and forced a smile. She could sense his unease at their mother's disgrace for her older daughter.

Mamita poured more coffee and sat at the table. "So, how's your boyfriend?" she quipped, her face contorting into a disapproving scowl. "How's his wife?"

Karina tightened her grip on her cup feeling her mother's judgment. She struggled to find the right words, the guilt of her relationship with Garza tearing at her conscience.

The lines on Emilio's forehead showed his discomfort.

"I raised you better, Karina." Mamita's tone reeked of rebuke. "Your life should reflect your family's values," she said crossing herself. "Not entertaining yourself with the likes of Cesar Garza."

Karina's throat constricted, and her chest tightened. She felt like a teenager caught coming in late once again. If only she could earn her mother's approval and for once, not trigger her reproach.

Karina tried to push back her shame. "I know you don't understand the choices I've made, Mamá." Karina's voice wavered slightly. "But I did what I did to survive in Juarez. Women in Aldama were disappearing by the dozens. I needed protection."

Mamá's expression seemed to soften, but disappointment lingered in her eyes. "Survival is one thing, mija." A note of sorrow colored her tone. "But at what cost to your soul? And what example are you setting for Sofia?"

Mamá's words struck a nerve. Karina knew she must deal with the consequences of her choices. But Sofia?

"What do you mean, Sofia?" Karina's voice trembled on the edge of silence, worried her sleeping younger sister might hear.

Mamá rose to tend to their breakfast in silence, as if enough had been said.

Could her mother be right? Did Karina's choice to become Cesar's lover have an impact on Sofia's worldview?

As the tension in the kitchen escalated, Emilio, who'd

been quietly sipping his coffee, set down his cup and uttered a heavy sigh.

"I can't help but feel you're unhappy, Karina." His eyes revealed his worry. "Men like Garza are never the answer."

Karina shifted uncomfortably in her seat. She knew her brother only wanted the best for her. But the nagging defiance that plagued her since grade school stirred. "I know what I'm doing. I can take care of myself."

"I don't doubt your strength, Karina," Emilio said gently. "But men like Garza are dangerous. They see what they want and take it, no matter who it hurts."

Karina bristled at her brother's comments. Her stubbornness flared. Emilio may be right, but she couldn't admit it. Couldn't admit that she'd seen Cesar at Diablos headquarters. She sat straighter and met his gaze head-on.

"Don't worry about Cesar," Karina insisted, her voice filled with defiance. "I can handle him. I've been doing it for two years."

Emilio ran his hand through his hair and exhaled.

The kitchen door creaked open. Sofia, rubbing her eyes and yawning, shuffled in. Her hair was tousled, and her pajamas were wrinkled. But when she saw her siblings, her eyes sparkled with anticipation.

"Buenos días," she said, her voice thick with sleep.

Karina's mother placed a glass of milk in front of Sofia and smiled. "Buenos días, cariño."

Sofia blinked before settling her gaze on Emilio. "What's going on?" she asked with piqued curiosity.

Emilio beamed. "Just a family discussion, hermana pequeña. Nothing for you to worry about."

"I heard you talking," Sofia said through a yawn. "Something about making the right choices. What was that about?"

"Nothing you need to worry about, *mi hija.*" Mamá's tone turned protective. "Just boring grown-up talk."

Emilio's phone buzzed in his pocket. The sudden sound cut through the tense mood and drew everyone's attention. "Hello." His eyes darted between Karina and Mamá. His expression tightened. "Where are you, Eli?" Lines rippled across his forehead.

Karina's muscles coiled like springs as she inched closer to Emilio, desperate to hear both sides of the conversation.

Her thoughts raced to Dakota. Her heart stuttered, confusing her. When had this brash American become so important? What would happen if she introduced this man, who risked his life to help children, to Mamá? Would she see his courage? Or just the danger he brought? Karina rubbed her temples, desperate to sort her feelings.

The sound of a chair scraping across the flooring jarred Karina from her thoughts. "What's happening?" said a wide-eyed Sofia.

Emilio held up a hand, signaling for them to hush as he continued to listen to Eli over the phone.

Anticipation roused Karina's heartrate.

Emilio terminated the call. "Señors Colt and Sutcliffe are in trouble," he said, his voice strained with concern. "I must go pick them up."

"I'll drive you," Karina said as cold fear formed inside her ribcage.

Mamá's eyes widened. "No, Karina, it's too dangerous." Her voice trembled with a motherly fear. "Stay here until your brother returns."

"I'm a big girl, Mamá," Karina said, standing and gathering her purse. "And it's my car."

"Can I go?" Sofia asked, her face alight with adventure.

"*No, mi hermana,*" Emilio said. "You stay here and

protect Mamá." He pulled their mother to him and kissed her forehead. "I'll take care of Karina, Mamá. She'll be fine."

Karina rushed out the door to her Audi. "I'm worried," she said as she climbed behind the wheel.

Emilio sat beside her and strapped on his seatbelt. "About Eli and Dakota?"

Karina's breath caught in her throat. "All of it." But what was *all of it*? Her family? Her soon-to-be-abandoned lifestyle? Sofia's safety? The two men who had upended her world?

Or maybe, just maybe, it was just one man in particular.

TWENTY-EIGHT

Tuesday, 8:15 PM—Aldama, Juarez City

Automatic rounds pelted the cobblestones just outside the alley's alcove. Eli reached for a flashbang grenade from his rucksack and hurled it at the pickup truck. A loud bang and bright light followed.

Eli's gaze flitted between the converging threats—the pickup with its machine gun and the two pursuers on foot closing in from behind. His mind raced for a solution. "I've got the truck. You take the two on foot," he shouted to Dakota while darting behind the rusted dumpster to shield himself from the machine gun.

Dakota's weapon erupted three times in sharp staccato bursts. One of their pursuers behind Eli cried out, "*Cuídate*," a warning not lost on anyone in the alley.

With no cover at his rear, Eli pivoted and unleashed a barrage of rounds at the shadows behind him.

A guttural boom from a single round sounded from Dakota's direction. Then, the sickening *pow-WHOP* of a bullet hitting living flesh.

A man crumpled from the shadows. His pistol clanked

and bounced on the cobblestone floor. The fading patter of soft soles hitting stone announced the surviving pursuer was retreating.

Eli turned to levy his weapon at the pickup. A stream of tracers from the truck streaked past him, whizzing like angry hornets.

Dakota emptied his clip at the truck. The machine gun turned its aim and tore through the bricks around him. An acrid whiff of gunpowder floated past Eli's nostrils as the volley of bullets assaulted Dakota's position.

Eli rose and fired a series of double taps at the muzzle flashes above the truck's cab.

The firing from the truck ceased. Eli and Dakota exchanged glances. And as if with a shared understanding, they bolted back to the alley's entrance.

No rounds followed. No sound but their ragged breaths and their boots pounding against the cobblestone.

Had they made it? Eli wanted to shout like the redeemed until a car turned into the alley.

WITH HER HEART thumping like a relentless drumbeat, and her fingers locked as a vice grip on the steering wheel, Karina pushed the Audi's performance through the winding streets of Aldama.

Beside her in the passenger seat, Emilio sat rigid. His gaze fixed on the road as he barked instructions to the location Eli Colt had pinned to Emilio over the phone. "Look for the barricade up ahead."

Karina's jaw clenched as she took a sharp turn, tires screeching against the pavement. Her eyes darted frantically between the road and the rearview mirror. "How much further?" she snapped, her voice tight with tension.

The distant sound of gunfire thundered. She gripped the wheel tighter, her knuckles whitened as she prepared for what she'd do when she got there.

They climbed a steep hill and came upon the barricade. Shots rang from inside an alley. A tremor crawled up Karina's neck. She slammed her foot on the gas, the engine roaring as they careened through the narrow passageway.

The gunfire stopped.

Emilio's hands clamped the edge of the dashboard, his eyes alive with alarm as they raced deeper toward the gunfight.

Then, they saw two figures with faces drawn with exhaustion and relief. Eli and Dakota, arms swinging, sacks jostling on their shoulders, legs pumping like machines.

Karina's heart leaped as she slammed on the brakes, the tires shrieking in protest. The Audi fishtailed, coming to a screeching halt mere inches from Eli and Dakota. They dove into the backseat, gasping as they slammed the doors behind them.

"Go, go, go!" Eli leaned his head between Karina and Emilio.

Karina shifted the transmission into reverse and floored it. The Audi lurched backward, the rear bumper barely missing the barricade as she backed out of the alley. With a quick shift into drive, she sped away, the engine growling as they merged into the evening traffic.

"Anyone hurt?" Emilio twisted in his seat, scanning Eli and Dakota.

"We're good," Dakota panted, his face glistening with sweat. "But we need to get off these streets. Fast."

Karina nodded, her eyes constantly checking the mirrors. "Where to?"

"Head downtown," Eli commanded. "We'll figure out our next move once we're clear."

The Audi ate up the miles as they sped toward the city skyline. Downtown couldn't come soon enough.

———

ELI'S FINGERS tightened on the Audi's headrest. "For heaven's sake," he muttered, the taste of failure bitter on his tongue. "We lost Ramirez."

Beside him, Dakota hissed through clenched teeth, "Yeah, and I caught a souvenir."

Eli whipped around. His partner's left sleeve was soaked crimson, blood oozing between his fingers as he clutched his arm. "For the love of— When did that happen?"

"Right before you neutralized that machine gun," Dakota groaned.

Thoughts ricocheted through Eli's head like stray bullets. Ramirez. Dakota's wound. Their cover blown. Each realization hit harder than the last.

"How bad is it?" The words tumbled out before Eli could stop them.

Dakota's face twisted, a grimace he couldn't quite hide. "It's only a scratch," he said, his voice strained.

Karina glanced back from the rearview mirror. The corners of her mouth fell. "Does he need a doctor?"

"What about a hospital?" Eli suggested, scanning Emilio and Karina for options.

Emilio shook his head. "Diablos would find him within minutes. They have spies everywhere."

"A clinic? Private doctor?" Eli pressed, desperation creeping into his voice.

"What about Mamá?" Karina interjected abruptly, her tone urgent. "She's been tending to our neighbors' ailments since I was a kid."

Eli glanced at Emilio. "Is she a nurse?"

"No," Emilio said. "She helps out where she can. Not everyone can afford a doctor in our neighborhood."

"Can she handle a gunshot wound?" Eli's stomach churned.

Dakota groaned. "Not sure we have many options here, partner."

"We could make a run for El Paso," Eli suggested, knowing how desperate it sounded.

Emilio's laugh was humorless. "Diablos will have the border bridge covered."

Options dwindled in Eli's mind like sand through an hourglass. He grasped at the last grains. "So, your mother's place?"

"No," Emilio said with finality. "I don't want to get Mamá and Sofia involved."

"I agree," Dakota said. "Get me to a place where I can rest and I'll be as good as new in a few hours."

"What about the hotel?" Eli inquired.

Emilio's face darkened. "From the information they'll sure to get from your Explorer, they're probably running down hotel guest lists as we speak."

Karina's eyes widened as if some light went off in her brain. "But they'll look for them in their room. I know a place they'll never look."

"Where?" Emilio said.

There's a storage room up there." She steeled herself with a deep breath and opened the car door. She stepped into the smoldering heat of the garage. The distant sound of a slamming car door heightened her senses.

Karina led Eli and Dakota through a maze of parked cars. She kept a safe distance, not wanting to explain to employees why she was with two Americans with one of them injured.

She reached the service elevator and jabbed the call button. The door sprang open with a sudden thrust, sending Karina a step back with a hand on her chest. Eli and Dakota stumbled inside and she followed, punching the button for the top floor.

Seconds stretched to an eternity between each passing floor. The door slid open with a soft ding, and Karina breathed a sigh of relief as they stepped out onto the top floor. They'd made it without incident, yet a nagging pressure pushed against her chest.

As they stepped to the door leading to the roof's stairway, the throbbing bass from the nightclub music pulsed through the walls. Bursts of laughter and party cheers blared through the club's foyer as she turned to Eli. "We need to pass by the guest elevators to get to the roof," she said. "You stay here until I make sure nobody is in the foyer."

She slipped through the doorway, her stomach dropping as she spotted Isabella waiting for a guest elevator. Panic struck. The door to the service entrance clicked as it closed.

Isabella turned to catch sight of Karina. Isabella's eyes narrowed, her expression unreadable. She approached with slow, deliberate steps.

A cold bead of sweat formed at Karina's hairline.

TWENTY-NINE

Tuesday, 10:17 PM, Hotel Celebracion, Juarez City

Karina's fingers tapped an erratic rhythm against the Audi's steering wheel as she scanned the hotel's garage. Beside her, Emilio sat scrolling his phone, searching for someone who could treat a gunshot wound. Behind her, Eli sat with a visibly drained and pallid Dakota, who slumped against the car door.

"He needs a doctor, now," Karina said, her stomach roiling, her voice near panic.

Eli's gaze shifted from Dakota to Karina. "I've fastened a tourniquet, but it's not helping much. The artery must be nicked."

"I may need a little help reaching the elevator," Dakota said, his voice barely audible.

Emilio raised a hand for silence, his phone pressed to his ear. "Thank you," he said, ending the call. He turned to Karina, relief evident in his voice. "I've reached a doctor who lives nearby. I can have him here in twenty minutes."

"Take the car," Karina said. "I'll get them to the rooftop.

"What brings you here." Isabella's tone bordered on insolence. "I thought you took the night off?"

Karina straightened her spine for confrontation. No time for a catfight with a rival female. "Excuse me?" Her voice was a venomous torrent. "When did I start answering to you?"

"I...uh...was just making conversation," Isabella stammered over her words as if trying to backtrack.

"Not with that tone, you weren't." Karina added an edge of authority to her inflection. "Go to the lobby bar and check for extra linens."

A puzzled frown creased Isabella's forehead. "But wouldn't they be in the storage room upstairs?"

Karina's body tensed at her mistake. She tightened her lips and pressed her fists on her hips. "Did I ask for your input?" Her tone rose as if her patience wore thin. "Follow my instructions or find another job."

A flicker of defiance flashed in Isabella's eyes. The elevator opened. Isabella hesitated, then scurried inside.

Karina waited until the elevator doors closed, then rushed back to the service entrance. Eli stood as if he'd been listening. There was blood on the side of his shirt.

Dakota sat on the floor with his back pressed against the wall.

"Let's hurry," she said as she reached to help Dakota stand. "I don't know how long before she returns." She led them to the stairs and up to the rooftop.

The door to the storage room creaked open, revealing a spacious area. Discarded furniture stacked in organized clusters and dusty brown boxes formed tall towers.

Eli helped Dakota onto a slightly worn burgundy couch. His face was ashen and drawn with pain. Karina's stomach swirled into a bubbling cocktail of nervous energy. How much time did he have before Emilio arrived?

Eli unwrapped the makeshift bandage, revealing the extent of Dakota's injury. The sight of his blood-soaked arm made Karina wince.

His eyes fluttered, and his body went limp. Karina leaned over him and placed a hand on his forehead, feeling a fever beneath her fingertips.

"We need to do something," Karina said, her voice shaking. "I can't just stand here and watch him die."

"It's just his arm, but I can't stop the bleeding. Can you get me something I can use for a better bandage?"

Karina searched throughout the storage room, finding the stack of linens Isabella mentioned. She grabbed a few from the top and tore them into strips.

The entrance door rattled. Someone was trying to get inside.

Karina's shakily stepped to the door.

Eli moved with silent urgency, dragging Dakota behind a stack of dusty crates and boxes.

"Who is it?" Karina gasped, her trembling hand hovering inches over the handle. What if it was Isabella, ignoring her instructions to go to the lobby bar? Or worse, what if it was hotel security alerted by an unseen security camera?

Karina buried her fear and grasped the door handle. "Who is it?" she said in an irritable tone.

"Karina, it's me." Karina's fear melted at the sound of her brother's voice. She swung open the door to find Emilio sporting a reassuring grin, relief flooding through her that he'd found the location she'd hastily texted him earlier.

"Why are you back so soon? You're supposed to bring back a doctor."

Emilio stepped to one side to reveal a short, balding man in a blue sports coat carrying a medical bag.

"This is Dr. Avila. He was waiting outside his home."

"*Buenos dias*," Dr. Avila said as he scanned the room. "*El paciente?*"

Karina's heart brimmed with elation. "It's alright, Eli. It's Emilio and he's brought a doctor."

Eli appeared from behind the boxes. "So soon?"

Dr. Avila rushed to Dakota and wasted no time in assessing his condition. "I need to get him horizontal and elevate this arm."

Karina dashed to the far end of the storage room, where she'd stored the fifty-foot red runner used for photo ops at the hotel's lavish gala dinners. "Help me!" she cried to Emilio and Eli.

The two men dragged the six-foot wide folded carpet to an area tucked out of sight from the entrance. They then rested Emilio gently, his blood darkening the rug's crimson surface.

"I need more light," Dr. Aliva said.

Eli rummaged through his bag and retrieved a small flashlight, its bright beam cutting through the darkness to illuminate Dakota's blood-soaked arm.

"Gracias." Dr. Aliva nodded. But his expression turned grave as he examined the wound more closely. "With all this bleeding, I'm sure he's nicked his brachial artery. He needs to be taken to an emergency room."

"Like I've already told you, amigo," Emilio said. "Our situation won't allow us to bring him to a hospital. Is there anything else you can do?"

Karina's optimism crumbled. She caught Emilio's eye, then Eli's.

From his bag, the doctor clutched two glimmering stainless-steel instruments. One, a scissor-like tool about six inches long, with a pair of slender, curved jaws at the ends. The other, a simple handle with a simple blade—a scalpel.

For five breathless minutes, the doctor worked on cutting tissue and positioning his clamping tool. Finally, he sat straighter, brushing a handkerchief across his brow. "That should stop the bleeding temporarily. I'll need to cauterize the artery to make this mend permanent."

"What do you need," Eli asked.

"A cautery pen," Aliva stood and pulled a notepad from his jacket. "Simple procedure really."

"Where can we get it?" Emilio stepped to Dakota inspecting the doctor's work.

"I have an associate who is discreet." Dr. Aliva scribbled on a notepad. "He owns a medical supply store nearby, and lives upstairs," he said, tearing away the paper and handing it to Emilio. "I'll call ahead to let him know what I need. Go to this address and I'll have him waiting for you."

Karina's fingers twisted the fabric of her shirt as the doctor's concerned gaze settled on Dakota's pale form.

Dr. Aliva studied his surroundings. "This is not the best place for the procedure, and I'm not sure that clamp will stem the blood flow for long. You best hurry back."

"Let's go," Eli said as he grabbed Emilio's arm and rushed him to the door.

They disappeared beyond the storehouse entrance. Karina turned her gaze to the doctor who leaned over Dakota as if assessing his work. "Let's pray your brother and his friend get back soon. This man has lost plenty of blood already."

Time slowed to a torturous crawl. How long would it take for Emilio and Eli to return with the instrument?

A low groan escaped Dakota's lips, shaking Karina from

her thoughts. "Dakota," she whispered in a low, almost loving tone. "Hang on. Just, hang on."

Clutching his hand with a desperate grip, her eyes lingered on his still form. Fear gnawed at her insides, a sinking sensation that his life was slipping away as his chest rose and fell.

THIRTY

As Eli steered the Audi out of the hotel parking lot into the hectic traffic, its chaotic flow mirrored the storm raging within him. Emilio sat beside him, a stalwart presence amid Eli's internal crisis.

Memories of Aziz, the young Afghan boy whose death tormented Eli's sleep. The narrow Afghan alley. The sickening sight of Aziz's small frame—his eyes glassy and vacant, his throat open in a crimson slit. Would Dakota be the latest of Eli's failures—another friend's life coming to an end?

If he'd struggled to forgive himself for Aziz—how would Eli ever forgive himself for bringing Dakota on this impossible mission? Eli was injured. Damaged. Not himself. The dizziness and memory lapses from his recent head injury should have been enough to send him home. But Eli had pushed on, convinced he could handle it. Now Dakota was paying the price for his stubbornness.

"You seemed lost in your thoughts?" Emilio's voice cut through Eli's self-degradation.

Eli sighed, grappling for words to express his remorse. "It's about a boy who died in Afghanistan and me not saving him," he confessed. "Aziz was just a kid who sold DVDs from a booth at the base every Wednesday. And every Wednesday I'd pull out my baseball and gloves and we'd play catch. But then I saw him in a small village..." Eli's voice trailed off, his guilt returning. "Now, seeing Dakota so close to death..." He sighed, then gazed at Emilio. "I came here to ease the hurt of my past sins. Now Dakota's life hangs in the balance."

"So, you feel responsible for bringing Dakota into this?"

"Sure. Wouldn't you?"

"You had to talk him into coming to Juarez?" Emilio asked.

"No. It's not that," Eli asserted. "Dakota is one of the bravest men I've ever known, and that's coming from an ex-ranger, trained as an elite light infantryman. But with the injury I suffered in Study Butte, I should have insisted we go home."

"And who would have saved me in the desert, my friend?" Emilio's words were soft but firm.

Eli shrugged with uncertainty. "I don't know?"

Emilio smiled gently. "We all must confront our past in our own way, Eli. I suspect your journey is Christ-centered, but I also suspect it hasn't reached the level of Christ-surrendered." Emilio pointed to an available parking spot. "Pull the car up here by the corner."

Eli parked the Audi with a swirl of conflicting emotions. "I'm not sure either," he admitted, his voice almost under his breath.

Emilio's expression softened with understanding. "No one's past is perfect. After my father's murder, I was consumed by fear. I ran, Eli. I ran as fast and as far as I could, leaving behind my family, my responsibilities, everything I held dear. I thought I could escape my own guilt, by drowning my demons in drugs," Emilio continued, his voice filled with regret. "But all I found was emptiness. A hollow existence that left me more broken than ever before."

Emilio's voice softened. "There was this girl, Maria, at the compound where you rescued me." His shoulders tensing as if he'd lost a good friend. "She reminded me so much of Karina at that age—fierce, scared, but with a spark of hope in her eyes. When I saw her there, caged like an animal, I felt a surge of protective anger I hadn't experienced since..." He swallowed hard, his Adam's apple flexing. "In that moment, I felt God confirming my calling. I whispered to her that help was coming..." he fixed his eyes on Eli, "that you were coming and that she needed to stay strong." His eyes dampened. "In that moment, I wasn't just trying to comfort her—I was trying to save the young Karina I couldn't protect years ago." He wiped his eyes. "It hit me then, Eli. This is where God has me. To show these children there's hope coming. And show Karina too."

Emilio's expression brightened slightly. "God's mercy is greater than any guilt we can carry. Our mistakes don't define us, Eli. God's mercy and grace do." Emilio opened the door. "I'll be right back." He bolted across the street to the medical supply center.

Something stirred inside Eli. The weight of his guilt seemed to lift, if for only a moment. Then he remembered Lindsey's sharing a scripture soon after he'd started Redemption Rescue. He opened his Bible app and scrolled to Proverbs 3 where a verse seemed to leap off the screen.

"Trust in the Lord with all your heart and lean not on your

own understanding; in all your ways submit to him, and he
will make your paths straight."

ELI SHOOK HIS HEAD. His military training and
experiences were his cornerstone, his way of controlling the
unpredictable. But now, with his body betraying him and
his decisions endangering others, that foundation seemed to
be crumbling. What was left when all he knew failed to
steer him through the twists and turns of this dangerous
profession? Could he surrender like Emilio said?

With trembling lips, he repeated the words on the page
over and over, memorizing them as if they were part of a
battle plan. And in that moment, a supernatural peace
warmed him from the inside.

He whispered those words once more, repeating the
simple instructions from a king, "Trust in the Lord with all
your heart."

THIRTY-ONE

Wednesday, 1:15 AM, Hotel Celebracion Rooftop, Juarez City

A faint tingling, like tiny pinpricks, crept up and down Karina's thigh. Adjusting her position ever so gently on the folded red runner spread across the storehouse's floor. She took care not to disturb Dakota, whose head rested on her lap.

Dr. Aliva knelt beside her on the mound of carpet, under the faint glow of sunlight filtering in through a skylight. He peeked at the wound and the clamp that staunched the blood flow. "We've kept the bleeding to a minimum, and he seems to be resting comfortably," Dr. Aliva said, breaking a long silence. "If your brother returns soon with the cautery pen, this young man should make a full recovery."

Karina glanced at Dakota's pale, peaceful face. "I feel so helpless. Is there anything I can do?"

The doctor's eyes drifted upwards as if he considered her question. "If he survives, he'll need to replace that lost blood. I can't give him transfusions so, you'll need to give him proper nourishment for blood regeneration."

"*Proper nourishment?*"

"Iron-rich foods like red meat and fish. Beans and raisins are good too. They need to be cut in small sections for easy digestion."

Karina nodded, grateful for the distraction. "There's a kitchen in the nightclub one floor down."

"Excellent. Get plenty of water and fruit juices for hydration too," Dr. Aliva said.

Karina replaced her leg with a pillow to support Dakota's head. Then she searched the storage room for something to carry the food.

She must hurry. Another hour and the nightclub's staff would be buzzing in the kitchen like angry wasps.

Two minutes later, with an empty tote bag slung over her shoulder, Karina slipped into the empty nightclub and hurried to the kitchen. The near-silent hum of appliances offered a vivid distinction to the nightly chaos of sizzling pans, clattering dishes, and frantic cooks.

Karina hurried past abandoned workstations and the lingering smells of grilled meats and exotic spices, remnants of the kitchen's late-night frenzy. Inside the refrigerator, she discovered an array of leftover fish and beef fillets, in the pantry—bottled water and fruit juices.

Distant murmurs too low to distinguish drifted into the kitchen from the nightclub. The voices grew closer and closer and solidified into recognizable tones—Cesar in a loud authoritative cadence speaking to someone else. Was it Raul who remained in silent submission? Or maybe Isabella. Karina narrowed her eyes and perked her ears, eager to hear their every word.

Something inside her said, "Stay hidden." Her heart seized. She turned off the light in the pantry.

The clickety-clop of footfalls on tiled floors signaled two people had entered the kitchen.

"Things don't always go as planned. You know this." The chilling voice of *La Serpiente* sparked an inferno of fear that seared Karina's core.

"But they shouldn't unravel like a cheap suit." Frustration seethed beneath Cesar's tone. "I can't afford these setbacks."

"I understand, *Patron*. It won't happen again."

Patron? Did La Serpiente just call Cesar his boss?

"Now, let's talk about Isabella," Cesar said. "I have a buyer. But he wants to take delivery in El Paso. Who can you send, your brother?"

"No, not Hector," *La Serpiente* said. "I need him to take care of the gringos."

"Gringos?"

"*Si*. We found two gringos outside our offices in Aldama."

"Why didn't you just kill them?"

"We tried, but they got away."

"How?" Cesar's tone flared with a scalding fury. "First, you lose the compound in Texas? Now you have Americans sniffing around your headquarters?"

Karina's breath caught, almost prompting an involuntary shudder. This confirms Diablos knew Dakota and Eli were in Juarez.

"It's only a temporary setback, Patron," Ramirez said in a submissive tone. "We'll find these gringos. We think we hit one. We have our men at all the hospitals and clinics."

"Who are these gringos?" Cesar's voice settled to an angry growl. "DEA? FBI?"

"I don't think so. Maybe mercenaries," La Serpiente said. "They're well-trained and well-armed."

"I don't need this, Carlos. I'm on the verge of selling Isabella to a very powerful American Senator from California."

"I thought she was for your friend in Los Angeles?" Ramirez said. "Why the change?"

"I need the political clout. You losing that compound in Texas has me worried."

"The border is open, Patron," Ramirez said with an air of confidence. "The desert is massive, and opportunities for new routes are unlimited. You don't need political clout from the gringos."

"Don't tell me what I need or don't need, Carlos." Absolute authority threaded through Cesar's words. "I want to triple the profits in our trafficking enterprise to America this year."

A pause lingered for several seconds, pregnant with an unspoken incrimination. Karina's mind struggled with the unthinkable. Ramirez took orders from Cesar.

"We need to address this gringo problem quickly," Cesar said. "I can't afford the stink of child trafficking to land on me. Not when I'm about to land a connection in the gringos' capital city. Anything on the preacher?"

"Nothing from the streets. He's a popular figure in Juarez. The people love him. They call him, '*Santo de las Calles.*'"

"I don't care what they call him. Find him."

Karina clutched the wall for support, her hidden corner providing no shelter from Cesar's cruel words.

"I remember his father," Cesar said. "He was a policeman who wouldn't take my money or heed my threats. He was a problem too and vowed to stop me. A problem is like an infection, Carlos. You let it persist, and it will spread." Cesar paused for several seconds. "If I let this *Santo de las Calles* persist, that policeman's son could give this city hope. And where there's hope, people resist."

Ramirez cleared his throat. "What do you want me to do?"

"The same thing I did with his father. Kill him."

The news hit her chest like a dagger, and cut clear to her heart. Cesar killed Papa?

Her mother was right. Karina was a *puta* who'd sold her soul for the safety of this killer's bed. The same killer who'd murdered her father, and now wanted her brother dead.

She took a steadying breath to ease her frantic heartbeat.

Her brother would be returning with Eli soon.

Where did that leave her mother and Sofia?

The murderous world she sought to escape had, once again, ensnared her.

KARINA WAITED thirty minutes after Cesar and Ramirez had left the kitchen. She stepped into the dimly lit club and scurried toward the stairway that led to the rooftop. But the guest elevator opened abruptly and Cesar stood inside.

She forced a smile to her lips, but it felt brittle, like glass on the verge of shattering. The weight of the tote bag over her shoulder felt heavier.

"*Mi amor,*" Cesar's voice sliced through the silence. His scrutinizing gaze pierced through her as he stepped out of the elevator. "How long have you been up here?"

Panic gripped her by the throat. "Not long." She struggled not to stammer. "I just came to grab a few things from the kitchen for my mother and sister. I didn't want to disturb the staff during the busy hours."

"I seemed to have left my appointment book in the kitchen," he said smoothly, his eyes never leaving hers. "Wait here, I'll ride down with you."

Karina didn't want to wait. She couldn't bear to face Cesar, knowing the darkness that lurked behind his charm. He'd killed her father. He'd just ordered Emilio's murder. A thought crossed her mind, fleeting yet tantalizing—she could use the knife she'd tucked away in the tote bag to kill Cesar. She pushed the thought away. Her hands trembled.

Cesar's eyes bore into her when he returned. "I heard you talked to two Americans in the lobby bar yesterday. What was that about?"

Fear roiled in the pit of Karina's stomach, but she met his gaze with feigned innocence. "They met my brother in El Paso. He asked me to take care of them once they arrived."

He regarded her with an unreadable expression. "And where is your brother these days?"

The elevator descended. The continuous thrum amplified the tension in the confined space. "I wouldn't know. We don't speak."

Just as Karina began to feel the walls closing in, Cesar's stern expression softened, and he sighed. "Uh, I get it. He's full of righteous indignation. Am I right?"

"Something like that."

Cesar nodded, his gaze lingered on her for a moment longer after the elevator doors opened on her floor. "You must be careful talking with Americans, my love. With Diablos all over the city, they may take your hospitality the wrong way."

"I didn't know being nice to tourists was a bad thing. After all, they're hotel guests."

"Just be more careful in the future. I wouldn't want to lose you."

Karina nodded, holding strong to her façade. The elevator doors opened on her floor. She kissed Cesar on his cheek before stepping into the hallway. "See you tonight?" she asked as if nothing was out of the ordinary.

"We'll see. I have to tend to some business quickly. An emergency at one of the plants."

"Oh no. I hope everything is all right."

"Nothing to worry about. These things have a way of working themselves out."

The elevator door closed. Karina let out a shaky breath, her pretense crumbling in the solitude of the hallway. She knew what she had to do—contact Emilio immediately to protect him from Cesar's wrath.

PART 3

THIRTY-TWO

Wednesday, 2:45 AM, Hotel Celebracion Rooftop Storeroom, Juarez City

Eli's phone buzzed with a text from Karina. "Coast clear. Come up now." He and Emilio made their way from the garage to the service stairs, up to the rooftop storage room. Eli paused, pressed his ear against the metal door, and listened. Nothing. He edged his way through the storeroom entrance, his eyes immediately seeking out Dakota.

His partner appeared wilted—a mere form draped across the mound of carpet stacked in the corner. Dakota's face was deathly pale, his skin waxy under a sheen of sweat. A sudden vertigo gripped Eli. How close had he come to losing his partner?

Eli crossed the room in a few long strides and leaned over Dakota. "Hey, partner," he said, his voice tight with contained dread. "How you holding up?"

Dakota managed a weak smile. His eyes were glossy and unfocused. "I've had worse paper cuts," he gasped through a wheeze. "Stop this leak in my arm, and I'll be ready to mount up in an hour or two."

Emilio passed the medical supplies to Aliva. He drenched a strategically positioned cart from a large plastic bottle, the sterile scent of alcohol overpowering the iron-heavy smell.

Dr. Aliva patted Eli's shoulder with a blue-gloved hand. "Let's stop this bleeding, shall we?" He unwrapped an IV catheter, swabbed the crook of Dakota's good arm with anti-septic, and inserted a needle into a protruding vein. He connected the IV line to a bag of solution, hanging it from a coat rack nearby.

Eli joined Emilio and Karina a few steps away. He glanced at Karina. "How's he doing?" he asked through a constricted throat, the words barely finding air.

"He's been in and out since you left three hours ago," Karina whispered with unmistakable concern. "I managed to get some food for his recovery. And I've learned some things you both should know."

After extending Dakota's wounded arm, Dr. Aliva applied a solution around the wound and probed the area using a flashlight and straight, thin forceps.

Eli leaned closer to Karina, but he kept his gaze on Dakota. "What is it?"

"Cesar Garza," Karina's voice wavered with a slight tremor. "He's the real leader of Diablos. Not Ramirez."

"Where did you hear this?" Emilio blurted like he'd been struck in the gut.

"I overheard them in the kitchen while gathering the food." She paused to draw a shuttered breath. "And just as we suspected, they know you and Dakota are in Juarez and have a room at this hotel."

A muscle ticked in Eli's jaw as he processed the new information.

Without looking, Dr. Aliva grasped a scalpel from the

cart, its stainless steel glinting under the dim light. "This is the tricky part."

Eli stood taller for a clearer view. "This Cesar Garza; he's supposed to be legitimate, right?"

Blood oozed slowly from Dakota's arm.

"Yes," Karina said. "But Dakota and I saw him in Aldama when you were rescuing Emilio in the desert."

"Anything else?" he said, hoping for better news.

Karina chewed at her lip. "There's a girl who works here, Isabella. Cesar is..." Her expression twisted in disgust. "He's selling her to an American senator."

Aliva left the forceps in Dakota's bicep and gripped the cauterizing pen in the cradle of his hand. A sharp hiss accompanied the heated tip touching tissue. Wisps of smoke spiraled upward.

Eli's focus hovered somewhere between Dakota and the gears in his brain assessing the new information. "Where's this Cesar Garza's office?"

"Here in the hotel," Karina said with wide eyes focused on Dakota. "On the fourth floor."

"And security?" Eli asked.

"No more than what you've already seen," Karina said. "Cesar feels safe here."

"He's stable for now," Aliva said as he stitched the wound. "I've cauterized the nicked artery and stopped the bleeding."

Eli gazed at his partner. Dakota's chest rose and fell in a steady rhythm.

"He'll sleep for a while. The IV will help replace fluids and stabilize him." Aliva began packing his bag and glanced at Karina. "Keep the wound clean and get that food down him when he wakes up. He should be good as new in a few days."

Eli exhaled, his chest easing with an internal prayer of thanks. Then, he returned his attention to Karina and Emilio and sharpened his eyes with purpose. "If Garza is a businessman, businessmen keep records. And his records may contain incriminating evidence. Documents. Transactions. Maybe even a ledger that records his trafficking activities."

Emilio's forehead furrowed over eyes that questioned. "Are you planning on breaking into his office?"

"I am," Eli said as he weighed the risks against the potential payoff. They needed hard evidence to bring down Garza and Diablos. An idea began to form.

Karina lifted a hand to her mouth. "What if you're caught?"

"It's a risk, sure." Eli stood a little straighter. "But Dakota and I didn't come here to sightsee. We came here to gather intel on Diablos. Now you tell me that this Garza is a silent partner of the cartel, and his office is in this building." Eli allowed a smile to spread to his temples. They'd already made progress—rescuing Emilio, gathering intel on the Diablos' operation, and now this lead on Garza. Each step brought them closer to their goal. "We take him down. We're on our way to taking the whole operation down."

"But what if you're caught?" Karina said. "Garza is powerful, and has connections everywhere. If he finds out what you're doing..."Fear flickered across Karina's delicate features before she continued. "There's more," she glanced at her bother, "Cesar is looking for Emilio. He wants him dead."

Emilio's eyes widened, but he quickly composed himself. "All the more reason to act fast," he said, his voice steady despite the news.

Eli held up a hand. "I know the risks, Karina. Believe

me, I know." His gaze shifted to Dakota sleeping. "But those girls I left behind at the compound and the ones from Honduras, and this Isabella, the one who works here. Garza's selling them like cattle..." He shook his head. "He can't be allowed to go on doing that."

Emilio reached his arm around Karina's shoulder. "Eli's right. If we can get proof of Garza's involvement, proof that he's been pulling the strings all along..."

"Then we can bring his whole operation crashing down," Eli finished Emilio's sentence with grim conviction. "I need to know everything about Garza's office. Security measures, schedules, anything that could help me get in and out undetected."

Karina swallowed hard. She stared at her brother. A silent understanding seemed to pass between them.

"Alright," she said softly as if the word was pulled from her mouth. "I'll tell you what I know."

Eli nodded as Karina laid out the details of Garza's office. She described the layout, the security cameras' blind spots, and the cleaning staff's schedule. As she spoke, a plan began to take shape in Eli's mind. He'd need a disguise, a way to bypass the electronic locks, and a quick escape route. It was risky, but with Karina's inside knowledge, it just might work.

"Okay," Eli said, his voice low and determined. "Here's what we're going to do..."

His gaze drifted back to Dakota's sleeping form, another casualty of this war. Would he be the last?

THIRTY-THREE

Wednesday, 8:45 AM—Hotel Celebracion, Rooftop Storeroom

Eli stood erect as Karina inspected his outfit. The jacket pinched his shoulders. The pants sagged at his waist. But despite the ill-fitting suit Karina had taken from Garza's wardrobe, Eli was slightly more comfortable he looked the part.

"It's the closest thing I could find that matches what Emilio said Cesar's wearing."

Eli nodded. Emilio had been holed up in the hotel parking lot all morning, just to describe to Karina what Garza wore to work.

Karina's phone buzzed. "It's Emilio. Cesar just left with his entourage."

"How long do you think I have before Garza returns?" Eli mentally reviewed the next step of his plan.

"No telling. But I wouldn't waste any time. He comes and goes quite frequently."

The warning in her tone was clear. Eli stuffed his Glock

tucked in its pancake holster into the back of his trousers. The added bulk helped anchor the loose fabric.

He peered outside onto the rooftop, ready to step into the lion's den. "Say a prayer that my pants don't fall down."

Eli hastened down the steps to the guest elevator, on the top floor. Certain that the cartel had caught wind of his recent notoriety in El Paso, he lowered his head before pressing the call button. With a soft lull, the elevator doors parted, revealing an empty carriage. A sigh of relief escaped his lungs.

The elevator halted at the eighth floor with an agonizing ding. Eli tensed. The doors slid open, revealing a middle-aged man with a slight paunch, clad in khakis and a loud Hawaiian shirt, sporting a dark mustache that curled at the ends. "*Buenos días,*" the man said, his eyes alight with recognition.

Eli returned the smile but said nothing, unwilling to give away his accent.

"*Te conozco,*" the man persisted, his gaze fixed on Eli.

Eli shrugged his ignorance. "I don't understand."

"Do I know you," the man tried again, switching to English.

"Walt Garrison," Eli said, extending his hand. "I'm in farming equipment."

The man took his hand, but his eyes remained suspicious.

"Arrived late last night. Any lunch recommendations?" Eli inquired casually.

"*La Casona*. Americans love it." A hint of disgust tinged the man's tone.

"Gracias," Eli nodded gratefully. The elevator descended to the lobby. Eli bolted for the men's room, where he waited several minutes, ensuring the man with the mustache hadn't followed. With nonchalance, he strolled back to the elevator and hit the call button.

Two minutes later, he strolled the fifth-floor hallway, it didn't take Eli long to spot what he sought. Tucked around a corner, adjacent to a room with its door ajar, was a maid's cart. Clipped to the cart's handle was his prize—a passkey that would grant him access to any room in the hotel.

Eli found the stairway and walked down to the fourth floor. Following Karina's directions, he navigated the hallway to Garza's office. He knocked on its door softly, then louder. No response. With a swipe of the key card, the lock clicked open. He entered the dimly lit room.

The room smelled of expensive leather and cigar smoke. It took a moment for Eli's eyes to adjust to the darkness. He surveyed the space more out of curiosity than necessity. Garza's desk stood as a centerpiece, adorned with intricate Aztec carvings. Photos of Garza's family stood to one side, a closed laptop to the other.

Eli sat on the plush chair, methodically opening drawers in search of intel. All were unlocked except the one at the center. He pulled his lock picks from a jacket pocket and within five seconds had the drawer open.

From inside, Eli pulled a bound book filled with several printed pages in ledger form. The headers and columns were a maze of Spanish—labels and symbols, numbers, and handwritten notes on the side.

The unfamiliar language obscured the details, but the layout and the sheer volume of entries told him it whatever it recorded had to be important.

Eli pulled his phone and tapped its camera, its flashes highlighting every detail from every page. A sudden knock at the door shattered the silence. Eli's heart seized.

Finished, he replaced the ledger and retreated to the bathroom, his hand instinctively reaching for his Glock. Eli's muscles tensed like coiled springs, as he stood motionless in the shadow of the bathroom door.

The office door swung open to a splash of light. The man with the curled mustache entered. "*Patron?*"

Eli took a deep breath and held it. He clutched his Glock's handle.

"*Patron? Estás aquí?*" The man entered.

Recognizing the potential intelligence value, Eli turned on his phone's recorder.

"*Creo que acabo de ver a uno de los hombres que estamos buscando. Jefe?*" The man stepped to the desk and hesitated. Then looked toward the bathroom. "*Patron? Estás aquí?*"

The man stepped toward Eli as if sensing something was wrong.

Eli raised his weapon.

KARINA'S FINGERS traced the edge of the red-runner carpet, her gaze drawn to Dakota's sleeping form. His steady breathing lifted the fabric of his shirt. His pale cheeks now a healthier hue. With a contented sigh, she settled into the chair beside him.

Dakota's curls fell across his forehead, and Karina's hand twitched with the urge to brush them aside. She coiled her fingers into her palm, resisting. There was something about him that awakened a yearning she'd long forgotten, both thrilling and terrifying. His unwavering commitment to helping the vulnerable, even at his own expense, stirred something deep within her.

The difference between Dakota and Cesar slammed into her consciousness. Where Garza was aloof and indifferent, Dakota radiated warmth.

Dakota stirred. A low moan escaped his lips as his eyes fluttered open and fixated on her.

Karina's heart leaped. Laughter bubbled up and escaped through her lips. "Dakota! You're awake!" Heat rushed to her cheeks. Her yes filled with moisture.

Dakota flashed her a lopsided grin. "How long have I been horizontal?" His voice rasped, thick with sleep. He pushed himself up by his good elbow, wincing as he moved.

Karina's hand shot out, gently pressing against his chest. "Oh no, you don't. You've lost too much blood." Her tone offered no room for debate. "Doctor's orders. You need to rest."

"I'm fine, Karina. Really. I've got to—"

"You've got to rest and let yourself heal." Karina softened her expression and lifted her hand from his chest. "Please, Dakota. Let me take care of you."

Something flickered in his eyes. He sunk back onto the carpet with a sigh, grimacing as he tried to find a comfortable position. "Alright, alright. You win." The hint of a smile tugged at the corners of his mouth.

Karina fluffed a pillow and slid it beneath his neck. "Are you hungry?"

"Starved." He rubbed his belly. "What's on the menu?"

"The doctor wants you eating red meat or fish. Which do you prefer?"

"Meat any way you got it. I'm dying for a cheeseburger."

Karina shook her head in mock exasperation. "I've got some medium rare steak. I'm afraid it's a little cold."

"You're talking to a bachelor. Half my meals are cold."

Heat blossomed in Karina's chest. "So no one cooks for you back in Louisiana?" she asked, aiming for a casual tone.

"Only my microwave and the neighborhood diner."

She stood up to serve his food. "No one special waiting for you back home?"

"Why?"

She shrugged and looked away. "Just curious. We've been through so much, yet I know so little about you."

"But I know a little about you," he said as his brow lifted. "Señor Garza, yes?"

"Señor Garza, no," Karina said, almost scolding. "You were out of it when I told the others. Cesar is the real leader of Diablos."

"No way."

"Si. I overheard him talking with Carlos Ramirez yesterday."

Dakota's eyes scanned the room. Lines formed across his forehead. "Where is everybody? Where's Eli?"

Karina peeked at her watch. "He's breaking into Cesar's office to see what he can learn." She glanced over her shoulder at the door. "But he should be back by now."

Her phone buzzed in her pocket. A text from Emilio flashed across the screen.

"Cesar's back," she said, her tone clipped with alarm. "His car just dropped him off."

IN GARZA'S OFFICE BATHROOM, Eli's palm slicked the Glock's grip. The mustached man drew closer, craning his neck.

"*Patron? Estás ahí dentro?*" His hand disappeared into his leather jacket.

Eli slipped his finger inside the trigger guard. The cool metal felt solid. Powerful. He steadied his breathing to steady his heart rate.

The footsteps ticked within three feet of the bathroom. The man's shadow darkened its doorway, accompanied by the erratic rhythm of the man's breathing.

Eli's trigger finger twitched. His pulse thundered. One shot—would it bring the whole hotel down on him before he reached the roof?

The man's hand emerged from his jacket. Eli fixed his aim at the man's heart.

A blue glow lit the man's face. Not a gun—a phone. "Hola."

Eli stopped breathing.

The man's brow shot up. *"Si. Enseguida."* He turned and hurried from the office.

Tension drained from Eli's shoulders. He closed his eyes, let out a shuttering sigh, and stood still for a moment, daring to believe in supernatural involvement.

One heartbeat passed, then two, then three. With quick, silent steps, he made his way to the door, pressing his ear against the smooth, cool surface. He strained to hear any sound, any indication that the man with the mustache might return. But the office remained still and quiet.

Eli cracked the door open, peering out into the hallway. The elevator doors at the end of the corridor were just sliding closed. He glanced toward the stairway, weighing his options, but the sudden whoosh of an ascending carriage made the decision for him.

The floor numbers above the brass doors blink upward —2... 3... 4... Adrenaline rushed through Eli's veins. The numbers came to a stop with a soft ding and the door slid open. Time seemed to slow as a shoe crossed the elevator's metal threshold. Eli's leveled his Glock and said a silent prayer.

A figure stepped fully into the hallway, revealing the last person Eli expected to see.

THIRTY-FOUR

Wednesday, 9:30 AM, Somewhere in the Chihuahuan Desert

Maria's chest relaxed to the sound of American voices outside the door of her prison. Hope flared—but her knotted muscles and empty belly testified of her cruel captivity.

Mamá's face, pinched with worry, flickered through Maria's mind. A stab of longing, sharp as a blade. Had her parents found her? Sent help? Or were these Emilio's promised Americans? Hope whispered, dangerous and sweet. Maria's heart ached to believe. Too sweet a possibility in a world that had turned so bitter.

She pressed her back against the cold metal bars, fingers absently rubbing the dirt-smudged hem of her jeans. If a rescue were at hand, wouldn't the clangor of gunfire, the chaos of a raid, the frantic cries of a defeated cartel have reached her by now? The voices grew silent—another form of torment, a void where she'd hoped relief would flow but didn't.

Then a familiar voice, speaking broken English, joined the Americans—Hector Ramirez. Maria's faith shriveled as quickly as it'd grown. Why did she allow herself to dream of salvation? Her captors' grip on her was like iron—tight and merciless. Overtaking them wasn't possible without a battle —a battle that clearly wasn't happening.

Maria glanced at the other girls in the room. Ana, the quiet one with haunted eyes, huddled in the corner of her cage. Tatiana, barely thirteen, silently wept into her hands. Their eyes met in collective mourning. Like Jonah, they remained in the belly of the whale that had no intention of spitting them out. At least not in a place of God's choosing.

Maria edged away from the bars, retreating to the back of her cage. The shadows beneath the door held no promise of deliverance, only more heartache. Despair settled back over her, heavy and suffocating.

The door swung open. Three figures silhouetted against a harsh light that forced Maria to squint.

As her eyes adjusted, she could make out two men, dressed like they'd come from an outdoor adventure— one maybe twenty, the other in his thirties, both unfamiliar. The younger man's gaze scanned the room before resting on Maria. He sauntered to her cage and stooped over. "Well, hello there."

His face—a boy's. Eighteen? Nineteen? But those eyes. Hard. Cold. Hungry. They crawled over her, leaving slime trails. Maria's skin shriveled, trying to hide from that familiar leer. The bodega flashed back—rough hands, bruising grips. The trunk's darkness swallowing her screams.

Maria pressed her nose between her knees, trying to quell the rising panic. But her heart sank like an anchor.

"Open the cages," Hector barked. The sound of foot-steps, heavy and purposeful, was followed by the clanging of metal doors wrenched open.

"Let's go. Let's go," Hector boomed, his command bouncing off the walls. "Out of the cages. Vamos."

The musky smell of desperate sweat mingled with the room's moldy odor. The clinging of shackles tethered them together as her captors forced her and her fellow prisoners into a single line.

Maria shuffled outside the compound with the others, to a raggedy bus that was covered in desert dust. She sat in the middle as the final girl boarded. Then the bus lurched with a raucous roar, the sudden motion snapped Maria's head back.

As the bus bumped along the desolate road, Maria strained to catch the conversation between Hector and the Americans. They were huddled at the front of the bus, but snatches of their words drifted back to her on stale air.

"...new place...this one is compromised..." Hector's voice was clipped and harsh.

"...a street preacher...so what?" The American's tone was indifferent.

The conversation made Maria's stomach twist. They talked about Emilio's execution.

As the barren landscape slid past the dirt-streaked windows, Maria retreated inward, her mind spinning into a future she couldn't comprehend. With each mile, the distance between the life she'd known—the girl she'd been— seemed to get farther and farther from her family.

Grim possibilities reeled in her brain—being trapped in a dingy room, her body no longer her own, subject to the lusts of strange men, the stench of sweat, and rough hands pawing her flesh.

A thousand horrors played out, each worse than the last. Would she lose control of her body, be forced into slavery, her spirit constantly attacked by her captors?

The dreams she'd once cherished of getting married and raising a family were now foolish fantasies, fragile hopes that would soon wither and die. What chance did she have against the Diablos traffickers and men who saw her as temporary pleasure?

But she'd survived this far, through horrors that should have broken her. She'd endured, and she would continue to endure, to fight, to hold fast to Jesus. In the end, even with Emilio gone, she still had her faith and the hope of seeing her family again—her father, poor but strong, her loving mother, her little brother worried about his big sister. She must guard her faith with prayer, for her and her family.

The bus lurched to a halt with a hiss, the sudden stop jarring Maria after endless minutes of motion. She blinked. Around her, the other girls stirred. Ana's face was a mask of quiet resignation, while Katiana's eyes darted frantically, searching for an escape. Maria reached out and squeezed Katiana's hand, offering what little comfort she could. Floodlights illuminated their faces. Faces that mirrored the same fear and curiosity that swirled in her own belly.

The bus door folded open. Hot air rushed in.

"Everybody out!" Hector screamed. The chains around her ankles rattled as she stumbled down the steps into the darkness. The cold asphalt of a parking lot that stretched out before Maria scratched against her bare feet. A hulking structure loomed ahead. A sharp pungent odor assaulted her nostrils. A white plume of smoke billowed from a brick smokestack on the building's rooftop.

A shadow emerged from the bright lights—a man, tall and broad-shouldered, his features obscured by the night. He raised a hand in greeting. Maria's throat tightened.

The girl behind Maria let out a whisper. Maria reached back and grasped the girl's hand.

The man beckoned to them, insistent.

Maria took a deep breath and a final glance behind her. The girl's face was pale and strained. Maria stepped forward, ready to confront what hell awaited inside this building.

THIRTY-FIVE

Wednesday, 10:35 AM, Hotel Celebracion, Juarez City

The knock at Karina's suite door echoed through the spacious living area. Though expected, the sound sent a small tremor to her belly. She'd counted on her plan to stall Cesar, giving Eli ample time to vanish into the storeroom's darkness. Smoothing her blouse, she opened the door slightly and took a glance, then flung it open fully.

Cesar drifted into the room. He closed the distance between them, grazing his lips along her neck. The scent of his cologne that once excited her now soured in her nostrils. "I'm sorry I haven't been around," his voice was smooth as poured honey, "work has me tied up." His hand slid down her spine, pulling her tightly against him.

Karina tensed, the heat from his unwelcome touch seeping through the fabric of her blouse. "Perhaps you're busy with someone else. Huh." Karina pushed him away with measured force. "Someone younger." She took a step back as if searching for signs of his guilt.

Cesar held his hands out, innocence etched on his face.

"Come on, Karina. Who's putting these thoughts in your head?"

She jabbed a finger at him. "*Quién?* You know exactly who." She elevated her tone to show hurt and indignation. "Isabella, the new hostess," she said to appeal to his ego and ease any suspicion. But her despair at being attached to such a man wasn't entirely feigned. "I see you looking at her. I hear the rumors."

He chuckled, but it did little to mask his dark nature. "What's got into you, *mi amor?* Believing idle gossip over what we have?"

With each step he took forward, Karina took a step back. She retreated across the plush carpet of the living area and into the adjoining kitchenette, anchoring herself against the cold marble countertop.

As Cesar approached, his arms outstretched like a peace offering she had no interest in accepting. "No, Cesar. You've made me too furious to even look at you."

Her heart thundered against her ribs, not from the nearness of the man who'd once charmed her, but from the threat of him going to his office too soon. Every precious second he spent trying to soothe her made-up jealousy was another second Eli had time to escape.

Another knock at the door. Another part of Karina's plan.

"Who is it?" Cesar's voice was a sudden crash of thunder.

A whimper seeped through the door too low to distinguish.

Karina shouldered past Cesar, making a show of being angry. "Let's see why you hired the little *puta*, huh?" She pulled the door open.

Raul stood there. His mustache was twisted up, but his

face hung low like the tail of a defeated dog. "Sorry to disturb, *Patron*." His eyes darted to Karina then back to Cesar. "But Karina said—"

Cesar's face flared to an angry red. "And who do you work for, Raul? Who signs your check?"

Sweat glinted on Raul's forehead. A sympathy pang flit through Karina. She had texted him that Cesar had called a meeting in her suite.

Cesar's face suddenly closed, shuttering any insight into his thinking. "Maybe I've been spending too much time away from the hotel, venturing into other investments." His gaze shifted from the cowed figure of Raul to Karina. His eyes softened, or rather their hardness turned from anger to coldness. "The money I pay you, Karina, is not just for you, is it? Don't you help support your mother and sister?" His voice was low and smooth like draped silk over sharp horns.

Karina felt the blood drain from her face at the veiled threat. Her heart quickened—not out of self-survival, but for Mamá and Sofia. His implication was clear—their welfare hinged on her compliance.

"Now, Raul," Cesar said low and firm. "Can we get some work done?"

Raul hurried out of the room and Cesar slowly followed. He turned to give Karina one last, disappointed glance. He shook his head, tramped out the door, and slammed it.

Karina dropped onto the plush couch, expelling a trembling breath. Did she give Eli enough time to flee Cesar's office undetected? Would her next encounter with Cesar have dire consequences for her and her family? Her phone buzzed. A text from Emilio.

"I'm in the storeroom with Eli and Dakota. You won't believe what Cesar found in his office."

THIRTY-SIX

Wednesday, 10:50 AM, Hotel Celebracion Storeroom, Juarez City

Eli stepped into the storeroom after his narrow escape from Cesar's office, focusing on his phone. A mix of numbers and Spanish characters glared back at him, mocking his efforts to make sense of them. He exhaled a flustered breath, massaging his temple with his free hand as he moved to the pile of mattresses where Dakota lay sleeping.

The IV drip, the empty plate, the flush of color in Dakota's face eased Eli's worry. He lifted his eyes and whispered, "Thank you," in a heartfelt prayer.

The creak of the door hinge drew his attention. Karina slipped into the room, uncertainty written in the lines across her forehead. "Cesar's not happy, not happy at all." Her tone was terse. "He ranted about me disrupting his busy day."

Emilio's expression tensed. "Does he suspect anything?"

She shook her head. "*Nada.* He's upset. Upset that I accused him of cheating with Isabella, the new girl."

Eli bowed his head slightly. "Thanks for helping me out of that office." Relief colored his tone. "I'm sorry if I put you at risk."

Karina waved off his apology, "No worries. Emilio tells me you found something. Anything useful?"

"Maybe." Eli sighed with frustration. "It looks important. But I can't make heads or tails of what's on it."

"Let me see," Emilio reached for Eli's phone. "How come you Americans never learn our beautiful language?"

"You spend enough time with me and Emilio," Karina's eyes sparkled. "We'll have you fluent in no time."

"I'm all for that," Eli said. "But let's see if this book has anything we can use first."

Emilio's thumb slid over the screen. "I think I found something. It's a ledger with transactions from banks in El Paso and Tegucigalpa, Honduras." He looked up to exchange glances with Karina. "There were girls from Honduras in the compound where I was held captive."

"Garza's buying girls from Honduras?" Eli asked.

Karina squinted over Emilio's shoulder. "It wouldn't surprise me now that I know what he does. Cesar's always been one to exploit any opportunity for profit."

"*Espera un momento.*" She paused as if a memory had just surfaced. "Just like a factory he bought last year in Tijuana. The workers were underpaid, and the conditions were horrible. But Cesar changed nothing. He didn't care as long as production kept rolling. I knew it was wrong." Karina's voice grew quieter. "But I said nothing, nothing at all. I was too afraid of losing the lifestyle he afforded me." She shook her head. Her eyes got glossy. "I should have said something."

Emilio placed a comforting hand on his sister's shoulder. "You're speaking up now, Karina. That's what matters."

Eli cleared his throat to bring the conversation back to their planning. "Morality aside, the move makes sense. With all these human caravans traveling north from South and Central America, Garza could easily supply the US with dozens if not hundreds of kids every month."

Emilio rubbed his face. "Since your federal government relaxed border policies," his words came out slow, "Garza has free rein to move these kids into America unfettered—like an eighteenth-century slave trader."

"And I suppose that pays more than auto parts." Eli took a deep breath and let it out slowly. "I'll get these numbers to El Paso. Blackwell can have a forensic accountant comb through this ledger. Then they'll know how much trafficking Garza's doing north of the border." He glanced at Emilio. "Think we should see what's up at that compound in the desert?"

"I'm sure Cesar closed it soon after you rescued Emilio," Karina said. Her eyes narrowed as if she'd been struck by a sudden revelation. "May I see those numbers?"

Emilio handed her the phone.

Karina's shoulders sagged. "*Qué coraje!* How do you see anything on this small screen." She strolled to the back of the storeroom and disappeared behind stacked desks and file cabinets. The sounds of rummaging followed.

Seconds later, she emerged with a laptop and cords and a determined glint in her eye. "Now we can really study these numbers." She set the computer on a nearby table, connected the cords, and the screen flickered to life.

Karina huddled over the laptop, her face illuminated by the screen's glow. Her fingers slid across the trackpad. "Wait a minute," she said, her voice rose with disbelief. "I recognize this address. It's an old plant Cesar shut down last year."

Eli crouched over her shoulder to study the screen. "Not very good business to pay utilities on an abandoned building. Are the costs substantial?"

"Substantial enough to pique my curiosity." She pointed to a figure listed in pesos.

"Indeed," Eli affirmed with a solemn nod. "These amounts are suspicious."

"It's not abandoned at all, is it?" Emilio said.

Karina's lips pressed into a thin line. "No, it's not. Cesar was supposed to demolish the building months ago. But these payments say something different."

"Where is this plant located?" Eli asked.

Karina tapped the keyboard and pulled up Google Earth. She zoomed the screen larger. "It's just a half mile from the Rio Grande River and the US border."

Eli's gut churned with a sickening realization. "It's the perfect location for a trafficking hub. Remote, close to the border, and easily accessible from both sides."

"Those poor girls," Emilio said, his face blanching, "being held in that plant like cattle."

"Text me detailed directions." Eli's moved to his bag and grabbed it. "If I can catch images of that building being used to transport young girls, we might have enough for the local authorities to bring Garza and Diablos down."

As if a switch flipped, Karina's features hardened. Gone was her sorrowful expression, replaced by a steely resolve. "I'm going with you. I can't sit back, not anymore."

"No, Karina," Emilio placed a hand on his sister's shoulder, "it's too dangerous. I'll go."

Her eyes locked onto her brother's. "I must do this. Don't you understand? For myself as much for those girls."

Eli's chest warmed with admiration for Karina. But no way was he taking her. "Who'll stay back and care for Dakota?" He kept his voice low and calm. "I can't go without knowing he's in good hands."

A sudden stirring from Dakota's bed. He was sliding his legs off the edge of his makeshift mattress. "Well, you won't have to. Where's my clothes?"

"Whoa," Eli cried, raising his hands palms out. "Hold on there, partner. You're in no shape to be running around."

"I'm fine." Dakota grimaced as he pushed himself to his feet. "I've been laid up long enough."

Karina's eyes flashed like a scolding nun's. "Get back in that bed, Dakota, and stop being ridiculous. You nearly died less than twenty-four hours ago."

"But..." Dakota blinked like a toddler caught with a bag of cookies. he said weakly. "Those girls need help."

"And they'll get it," she fired back. "But not from someone who could collapse because he reopened his wound."

"Karina's right, man," Emilio said with a grin, as if issuing a warning. "You better do as you're told, or Garza won't be the only one in trouble."

Dakota's shoulders slumped. He collapsed on the mound of carpet.

"If I'm staying," Karina eased in beside him and rested her hand on his chest, "you're staying. Understand?"

"*Si, Senorita*," he said in a submissive tone.

Eli chuckled at the exchange. "Listen to the lady, Dakota," he said, his voice light but firm. "We'll be back before you know it. Rest up and heal up. Who knows when the real fighting will begin."

Dakota let out a long sigh. He closed his eyes in quiet resignation. "Fine," he grumbled, his voice taking on a child-like sulkiness.

Eli slung his rucksack over his shoulder. "Dakota, if you

feel up to it, work with Karina to get those ledger numbers to Blackwell."

"Consider it done." Dakota waved with his good arm.

"See you soon." Eli stepped to the bed, and offered Dakota his hand. Take care of yourself."

His farewell carried a heavy finality, hinting at the possibility that it could be their last.

THIRTY-SEVEN

Wednesday, 1:30 PM, Five Miles Outside Juarez City

Eli lay low behind a cluster of lush shrubs in the fertile Rio Grande Valley, his eyes fixed on the abandoned auto-parts plant a hundred yards away. Tangles of green grass brushed against his jeans as he shifted slowly, careful not to rustle the leaves. Dawn spread across the horizon, offering scant light as he framed the plant's entrance through his binoculars.

Stirring beside him, Emilio wiped the sleep from his eyes. "Anything happen while I was out?" His whisper was coarse as gravel.

Eli massaged his forehead. "A school bus in at midnight, out by two. The guards are rotating now."

Emilio lifted his field glasses to eye level. "Who's that by the gate."

Eli eyed the solitary figure who detached himself from the shadow of the perimeter wall—a guard, complete with radio crackle and the casual swing of a flashlight beam. "He's been there for hours. Should be getting off about now."

Emilio tensed. An intake of sharp breath cut through the calm. "Mateo..." Recognition threaded in the name.

Eli lowered his binoculars. Emilio's shoulders were rigid, his lenses locked on the man below—an obvious connection.

"You know him?" Eli whispered.

"Used to be hooked on the needle. Heroin was eating him alive." Emilio's voice was a light murmur, but heavy with satisfaction. "I helped him find his faith. Faith in Jesus to kick his addiction."

Eli scratched his scalp. Heroin? Could they use this man? Faith was a currency Eli seldom dealt with, yet Emilio's conviction was somewhat convincing. "How long have you known him?"

"Since we were kids playing in the streets of Aldama." Emilio's gaze never wavered from Mateo. "He's turned his life around. I'm sure he took this job to support his little girl, Marisol. She's only five."

"Can you trust him?" Eli said above the rising wind fluttering against Eli's shirt sleeves.

"With my life," Emilio said with steadfast confidence.

Eli searched the preacher's expression for a hint of doubt. Then Eli signaled his trust in Emilio's judgment with a nod. "Okay then. Go have a word with your friend before he clocks out."

Eli held his breath and his position.

Emilio's boots beat against the hard-packed dirt as he moved to the building's perimeter. Eli watched through his binoculars as Emilio's figure cautiously approached the fence line. The landscape came alive with the emerging sunlight that glimmered behind the distant hills. Emilio scurried along the perimeter's edges, hunched low to avoid detection by any other guards. "Mateo." His hushed call barely reached Eli's ears.

Eli tightened his grip on the binoculars as uncertainty crossed Mateo's features. The man's posture grew rigid with readiness. Then, recognition sparked in his movements—evident even from Eli's distance, thanks to many surveillance missions studying body language.

Mateo edged closer to Emilio's position. Distant murmurs followed—snippets of conversation carried by the brisk wind. Then silence except for the breeze swishing through green bushes and shrubs.

Emilio returned, his eyes alight with a glow that something might have shifted in their favor. "He doesn't know much—hasn't set foot inside. Guards the perimeter only." He paused to catch his breath.

"And?" Eli said with an impatient itch.

Emilio's brow knit, then relaxed as he steadied his breathing. "He knows a way in—an old drainage tunnel they've barely been watching."

"What do you think," Eli murmured. "Do we move on this information?"

"I'm just a street preacher, but I trust him. He thinks he owes me a lot."

Eli breathed out slowly, like releasing a revolver's hammer to prevent a round from firing too soon. Such threads were a risk and a gamble. Did they dare hang their trust on Emilio's ex-addict friend?

With a nod, more to himself than to Emilio, Eli made the call. "All right. But I want to talk to him first. And not huddled out here in the shadows."

"He said the same. He's leaving in a half hour. Wants to meet us at a diner nearby. Says it's a safe place to meet."

"Let's make sure," Eli said, "and get there before he does."

ELI SAT with his back to the wall in the diner's corner booth, his gaze sweeping the room. Across from him, Emilio watched the parking lot through grime-streaked windows. Forgotten menus lay beside their cold coffee, and the buzzing hum of dying fluorescent bulbs harmonized with the hubbub of blue-collar patrons as the afternoon sun filtered through the front glass.

Mateo arrived on time and slid into the booth next to Emilio, his uniform hanging loosely on his frame. Flickers of tension pulled at his eyelids as he looked over his shoulder, once, then twice.

Emilio made brief introductions without ceremony. Eli started, his voice steady, "How well are you known at the plant, Mateo?"

Mateo's Adam's apple bobbed with a nervous gulp. "Not much. I'm mostly invisible—just part of the scenery."

Eli sharpened his gaze, studying every twitch and flicker in Mateo's expression. "Are you absolutely sure the tunnel won't be guarded tonight? That we'll have a clear path?"

"They're stretched thin as it is." Mateo's words seemed to fight their way out. "I checked the roster. It's my area, my responsibility. No shift overlaps. No surprises."

"And the cameras?" Eli's question hung heavy between them.

Mateo's gaze flickered to Emilio, then he repositioned the salt and pepper shakers. "Old. The ones that still work in that area are pointed at the plant—nowhere near the tunnel entrance."

"You've seen nothing out of the ordinary?" Eli narrowed his eyes on Mateo. "Extra security, new faces?"

Mateo's fingers found a loose thread on his uniform cuff, worrying it between thumb and forefinger. "Nothing. It's business as usual."

Eli scanned the diner, noting the blissfully ignorant patrons, then leaned back, his mind whirring with apprehension. "We're trusting you with our lives, Mateo. Don't let us walk into a dead end."

"No, *Señor*. Never." Mateo's eyes, hollow but sincere, locked onto Eli's. "I owe my life to Emilio Castillo. My daughter's too. I'll never forget that, never." Each word carried the weight of a vow, etched with the gravity of life and death.

The conversation ended. The trio sat in uneasy silence. Eli replayed Mateo's answers, probing for any sign of deception or hesitation.

Breaking the silence, Emilio finally spoke, his voice slightly shaking, "Mateo, you know what's at stake. We can't afford a mistake."

Mateo nodded fervently. "I know, Emilio. You have my word."

With a final nod to Mateo, Eli stood, signaling the end of their meeting. "We'll see you tonight," he said, his doubts lingering, each one asking the same question—could he truly trust Mateo as Emilio did? Or were they about to fall off a cliff and into the hands of Ramirez and Garza and the Diablos cartel?

THIRTY-EIGHT

Wednesday, 1:45 PM—Hotel Celebracion Storeroom, Juarez City

Perspiration beaded on Karina's skin as she perched beside Dakota's makeshift mattress. The storeroom's stifling air was thick with the smells of antiseptic and sweat. A rickety fan wheezed. Dust motes danced lazily in the midday light streaming in through the skylight. Twelve stories below, sounds from Juarez's traffic filtered up—a world beyond their precarious sanctuary.

As Karina's fingers hovered over Dakota's tousled hair, her phone buzzed across the battered nightstand. She snatched it, her mother's text glowing ominously on the screen— "Sofia has disappeared."

Dakota stirred beside her. He blinked slowly, then his eyes focused on her. "Karina?" His voice was thick with concern. "What's wrong?"

The words got stuck in Karina's vocal cords. "It's Sofia," she managed. "She's missing."

Sitting up abruptly, Dakota winced. "What?"

"My mother just texted me." Karina held up her phone,

the message still glowing on the screen. "I don't know what to do, Dakota. I'm scared."

He laced his fingers with hers. "Call your mother," he urged with a calmness Karina didn't feel. "Find out what happened."

Dakota slipped out of the bed.

Karina pressed redial. The phone rang once, twice, three times. "Please, Mamá, just answer."

"Oh, God, Karina." Mamá's words came in a rush of panic.

"Mamá, what happened? Where's Sofia?" Karina's vision blurred at the edges.

"The school called." Her mother's voice broke. "They say Sofia disappeared after lunch. No one has seen her since. I don't know what to do, Karina. I'm so scared."

The ground tilted beneath Karina. "I'll find her, Mamá." Her voice shook but was determined. "I'll do whatever it takes to bring her home." Karina terminated the call.

"I have to go," Karina said to Dakota.

"Of course you do, and I'm coming with you." His tone was unyielding, like an unbreakable promise.

Karina shook her head. "You're still injured, Dakota. You need your rest."

"I can't rest while Sofia's missing, and you're out there alone."

At that moment, Karina felt the full force of her vulnerability, that she'd be lost without Dakota being there. "Oh God, please give me wisdom," she breathed, a plea in desperation.

Dakota pulled her into a fierce, reassuring hug, his arms encircling her as if to shield her from the uncertainty ahead. "We'll find her," he whispered.

WEDNESDAY, 2:45 *PM, Escuela Primaria Aldama, Aldama, Juarez City*

Karina rushed out of the back seat of the Uber that Dakota had hired. The once cheerful exterior of the school of her childhood was now another ominous monument to the darkness that terrorized her family.

As she and Dakota rushed through the door of the principal's office, Karina's palms grew moist. The principal, a young, kind-eyed woman, greeted them with an earnest nod. "Señorita Castillo, I'm so sorry about Sofia." The principal was on the verge of sobs. "We're doing everything we can to help find her."

With a shaky inhale, she pressed a hand to her chest. "What happened?" Her voice breaking.

The principal hesitated, then shot her gaze at Dakota before settling back on Karina. "One of the teachers mentioned seeing a man in the area before lunch. He seemed out of place, but she didn't think much of it at the time."

"Who was it?" Karina said, fighting to steady her hands.

"Hector Ramirez," the principal said the name like a curse.

Hector Ramirez, the notorious cartel captain, had been near her sister's school? Karina shook and sweat seeped from her pores.

"Hector Ramirez?" Dakota's voice snapped. "What would he be doing here?"

Before the principal could respond, a timid knock sounded at the door. A young girl, no more than seven or eight, peeked into the room, her eyes a kaleidoscope of terror.

"Come in, Luciana," the principal coaxed gently. "It's okay. These people are here to find Sofia."

The girl stepped into the room. Her small frame shuttered. "During lunch," her voice was barely a whisper. "I was by the fence. I saw Sofia."

The girl's report thrust Karina's heart into her throat. She lowered herself to the girl's level and willed her voice to remain gentle. "What did you see, Luciana?"

Luciana's lower lip trembled, tears welling in her eyes. "*Había hombres. Llevaban camisas blancas y pañuelos azules. Agarraron a Sofía y la pusieron en un coche. Ella estaba llorando, pero a ellos no les importaba.*"

"She said there were men who took Sofia," Karina said in English for Dakota's benefit. "They wore white shirts and blue bandanas."

"Diablos," Dakota said with tight anger.

With each moment, Karina's throat grew tighter. Words wouldn't come, but she managed a nod, a silent thank you for Luciana braving her fears.

"You're a brave girl for telling us, Luciana." the principal said. "Thank you."

Luciana's eyes glistened. "I hope you find her," she whispered, before turning and slipping from the room.

Karina stood. Her legs shook beneath her. "Diablos has my sister," she said to Dakota. "And I don't know what to do."

Dakota placed his hands on Karina's shoulders. "I do."

THIRTY-NINE

Wednesday, 3:00 PM—El Paso, Texas

The afternoon sun illuminated the corner booth at Café Mayapan where Morales sipped his coffee. The rich aromas of sizzling fajitas and spicy salsa reminded him of weekend lunches with his wife and children. The soft strains of mariachi music spilling from unseen speakers tried to infuse him with a sense of celebration he couldn't feel. He missed the shared meals with his family, helping his kids with homework, and falling asleep beside his wife. A week had passed since he'd sent them away for their safety, and the separation gnawed at him. How much longer must this separation last?

Outside, the bustling streets of El Paso hummed with activity. Yet inside, Morales remained in the dark about why he was asked here for a late lunch. Was it about Diablos bringing more children across the Rio Grande? Or news about Marco Domingo?

Special Agent Marcus Blackwell strode into the café, his tall frame and weathered face commanding attention.

Sweat glistened on his forehead, and his crisp white shirt was slightly rumpled from the afternoon heat. With a nod here and a pat on the back there and a wave to the nearest server, he said, "Coffee, please. The strongest you've got." He slid into the seat across from Morales. "Counselor. Been here long?

Morales shrugged. "A few minutes. I take it you asked me here not just to enjoy the fajitas?"

The server appeared and barely finished pouring the coffee when Blackwell reached inside his jacket and withdrew a thick envelope. "Let's just say I wouldn't have pulled you away from the office without it being worth your while." He slid the envelope across the table. A smirk formed on his lips, suggesting he held a secret.

Morales's hand hovered over the envelope for a split second before seizing it. His fingers flipped open the flap and withdrew several pages.

"This is why I called you here," Blackwell said over the restaurant's casual chatter.

Morales thumbed through copies of a ledger for Oceanic Holdings, the shell company that posted Domingo's bail. Each entry, each name, each date, and cash transfer, some amounting to millions, some involving American celebrities and politicians, painted a vague map of children being auctioned—Garza's hidden empire.

The connections were too breathtaking, the patterns too clear. Every entry corroborated a conspiracy to use children for extortion, bribery, and slavery. Maybe, just maybe, Morales could use this information to shine a light on America's most secret yet vilest criminal enterprises.

How could he enter these pages into evidence that would frame a case against a Mexican billionaire? Garza had been beyond American jurisprudence, yet now Morales had solid evidence. But wealth means power, plus the billionaire was shielded by a border. A border he disregarded continually to sell innocent children to American pedophiles.

"Oceanic Holdings," Morales said with some reservation. "Can we confirm these transactions lead to Garza?"

"The ledger was found in his office," Blackwell said with confidence.

"And the source?"

"The two civilians we discussed last week."

Morales set the pages down and leaned back. "Civilians operating in Juarez? Aren't you outside your lane, Agent Blackwell? I thought deploying spies was under the purview of the CIA."

"The world we've stepped into plays by a set of rules that give them an advantage," Blackwell's voice was a low thrum that captured urgency. "But as I see it, what we've got here is a lever for us to clutch onto. We'll lose if we try to fight Garza and his minions in Diablos with conventional tactics. But if we pull this lever with a different mindset by incorporating tactics that are just as cunning, yet legal, we'll have Garza behind bars and Diablos dissolved, real soon. Now, do you think we've got enough to indict Garza with this?"

Morales met the special agent's question with a steel-edged grin. "You've heard the expression, 'I can indict the proverbial ham sandwich.' That's not the problem, is it?"

Blackwell's sharp nod was his silent acknowledgment.

"Indicting him isn't the trick," Morales said. "It's how to smoke him out, how to get him from Juarez and into our jurisdiction where we pull the strings."

"And your plan?" Blackwell's eyes were as focused as a feral cat near an unsuspecting bird.

"Oceanic Holdings has an account here in El Paso." Morales paused. His mind clicked like a metronome in sync with his prosecutorial discretion. "It was used to post bail for Marco Domingo. And with Domingo jumping said bail set by a certain judge, I'm sure I can attain a warrant to review all accounts related to Oceanic Holdings."

Blackwell's gaze didn't waver from Morales.

Morales continued. "Then, we'll need to convince Garza that his castle could crumble if he doesn't come to El Paso to take care of some aspect of his business in person."

Blackwell's eyes narrowed for a short second. Then, the edge of his mouth stretched up to his cheek. "Get your warrant, but not for the bank accounts, not yet. Get one for a wiretap on Garza's banker instead. But hurry up. I'm retiring in a couple of weeks."

"Your impending retirement means we need to hit the ground running. Your connections, your resources...I can't afford to lose that edge."

Rising from the booth, Blackwell extended his hand and winked. "Get that warrant and I'll line up the best electronic surveillance team we have in the area. Then we'll get enough evidence so Garza can room with El Chapo at Florence Supermax Prison." Blackwell's phone rang in his pocket. With a curt nod, he answered the call and left the restaurant.

As the door swung shut behind him, Morales allowed himself a moment of stillness as the server cleared the table. He pressed his fingers to his temples, then folded and slipped the pages inside the envelope. The ledger copies nestled in his jacket pocket pulsed with a raw energy, sending tingles across his skin.

Rising, he shouldered the weight of his briefcase and

stepped out into the burgeoning El Paso sun, its rays a sharp contrast to the shadows he was about to invade.

His battle for justice was just beginning. With God and Blackwell and his two spies in Juarez fighting with him, he was poised to battle against an evil that spanned across the two nations.

FORTY

Wednesday, 3:05 PM—Five Miles Outside of Juarez City

The stench hit Eli like a punch to the gut—mold, decay, and stagnant water filled his nostrils as he approached the drainage tunnel's rusted metal grate. His eyes watered, adjusting to the dim light that seeped through the slats. Slivers of illumination cast linear shadows along the ditch running to the river. Eli's fingers twitched, finding comfort in the familiar polymer frame of his Glock.

"You sure about this, Emilio?" he muttered, glancing at his companion. "Mateo's intel better be solid, or we're walking into a death trap."

Emilio nodded, but his expression showed uncertainty. "It's our only lead on the cartel's operations and where we can find those girls. We have to try."

"Alright," he said, nerving himself. "Let's do this." Eli stepped to the blocked opening. The grate groaned, like the gasp of a dying man, as he pushed the tunnel gate open.

The dark engulfed Eli, thick and oppressive. The beam of his flashlight struggled against the tunnel's inky blackness, barely revealing the path ahead.

Mere steps in, and a wave of vertigo crashed over Eli. His recent head injury flared with a sickening swirl. The tunnel tilted. Eli stumbled, slamming his shoulder into the water-stained wall. The impact startled every nerve in his body. But it was nothing compared to the tumult that erupted in his brain.

A high-pitched ringing filled his ears, drowning out the sound of his own ragged breathing. He pressed a hand to the cold, gritty surface, his fingers scraping, trying to ground himself against the rough concrete. But his vision doubled, then tripled. The tunnel warped and twisted, his injured brain struggling to process the surroundings.

"Eli?" Emilio's distant and muffled voice found him. "Are you okay, man?"

Eli blinked, trying to focus on Emilio's face. But his features blurred and shifted and melted into the shadows.

"I'm fine," Eli gritted out. The words passed through his throat like broken glass. "Just... just give me a second."

"You don't look fine, *Hermano*. Maybe we should— "

"No," Eli snapped. "I'm fine, I said. We'll keep going. I can handle it." He pushed himself off the wall, ignoring how his legs wobbled beneath him. The ringing in his ears shrilled like a fire alarm.

Emilio's hand clutched Eli's arm in the darkness. "Eli, if you're not up for this—"

"I said I'm fine," Eli growled, a hot, prickly heat rising in his chest. "We don't have time for this."

Emilio let go. "Okay, okay. But if it gets worse, you tell me, *por favor*."

Eli nodded, not trusting himself to speak. He knew Emilio had every reason to be concerned, but his worry only fueled Eli's frustration. He was supposed to be the one in control. But even his own body and mind refused to obey his commands.

He took a deep breath. Dank air filled his lungs. Thankfully, the ringing in his ears faded to a dull roar, and his vision cleared enough to make out the path ahead.

Emilio fell into step beside him, the beam of his flashlight joining Eli's to pierce the dark. But as they moved deeper into the tunnel, the blackness beyond seemed like a living creature, hungry, waiting to devour them.

The tunnel forked ahead, two gaping shadows framed by moldy walls. Eli paused. His flashlight beam danced between the two openings. The sound of running water, a faint trickle that had been their constant companion, seemed to fade as they approached the divide.

"Which way?" Emilio asked, his voice low and tight.

Eli studied the openings. The left tunnel seemed to be the source of the running water, the sound growing louder as he focused on it. But the right tunnel was silent, a stillness that made the hairs on the back of his neck stand at attention.

He stepped inside the right tunnel. Its silence pressed in on him.

"You sure about this?" Emilio's tone showed little support. "Maybe we should stick with the water. At least we know where it's coming from."

Eli shook his head, immediately regretting the motion as a fresh wave of dizziness hit him. He gritted his teeth, willing the feeling to pass. "No," he said, his voice rough. "The water's too loud. It could be masking other sounds. We need to be able to hear where we're going since our visibility is low."

Emilio's flashlight beam wavered with uncertainty. "I don't know, man. This feels like a bad idea."

Eli rounded on him. "You got a better one?" His voice bounced off the tunnel walls. "Because I'm all ears."

Emilio held his gaze for a moment, then looked away. His shoulders fell. "No," he said quietly. "I don't."

Eli jerked his chin to the right. "Then we go this way." He turned back to the silent tunnel, passing his fingers across his Glock.

Each step now felt like a gamble, a roll of the dice that could end in disaster. But Eli couldn't shake the feeling that they were running out of time. That each second they spent in this damp, dark hellhole was a second too long.

The darkness seemed to swallow them whole, the beams of their flashlights the only points of light.

He could feel Emilio behind him, probably shaking his head about Eli's decision. They were flying blind. He was navigating by his instincts when he didn't trust his instincts. And as the tunnel walls closed in around them, his doubt became more real.

As they ventured deeper, Eli's skin crawled with the creeping sensation of being watched—a feeling he knew too well—a sixth sense honed by years of combat and covert operations. But it felt different down here in the damp darkness. Alien.

He tried to brush it off as paranoia, a byproduct of his injured brain misfiring signals. But the feeling persisted, growing stronger with each step. There was an itch between his shoulder blades, a target he couldn't quite scratch.

Emilio must have sensed it too. His movements were tighter, more controlled. His flashlight beam darted into every crevice and shadow. They moved in silence, the only sounds were the scuff of their boots and the occasional drip of water from the tunnel's ceiling.

As they neared what Eli hoped was the end of the

tunnel, a stillness settled. An unnatural quiet. Even the dripping water stopped as if the tunnel held its breath.

And then, without warning, a cold draft brushed past them, ruffling Eli's hair and sending a shiver across his skin. It carried with it a faint sound, a distant hum that had no place in the depths of the earth.

Eli froze and held up his hand. "You hear that?" he whispered, his voice sounding too loud in the stillness.

Emilio nodded, his eyes wide in the beam of his flashlight. "Sounds like... machinery?"

Eli strained his ears, trying to make sense of the noise. It was faint, almost imperceptible, but it was there. A low, rhythmic drone that seemed to vibrate through the soles of his boots.

He swung his flashlight in a slow arc, searching for the source of the sound. But the beam only illuminated more damp concrete. The tunnel extended ahead of them, an endless stretch into darkness.

"I don't like this," Emilio muttered, his voice tight. "We should turn back."

Eli shook his head, ignoring how the motion made his vision swim. "Not now."

He took a step forward, then another, his heart pounding in his chest. The sound grew louder as they moved, the thrumming taking on a metallic edge. Then there was—

"Voices," Emilio breathed. "I hear voices."

A chill ran through Eli, a cold that had nothing to do with the damp air. He knew that sound, had heard it a thousand times before. The distant, muffled murmur of orders being given and received.

But here, in the depths of this tunnel, with this plant

being closed, it made no sense. There should be no work down here. Human voices, yes. But machinery?

Unless...

Eli's pieced together the fragments of information they'd gathered. The cartel's operations, the girls in the desert compound, and the abandoned plant above.

A blinding light flooded the tunnel. *"Para o dispararemos,"* boomed a voice from behind.

"Stop or we'll shoot," Emilio translated quickly, his voice tight with fear.

Eli's heart slammed against his ribs. His mind reeled. The gut-wrenching realization struck him—his resolve to push forward despite his injury had led them into a trap. Clutching his Glock, he poised his finger over the trigger.

Should they run or fight to get out of this tunnel alive?

FORTY-ONE

Wednesday, 3:30 PM—Aldama, Juarez City

As the Uber pulled away from the school, the ache that had penetrated Karina's chest at the mention of Sofia's capture persisted. The car's air conditioning chilled her skin, but it did nothing to cool the panic that raged within her.

The car's interior seemed to shrink around her. Karina's breathing came in short, shallow gasps. Her nails dug into her palms. Her mind replayed a vivid image of Sofia—her cheeks stained with tears, her hands pushing against the rough hands of her evil captors.

Dakota's presence failed to calm Karina, his voice muted against the roar of her trauma. She stared unseeing at the passing streets, the colors outside her window blurred into a lifeless gray.

What if they were too late? What if Sofia had already been sold? What if her fate was already sealed by the twisted desires of one of Cesar's clients? The idea of her sister alone and abandoned, while Karina had been enjoying her time with Dakota, filled her with suffocating guilt.

Her eyes burned. Her vision blurred. Tears trickled down to her chin. She'd first failed her mother, now she'd failed Sofia, failed to protect her from a known evil—another unforgivable sin.

She buried her face in her hands. *Please, God. Let Sofia be safe. I'll do anything, give anything, be anything You want if You bring her back to our family.*

The jarring vibration of her phone snapped Karina out of her prayer. She fumbled inside her purse. Her mother's name on the screen sent a jolt that touched every nerve ending.

"Mamá?" Karina's voice quivered.

Her mother's voice crackled through the line. "Karina, mi hija. I found a note from the monsters who took Sofia."

The phone almost slipped through her fingers as she thumbed the speaker on so Dakota could hear. "What does it say?"

"They want to trade Sofia," Her mother choked out between sobs. "For Emilio. They want to trade my daughter for my son."

Karina's focus narrowed as her mother's message settled in. The cartel wanted her brother in exchange for Sofia's life. Why? Because he'd escaped from their clutches?

"Mamá, listen to me," Karina said. "Don't do anything; don't go anywhere. I need to think about this." She glanced at Dakota who'd leaned in closer.

Her mother's whimpers had sharp edges that cut Karina deep. "I can't lose her, Karina. I can't lose my baby girl."

"You won't, Mamá," Karina promised without knowing her next move. "I won't let that happen. Emilio won't let that happen. Just try to calm down, and I'll call you as soon as I have news."

Karina ended the call and turned to Dakota. "Did you hear? We have to do something."

Dakota squared his jaw and reached for his phone. "I'll call Eli. You call Emilio. Let them know what's happening."

Karina's fingers shook and she punched Emilio's name on her call log. Each ring that went unanswered struck a blow to her fragile hope. "He's not answering," Karina said, her voice thick with impatience. "What if the cartel already has him, Dakota? What if we're too late?"

Dakota reached to squeeze her hand. "You need to stay focused for Sofia's sake."

Karina nodded, drawing strength from his touch. "What do we do now?" she asked, her voice so very small.

Dakota lowered his phone and shook his head. "Eli doesn't answer either." He hesitated as if devising their next move. "Take us to the airport," he said to the driver. "I need to rent a car." He rubbed his chin, then ran his thumb down his phone screen.

"What are you doing?" Karina asked.

"I just remembered. When we sent those files to Blackwell, you said there were other properties apart from the so-called abandoned plant."

Karina's pulse jumped to a drumroll's tempo. She chewed on her lower lip.

"There." Dakota handed Karina his phone opened to Cesar's ledger. "Can you find them?"

It took a second to register. Properties. The deeds of three other properties in Juarez owned by Oceanic Holdings. "What are you thinking? That Sofia could be in one of these?"

"What I'm thinking is that it makes sense for us to check

them out. Eli and Dakota have the plant covered. Let's check out these locations and see what's what."

Karina rubbed her temples. What were the chances of Sofia being at one of these properties? Would it be a waste of time to check them out? But what else could they do? Go to her mother's to worry with her?

"It's a lead," he said. "Three in fact. Let's see where they take us."

As they exited the Uber at Dollar Rent-a-Car near the airport, Dakota's hand slipped through the crook at Karina's elbow. "I'll rent something a little more practical than your Audi."

Her Audi? Emilio had it. Where was he and why didn't he answer his phone?

FORTY-TWO

Wednesday, 3:45 PM—Garza's Plant Five Miles Outside of Juarez

The blinding bright light had Eli blinking. He positioned himself in front of Emilio and readied his Glock. "Stay behind me," he commanded. He scanned the area, searching for an escape route. The beam lit up a nearby turn in the tunnel. "Move."

Eli sensed Emilio's hesitation behind him. "Now." Eli clutched Emilio by the shoulder and pushed him to the turn.

The voices behind them grew louder, bouncing off the damp tunnel walls.

Eli turned and fired blindly, sending off strobing bursts until the last casing ejected and the slide locked back.

"Keep moving," he shouted at Emilio, jerking his head to continue into the tunnel. "Find out where this tunnel ends."

Emilio's eyes widened. He hesitated for a split second.

"Go!" Eli prodded, giving Emilio another push. Emilio disappeared into the darkness.

With practiced precision, Eli pressed the magazine release, then replaced it with a full clip. The familiar rush of battle sent his head throbbing with the onset of another migraine. He squared himself, pushed through the pain, and trained his weapon—

...but the light was gone and nobody came. *What the...*

He sprinted after Emilio. His boot soles slipped against damp concrete. He held his breath, straining his ears for any sign of pursuit, half-expecting the bright beam to reappear at any moment.

"Eli!" Emilio's urgent call clamored through the narrow tunnel. "Over here!"

Turning corner after corner, Eli finally stumbled upon Emilio, visible in diffused light seeping through another grate—the din of machinery now closer. Louder. Enveloping.

"The end of the tunnel," Emilio said with a tight voice.

Eli nodded and peered back the way he'd come—no shouting voices, no foreign light beam, no other signs of someone following. "Let's not send them an invitation." Eli rushed to the opening.

Rusted metal bit into his palms as he grasped the grate and pulled. He took a deep breath, pressed his heels hard against the concrete to gain purchase, and heaved the grate open with a heavy grunt.

KARINA WATCHED the sun-bleached street stretch like an endless ribbon into the Juarez industrial section. With each block they drove, her heart brushed against her ribcage like a fluttering wing against a birdcage. Dakota navigated the rented Suburban in silence, his eyes hard on the road.

Karina searched his features for reassurance, but his expression remained set in stone.

A decrepit warehouse appeared. The structure stood alone, a relic at the end of a dusty road. Its walls bore stains of neglect and cracks that snaked like vipers.

With each breath, the knot in Karina's stomach cinched tighter. Could Sofia, alone and terrified, be trapped within these decaying walls? Was she huddled in a corner, with her body bruised and broken?

Finally, Dakota reached his fingers to brush against her arm. "Hey," he said softly. "Don't give up. We'll find her, I promise."

Karina took a shaky breath. It was the same thing she'd said to her mother. Was Dakota as unsure of his promise as she was of hers? The guilt she'd suffered since Sofia's disappearance surged. Bitter bile rolled on her tongue like a relentless tide. She fought it back with a hard swallow.

The car rolled to a stop. "Stay here," Dakota said as he exited the car. He surveyed the building and the road, then rushed to the warehouse, crouching behind overgrown plants and scattered piles of discarded parts and equipment. He disappeared behind the building with wary movement, then reemerged a minute later with no concern.

"No tire tracks," he muttered as he opened the door and sat behind the wheel. "And the ventilation fan isn't running. A person couldn't stand it for more than a few minutes inside."

The fragile flame of hope had slightly smoldered. She looked up at the warehouse. Its broken windows stared back, mocking her despair.

Dakota placed a hand on her shoulder. "What's next on the list?"

As Dakota steered the car away from the warehouse, the

sun was high in the sky. The more places they searched without finding Sofia, the less likely they would.

ELI AND EMILIO emerged from the damp tunnel into a muddle of decrepit machinery. The plant stretched before them, a maze of relic equipment and rusted parts. The air hung thick with a cloying stench of chemicals and decay. They moved through the shadows, their footfalls sounding off the metal walkways.

They passed row after row of old equipment. Countless conveyor belts, their rubber surfaces flaking and peeling, stood silent and still.

As they ventured deeper into the building, the sounds of production grew louder. The chatter of voices and clanking of metal swelled from a cacophony, then to a roar.

"What is that?" Emilio said above the din.

Eli narrowed his eyes and shook his head. "Couldn't tell you."

They rounded a corner, climbed up a set of stairs, and found themselves on a catwalk overlooking a vast, open space. Below them, a sea of machinery stretched out in every direction, covering an area nearly the size of a football field. A complex network of pipes, vats, and hissing valves filled the space. In the center of it all, figures in hazmat suits labored, their forms indistinct beneath the bulky protective gear, faces obscured by plastic visors fitted over hard hats. Two armed men stood at a doorway, engaged in relaxed conversation.

Eli breathed in the sharp, chemical tang that stung his nostrils and the back of his throat, mingled with a sickly sweet odor that made his head swim. His stomach churned.

Emilio clutched Eli's shoulder. "They're making fentanyl."

KARINA SAT in the sweltering heat beside Dakota in the Suburban parked in a working-class neighborhood. They sat across from a run-down house, its faded yellow paint against sprawling brown shrubs. The street was quiet, save for the distant laughter of children playing in a nearby park. Karina's heart clenched at the sound, a painful reminder of the innocence that'd been stolen from her sister.

Dakota cut the engine. Karina studied the house searching for a sign someone was inside. The windows were boarded with weathered planks, their gray edges splintered. Paint peeled from the walls in long, jagged strips, revealing green patches beneath. The yard was overgrown with weeds, their dying stalks straggling in every direction as if even nature had given up on this place.

Dakota stepped out of the car, his hand resting on the gun at his hip. "I'll be right back."

Karina nodded, her mouth dry with anticipation. Her gaze followed Dakota up the cracked concrete path.

Movement.

Dakota froze and clutched for his gun. Karina's lungs seized.

A group of children, no older than ten or eleven, crawled out of a broken window. They giggled and whispered, their high-pitched voices carrying on the stifling air. Their faces were smudged with dirt, their clothes tattered and torn in a rainbow of faded colors. Their eyes caught Dakota and they scampered away, a blur of small bodies and flailing limbs.

Karina's hope deflated like a punctured balloon. She slumped back in her seat, the leather cooled her flushed skin. Dakota managed to stop one child, speaking briefly before returning to the car. His footsteps seemed heavier now, matching the weight settling in Karina's chest.

"Those kids have been playing in that house for months." He turned his grim expression to Karina. "This isn't the place."

She settled back in her seat. "No," her voice faded. "Only one place left."

FORTY-THREE

Wednesday, 5:16 PM—Garza's Plant Five Miles Outside of Juarez City

Eli led Emilio across the catwalk to a morass of metal piping and tubes and they crouched behind them. The chemical fumes were stronger, yet, despite his blurred vision, he managed to see a tangle of wires emerging from a large metal box.

They were here to find the girls Emilio had encountered at the desert compound, but they found boys instead. How large was this operation? Trafficking—now fentanyl? Could they shut down this lab and rescue these children without getting anyone killed?

"See that control panel over there?" He traced a path to the box and wires with his finger. "I think we can shut this place down."

Emilio cocked his head and squinted. "How will that help us?"

"We create confusion, secure the guards, and then we get these kids out of here."

"But won't that alert the plant we're inside?"

"They already know we're inside from our friends in the tunnel." Eli scanned the egress where they'd entered the lab. "Stay here and keep watch. If you see anyone coming from the tunnel, create a distraction."

Emilio's lips parted slightly. "How?"

"Throw something, make a noise, anything to let me know."

"I can do that," Emilio said with a threadbare whisper.

Considering each step and potential obstacle, Eli formulated a plan. "Once I shut down the machinery, we'll need to move fast." He pictured the commotion that would ensue —the guards scrambling, the children's panic. He thought about the layout and the best route to the exit. "I'll deal with the guards, you get the kids. Understood?"

"What about the alarms?" Emilio asked, glancing at the lights on the walls.

Eli followed Emilio's gaze and crinkled his forehead. "I'll have to disable those too, I guess."

He moved with his Glock trained, his footsteps careful to avoid kicking over stray debris that might reveal his location. As he crept closer to the control panel, every flicker of light, every distant sound, every chemical smell registered with crystal clarity. He slowed his breathing. His heart thumped in a steady rhythm.

He scanned the room below, marking potential escape routes. The sight of the children, their small bodies burdened with the toxic fruits of adult greed, fueled his warrior spirit. He clenched his jaw, channeling his rage into his next move.

The control panel appeared larger. Eli drew in a deep breath, hardening himself for what was to come. He would shut this place down. He would save these kids. And God help anyone who tried to stop him.

He scampered, hunched low in the dark shadows to the control panel. His eyes studied a patchwork of old equipment and new technology, its levers all labeled in Spanish. Which to push? What to pull? He seized a promising switch by its handle.

A shout rang out in excited Spanish. His head snapped to the sound. One of the guards had spotted him. His rifle was raised and he was ready to fire.

WITH TWO DEAD ends behind them, Karina's desperation soared. The silence between her and Dakota, broken only by the engine's hum, was deafening. As they left the neighborhood behind, buildings blurred past, numbing her mind with exhaustion. The sun dipped below the American hills.

Dakota beside her was more than a small comfort, but it couldn't erase the guilt that consumed her. The urban landscape gave way to open farmland. Karina slunk deeper in her seat.

"One mile to your destination," the car's GPS said.

One mile to their third location. One mile to their last hope. One mile to a remote farmhouse in the Rio Grande Valley that appeared, from a distance, well-maintained.

The fields they passed were freshly plowed. The lawn surrounding the farmhouse was freshly cut, the hedges neatly trimmed. More alive than the abandoned warehouse and the dilapidated house where the kids played.

"Signs of life," Dakota said, pointing to two vehicles in the circular driveway.

Renewed hope had Karina straighten in her seat.

Dakota parked behind an outbuilding, hiding the

Suburban down a gentle slope. He collected two sets of binoculars from the back seat and swung his door open, "Let's have a look." His voice carried a hint of excitement. "Shall we?"

———

ELI COILED and vaulted over the catwalk railing. He plunged on the oblivious guard below, cracking his skull against the concrete flooring.

Eli whirled to face the second guard, already sighting down his weapon. Eli's gut clenched as the guard's finger twitched on the trigger.

Should Eli surrender?

Not likely the guard would understand English and less likely he'd show mercy.

What about a bum rush?

The space between them was too far and he'd be dead before he could close the distance.

Or...Eli positioned himself behind the guard's torso. His partner hesitated, showing an unwillingness to shoot. Eli leveled his Glock, placing the aim on the guard's forehead. Time was ticking. Should Eli kill this man?

Movement flashed in Eli's periphery. Something hurled from the catwalk spinning like helicopter blades in flight. It seemed to suspend for a surreal second before connecting with the man's head with a sickening crack.

A crimson stream spurted from the man's hairline. He crumpled to the ground like a puppet with its strings cut.

Eli dropped his human shield and bolted to the twitching guard in three strides. The man shuddered and groaned as he clung to consciousness.

Eli rammed his fist into the man's temple, snapping his head back. His body went still.

The suddenness of the spinning pipe's appearance, the brutality of its impact, and his near-death experience had Eli's chest heaving, searching for air. He signaled a thumbs up to Emilio, his unexpected savior, then pointed at the control panel. "Shut the whole plant down."

Emilio ran to the panel, studied it, and then pulled a lever. The constant drone that'd filled the space, sputtered and died. An eerie silence descended, broken only by the soft gasps of the young boys who pulled up their plastic shields.

Then, a piercing alarm split the air.

Eli's flinched and covered his ears. A pulsing red emergency lighting cast a menacing glow over the boys.

He turned to Emilio, ready to shout instructions, but the words died on Eli's lips. Emilio's eyes blazing with an unexpected fire. The street preacher's usual gentle demeanor had transformed into something harder, more resolute.

He nodded at Eli and Eli realized he wasn't alone in this fight. The weight of responsibility, though heavy, was now shared between them. Emilio's unexpected bravery sparked a renewed sense of hope in Eli's chest.

They were outnumbered, outgunned, and now, with the power cut, trapped inside shadows and echoes. But, together, they might have a chance at getting these kids out alive.

The kids, huddled together in small groups, looked to Eli with terrified expressions.

The cartel would be on them in seconds. Eli needed a next move—a miracle to save them.

He searched for something, anything, that could twist this turn of events into a story he could tell his grandchildren. His eyes fell on a shelf of canisters and barrels of toxic sludge.

We need to create a distraction!" he screamed at Emilio, who'd jumped down from the catwalk. "Something that will buy us enough time to get these kids out."

The sickening sounds of boots pounding, weapons clattering, and men shouting started faint but grew increasingly louder. Diablos was coming, and they were coming fast.

FORTY-FOUR

Wednesday, 5:30 PM—Rio Grande River Valley Outside Juarez City

Karina pressed the binocular lenses against her brow, scanning the farmhouse windows for movement. From their vantage in the scrubby brush about one hundred yards away, she and Dakota had been surveilling the house for twenty minutes from a clear line of sight. The Suburban was parked behind a small rise.

A soft light flickered on in the corner, illuminating a figure she knew all too well. The curtains parted and the shadow became clearer. "Sofia?" she whispered, thoroughly convinced. "It's her. It's Sofia."

Dakota rushed back to the Suburban. Karina kept her gaze fixed on the window where her sister remained. Every fiber, every nerve, every muscle screamed—run to the house, burst through the door, gather Sofia up in her arms. She watched as the shadow moved again. "Please," she said, barely over her pounding heart. "Please, God, keep her safe."

Despite the cool breeze, sweat spread across her forehead and lower back. Sofia was gone from the window. Other shadows emerged. Larger shadows. Men. Her captors.

The crunch of footsteps behind Karina had her flinch. She whirled to find Dakota approaching from the SUV.

"Here," he said, holding out a pistol. "Just in case."

She stared at the sleek metal. Her body quaked. But she reached for the weapon regardless. "What do I do with this?"

"I'm going to check out the farmhouse," he replied, his voice low and steady. "That's in case somebody comes before I get back."

Sweat seeped down Karina's spine more freely. Dakota was leaving her, but only to rescue Sofia. She nodded her unspoken approval.

She glanced at the farmhouse. Somewhere inside, her sister was waiting for someone to save her. Karina tightened her grip on the pistol, the metal cold against her palm. "Be careful."

He stepped to her and leaned in.

Her heart clenched. Her breath became more rapid. "Go," she said. "Go get my sister."

———

THE ACERBIC STENCH of chemicals burned Eli's nostrils. The swirling lights cast a sinister red gleam across the makeshift lab's rusted pipes and decaying walls. His heart hammered in sync with the intermitting shrill of the alarm. The faint shouts of the incoming cartel soldiers unleashed a torrent of adrenaline, firing his senses into overdrive.

The boys huddled. Their eyes widened with terror.

Their fear twisted a knot inside Eli's gut. He needed to get them out. Now.

But the lab was a maze of machinery and pipes, and the only known exit was the tunnel he and Emilio had come through. And between them and that tunnel, men marched in a hurried pace. Voices blared commands in Spanish.

Moving to the assortment of glass containers filled with various colored liquids, Eli was ready to execute his crazy idea. His world narrowed to pinpoint focus. It was risky, but it could be their only chance.

Emilio's shoulders slumped. He glanced at the containers filled with chemicals, then back at Eli. Understanding dawned in his eyes, as did a grim frown. He clenched his jaw and nodded.

The trembling boys pressed closer together. One of them broke down, his whimper silenced by the blaring alarm. Emilio's posture slackened. He placed a comforting hand on the boy's shoulder.

Eli swallowed what little moisture remained in his mouth. The sounds of footsteps grew closer. *God, give me strength to get these kids out alive.*

He moved to the containers. Their labels—pictograms of bright red diamonds and orange flames screamed danger. Sweat dampened Eli's temples.

Emilio's gaze darted to the dark tunnel entrance, then back at Eli. "What do you need me to do?" His voice was surprisingly calm.

Eli inhaled through his mouth to steady his nerves. It was a gamble, but it could be their only chance. "Get the boys ready to run and pray that this works."

Just as the thundering sound of boots against concrete reached a crescendo, close to entering the lab, one of the boys let out a high-pitched scream. *"Conozco una salida.*

Conozco una salida. Hay un pasaje secreto escondido detrás del equipo." His words tumbled out in rapid Spanish.

Emilio's brow shot up. "He says he knows a way out. A secret passage behind the equipment."

Eli ran a hand over his brow. A secret passage? Trusting the boy was a gamble, but better than the alternative.

The footfalls grew louder. Harsh voices, tinged with fury, blared out commands. They were close. Too close. Only seconds now before these men burst into the lab.

"Have him show us," he said to Emilio. "Quickly."

Emilio translated.

The boy, no more than fifteen, hesitated. His dark eyes, set in a face still rounded with youth, darted between Emilio and the approaching sounds. With a quick nod, he bolted for the back of the lab.

Dozens of footsteps turned the corner. No choice but to trust the boy now.

Emilio herded the boys to follow their comrade.

Eli grabbed a chemical container with a flame on its label.

As they moved deeper into the plant, the sounds of the approaching men faded slightly. The boy led them to a stack of crates and, with shaking hands, pushed them aside. And there, behind the crates, was a narrow opening—a secret passage, just as he'd said.

Eli's heart soared. The passage was dark and cramped, and there was no telling where it led. He turned to Emilio. "Get the boys moving in there. I'll buy us some time."

Emilio nodded. He ushered the boys into the opening, their small forms disappearing into the darkness.

Eli breathed in and gripped the container. With a sense of calmness that only comes with the experience of battle, he turned to make a stand.

His pulse surged. Every muscle, every tendon, every sinew in his body was primed with a readiness to spring.

A rag-tag mass burst around the corner. Men in white shirts and blue bandanas. A dozen fanned out across the lab. Pistols. Shotguns. Rifles. Wild eyes. Contorted faces. Angry young men seeking violence.

Shouts echoed off walls.

Eli spotted a red barrel near a stained table. Skull and crossbones. He hurled his flame labeled container. Glass shattered. Orange liquid spilled.

A moment of stillness.

Then, chaos.

The barrel erupted. Yellow geyser. Men screamed. Acid ate through clothes and flesh. They fell. Writhed. Convulsed.

Panic spread. Gunfire erupted. Bullets pinged off equipment. Some men fled back to the tunnel.

Whoosh. The lab ignited. Heat blasted. Smoke thickened. Chemicals and flesh burned.

Eli slipped into the narrow opening. Crawled. Scraped palms. Tore pants. Lungs burned.

Behind him, flames roared. Screams and fizzling fire mixed like a symphony of terror. Eli pushed the thoughts away. Focus on the boys. Get them to safety.

DISTANT GUNFIRE WOKE Maria Perez in the confined space of her cage in the isolated room of her new prison. She bolted upright. The girl in the cage next to her stirred—her face etched with lines of uncertainty. Then a muted boom like a distant thunderclap rocked the room.

Dust and debris rained down from the air ducts. Her eyes stung and she tasted ash.

The smell of chemicals flooded her nostrils. She coughed and squinted through a smokey haze. Wide-eyed with terror, the girl next to her had her mouth open in a silent scream.

The whole building shuddered with a series of smaller explosions. Maria's ears rang. She gripped the cage wire that confined her to steady herself.

Through the grimy window on the far wall, angry flames licked the night sky. Plumes of thick smoke billowed upward, like clouds swallowing the stars. Shouting and gunfire mingled with the whooshing from the fire.

Ana from across the room rattled her cage's gate. "What's happening?"

Maria shook her head, unable to formulate an answer. What was happening? Was this a rescue attempt? Or had something gone horribly wrong?

FORTY-FIVE

Wednesday, 5:57 PM—Rio Grande River Valley Farmhouse, Outside Juarez City

Karina crouched in the shadows, 100 yards from the farmhouse. Beside her, Dakota pulled his pistol. Metal clicked against metal as he slid something from the handle, inspected it, then locked it back in place.

The farmhouse door flew open with a bang. She instinctively shrank lower, her pulse quickening. Five men charged out, their voices raised in rapid, urgent Spanish—too far away for her to decipher. The stillness of the night shattered into a frenzy of movement. Karina's grip tightened around the gun Dakota had given her. "What's happening?" she whispered, a tremor in her voice.

Dakota's gaze remained fixed on the house. "I'm not sure yet."

The men jumped into one of the cars. The engine roared to life, tearing down the driveway, gravel spitting from beneath the tires in a cloud of dust.

"But our odds just improved," Dakota muttered, pointing to a spot a few yards from the farmhouse where moonlight glinted off a metallic surface. "And I'm about to make them even better."

"Dakota..." Karina began, but her words were cut off as his warm lips met hers—firm, commanding. The kiss was brief, but it sent a tremor of reassurance through her. For that fleeting moment, the fear melted away.

Then, he pulled back, a soft smile brushing his lips. "I won't be long." He checked his gun again, then vanished into the shadows with long, purposeful strides.

The night closed in around her, every nerve on edge, every sound magnified. She raised the binoculars to her eyes, heart thudding, her mind a whirl of terrifying scenarios—what could they be doing to Sofia? She strained to see any movement inside the farmhouse. What was happening behind those walls?

Through the binoculars, Dakota moved stealthily, his silhouette low and deliberate, like a predator in the hunt.

He pressed himself against the farmhouse's weathered boards, inching his head up to peer into a window. Karina's breath hitched. What was inside? Were there more men? Did they have weapons trained on him?

Dakota crept from one window to the next, his movements in sync with the rhythm of Karina's breath. Finally, he made a break for the satellite dish. His fingers curled around the metal as he twisted it sharply to the side. The sound of groaning metal carried across the distance to her. He'd severed the farmhouse's connection to the outside world.

A figure stormed out of the house, his silhouette menacing in the dim light spilling from the open door. Karina's heart pounded in her ears. Had he spotted Dakota?

She watched, frozen, as the man stalked toward the dish, his eyes scanning the shadows.

Like a ghost, Dakota materialized behind him, his arm snaking around the man's neck. There was a brief, violent struggle, but Dakota's grip was iron. The man went limp, his body collapsing into Dakota's arms, where he was lowered gently to the ground.

Karina let out a shaky breath, but the tension in her chest refused to release. Dakota's eyes found hers across the distance, his hand rising in a silent signal for her to follow. For a moment, fear held her in place, her legs stiff. But Sofia's face flashed in her mind, and her resolve hardened.

She lowered the binoculars and steadied her trembling limbs. Sofia needed her.

With each step, the cool night air bit at her skin, but her focus was singular. She passed the unconscious man, her heart in her throat, fingers clenching the pistol. Her mind was racing, but her legs carried her forward.

She reached Dakota, crouching beside him in the farmhouse's shadow, the rough wood scraping through her shirt. His presence—steady, warm—was the only thing keeping her anchored.

"Stay here," he whispered. "I'll be back before you know it." Then he slipped away, vanishing once again into the night.

Seconds stretched into eternity. Every nerve screamed with tension as horrifying possibilities churned in her mind. What if the men were waiting for him inside? What if they'd already killed him? She swallowed against the rising bile, her stomach twisting in knots.

A floorboard creaked inside the house. Karina's head snapped up, heart hammering. Was it Dakota? Or had someone found him? Her grip tightened on the pistol as her body tensed.

Suddenly, the door swung open. Karina gasped, staring

at the small figure that emerged—slight, fragile, illuminated by the faint glow from within.

"Sofia," she breathed, hope flooding her chest.

Sofia's wide, frightened eyes found hers. For a brief moment, they stared at each other, disbelief and relief crossing the distance. Then, Sofia broke into a run, her bare feet flying across the grass. Karina surged forward, her legs feeling impossibly heavy, but her need to reach Sofia stronger.

They collided, arms tangling, sobs wracking their bodies. Karina clutched her sister, tears streaming down her face, her heart threatening to burst with a mix of love and anguish. Sofia's face pressed into her chest, her sobs muffled against Karina's body.

"You came," Sofia whispered, her voice trembling. "You really came."

Karina's throat tightened, her words choked by emotion. "Of course I came, hermana. I will always come for you."

Movement at the door drew Karina's attention. Dakota appeared, shoving a battered, bruised man to his knees. The cartel soldier's eyes flickered with defiance, but the fire had dimmed.

"One of Ramirez's soldiers," Dakota said, voice grim. "Found him trying to watch a soccer match with bad reception."

Karina's arms tightened around Sofia. Her heart surged with fierce protectiveness, glancing between Dakota and the man he'd captured. They'd done it. Sofia was safe.

Dakota crouched in front of the soldier, his voice low, cold. "Why did the others leave? Where did they go?"

The man spat on the ground, refusing to answer.

"*Por qué se fueron los demás?*" Karina screamed, her voice shaking. "*A dónde fueron?*"

"*Púdrete en el infierno*," the man growled, the curse rough and venomous.

Dakota leaned closer, his voice dropping to a dangerous whisper. "Tell him he has two choices. He can talk, or I'll hand him over to the Texas Rangers. And trust me, they don't take kindly to men who hurt underage girls."

Karina translated with a steely tone.

The man's bravado cracked. Fear flickered in his eyes.

Dakota's lips curled. "You'll be labeled a pedophile in prison. It's a death sentence, and you won't last a week."

Karina shivered, trying to suppress the rising anger. Men like this deserved worse.

The cartel soldier's gaze flickered between them. "*Yo... yo no...*" he stammered, but Dakota silenced him with a cold glare.

"Last chance," Dakota growled. "Talk, or you'll regret it."

Karina repeated the threat in Spanish.

Finally, the man's shoulders slumped. "*Hubo un problema*," he muttered. "*En la planta abandonada del Señor Garza. Alguien irrumpió y liberó a la mano de obra esclava.*"

Karina's heart stopped. She struggled to breathe. "He says there was an issue at Señor Garza's abandoned plant. Someone broke in and freed the workers."

Her eyes met Dakota's, fear rising anew.

"Emilio. Eli," Karina whispered. "They're in trouble."

FORTY-SIX

Wednesday, 5:58 PM—Garza Plant, Rio Grande River Valley Outside Juarez City

Eli crawled through the passageway faster, his breath shallow, his mind focused only on survival. The faint pinprick of light ahead grew brighter with each strained movement. Finally, he pressed through the opening and gasped for air. With a final push, he burst through the opening and gasped for air, stumbling to his feet. His legs felt unsteady, but he stayed upright—no time to rest. Emilio and the boys were there, wide-eyed, fear etched into their faces.

An earsplitting boom shook the plant's foundation. Blistering heat slapped against Eli's exposed skin. The stinging scent of combusting chemicals and melting metal filled his nostrils. Sweat poured down his back, mingling with the grime of the escape.

Eli spun toward the eruption, eyes burning in the thick, advancing smoke.

The boy tugged at Emilio's sleeve, screaming with urgency.

Emilio nodded. "He says we need to follow him. Now."

Eli urged the group forward through the corridor's twists as the searing heat warmed the back of his neck.

Suddenly, the boy skidded to a halt, his small hand grabbing the knob of a metal door. "*Salida*" blazed in bright red letters above.

But the knob didn't budge. The boy whimpered, pushing against the door in desperation. Emilio shoved him aside and yanked on the handle. His muscles tightened through his shirt. "It's locked," he rasped, panic clear in his voice. The roar of the fire was closing in, its breath hot and furious.

KARINA HELD Sofia tight as the Suburban sped toward the plant. The sense of urgency pulled them closer. thickening the air inside the car. Gravel crunched beneath the tires, the sound grating against Karina's already frayed nerves. As Dakota swerved off the trail, the vehicle jerked and jolted, brushing against low-hanging branches.

Her heart pounded as they crested a small rise, the factory sprawling out before them, a scene of pure chaos and terror. Through the tinted windows, Karina could see thick, black smoke pouring from shattered upper-story windows. The flames within glowed like malevolent eyes, threatening to devour everything.

"This isn't just an abandoned plant," she whispered. "It's a hellhole."

Dakota's hands tightened on the wheel, his knuckles white with tension. Without a word, he glanced over his shoulder, meeting Karina's wide eyes. "Stay here with

Sofia," he said quietly, his voice laced with an urgency that struck her core. "I'll bring Emilio back."

Fear for her brother gnawed at Karina's insides, but she nodded, too choked with emotion to speak. Dakota's hand briefly brushed hers, his warmth grounding her before he pulled away. She watched as he leaped from the Suburban and disappeared into the smoke-filled night.

ELI GRITTED HIS TEETH, pushing past Emilio to grab the door handle. The metal burned against his palm, but he ignored the pain. He braced his foot against the wall and pulled, muscles straining with the effort. "Come on!" he growled through gritted teeth, adrenaline fueling his every action.

The door wouldn't give. The heat pressed closer, and the smoke—thick and suffocating—stole the air from his lungs. Panic gnawed at him, but he refused to let it show. The boys' wide eyes bore into him, looking to him for protection.

Behind them, the fire's roar grew louder. A hellish reminder of their dwindling time.

Eli's heart slammed against his ribs. He had to get them out. Now. His pulse thudded in his ears, drowning out the cries of the boys and the roaring flames.

Emilio stood by, his head bowed, lips moving in silent prayer. It should have been a comforting sight, but in that moment, Eli felt only helplessness.

Then, the unmistakable sound. A soft, metallic click.

The door unlocked.

FORTY-SEVEN

Wednesday, 5:58 PM—Garza Plant, Rio Grande River Valley Near Juarez City

Karina's eyes couldn't leave the spot where Dakota had vanished. Her chest tightened, each breath a battle. "Please, God. Bring him back to me. Bring them all back."

Sofia's small hand clung to Karina's blouse, her fingers digging into the fabric like talons. Karina's arm encircled Sofia's trembling frame, pulling her close. The rapid flutter of Sofia's heartbeat echoed Karina's own frantic pulse.

Karina swayed, the motion instinctive, a futile attempt to calm them both. "Shh, it's going to be okay." The words tasted like ash in her mouth, hope warring with despair. "Dakota will find Emilio. He has to." But the roar of flames and distant screams mocked her assurance.

Sofia whimpered, burying her face in Karina's shirt. The dampness of her tears seeped through, a stark contrast to the heat radiating from the inferno before them. Karina's vision swam, but she blinked furiously, willing the tears away. She had to be strong. For Sofia. For Emilio.

Smoke stung Karina's nostrils as flames licked at shattered windows, casting eerie, dancing shadows. Then, movement caught her eye. Dakota, a lone figure against the chaos, sprinting to the building. Karina held her breath. A mix of terror and desperate hope tore at her throat.

He approached a side door, barely visible through the billowing smoke and panicked workers. His hand grasped the handle, and Karina's muscles tensed as if she could will the door open.

"Lord," she whispered, her voice raw, "if you're listening, please... keep them safe. Bring them back to us."

The door burst open. Karina's heart leapt to her throat. A figure emerged from the smoke-filled doorway. Emilio—alive and uninjured. A sob of relief spilled from Karina's chest, leaving her dizzy and lightheaded.

Close behind, Eli, his broad shoulders hunched protectively as he ushered a group of young boys through the doorway.

"Thank God," Karina breathed, the words a prayer and celebration in one.

The children stumbled into the harsh glare of floodlights, their eyes wide with shock and confusion. Soot streaked their faces, tears carving pale tracks through the grime. Dakota and Eli gathered them close, checking for injuries and murmuring words of comfort.

Sofia's grip on Karina's hand tightened painfully. "Those boys," she whispered, her voice quavering. "They're... They're my age."

Karina looked down at her sister, truly seeing her for the first time since this nightmare began. The reality of what could have been—what still might be for others—carved an ache in her chest. She nodded, unable to speak past the lump in her throat.

The rescued boys limped to the gate, each step a victory

against exhaustion and terror. Eli, Dakota, and Emilio formed a protective barrier around them. Karina's heart swelled, a fervent "thank you" rising to her lips.

But as the others passed through the gate, Emilio turned, his posture suddenly alert. Karina followed his gaze, dread pooling in her stomach. About twenty meters to his right, near the plant entrance, an old yellow school bus stood out against the chaos. A piercing girl's scream cut through the air, raising goosebumps on Karina's arms.

Her blood ran cold as she recognized a figure at the bus door. Hector Ramirez, Carlos' younger brother, his face twisted in a cruel sneer as he yanked a young girl's arm.

"No," Karina whispered, her momentary relief evaporating. "Dear God, no."

MARIA'S FINGERTIPS scraped against bare skin. Her muscles screamed as she strained against Hector's iron grip, desperate for her last chance at freedom.

"*Suéltame!*" she hissed, the Spanish rolling off her tongue, pleading. "Let me go!"

Hector's hands pressed harder, bruising the flesh already mottled in her arm. Maria's ears rang with a high-pitched whine, the world muffled as if she were underwater. She squinted through the thick, black smoke that stung her nostrils, searching for a miracle in the chaos.

And there—like an answer to her unspoken prayers—she saw him.

Emilio Castillo, alive and unbroken, was herding a group of young boys to the compound gate. Relief and terror warred in her chest, hope blooming even as dread threatened to choke her.

"Emilio," she screamed. Hot tears spilled down her cheeks. He was here, not dead in the desert as she'd feared, but saving others—just as he'd once saved her mother from breast cancer.

"Por favor, Dios," Maria whispered, her faith a fragile thing in this hell. "Please, God, let him see me."

She thrashed, every movement a rebellion against Hector. If she could break free, run to Emilio, throw her arms around him, and never let go.

"Emilio," she called above the din. *"Ayúdame! Estoy aquí!"*

As if he'd heard her, Emilio's head swiveled, scanning the turmoil. His gaze locked with hers across the sea of panicked faces and billowing smoke. In that moment, Maria saw everything she'd lost—and everything she could regain. Home. Family. Safety. A future free from fear.

A deafening crack split the air. Maria flinched, her ears ringing anew. Hector had fired his pistol.

Emilio shoved the boys to two unfamiliar men. Then he turned, sprinting toward the bus—toward her and Hector.

Terror seized Maria's heart, squeezing until she could barely breathe. "No, Emilio!" She redoubled her efforts to break free, twisting and clawing at any exposed skin she could reach. If she could just make him understand, make him turn back before it was too late.

"Vete!" she screamed, her voice breaking. "Go! Please, Emilio! It's a trap!"

But Emilio kept running, his eyes fixed on her with grim determination. And in that moment, Maria realized the price of her salvation might come too high.

KARINA'S FINGERS dug into the Suburban's door handle. What was Emilio doing? "Go back!" she yelled, her voice lost in the cacophony of gunfire and screams. "You can't save that girl!"

Emilio sprinted across the lot, concrete dust puffing up with each desperate stride. He kept advancing, ignoring the danger.

"No!" Karina cried out, her throat raw from the smoke that hung in the air.

A shot rang out, sharp and final. A crimson mist puffed from the top of Emilio's shoulder, suspended for a split second.

He staggered. His face contorted. But he kept moving toward Hector and the girl. Another crack split the air. Then his body jerked as if yanked by an invisible cord. He crumpled like a deflating balloon.

"Emilio!" Karina's agonized scream tore through her. She lurched forward, her body moving of its own accord.

Sofia sobbed beside her, her small frame shaking violently. "Is he... is he dead?"

Karina couldn't answer. She couldn't breathe. The world narrowed to her brother's still form on the ground.

THE CHAOS around Maria faded as Hector loosened his grip on her arm. She broke free, her legs propelled by some invisible force as she ran to reach Emilio. *"Emilio, soy yo, Maria!"* The words barely left her lips before two more shots rang out, echoing through the lot like a death knell.

Emilio's body jerked once, twice. Then he crumpled and fell.

A scream of pure anguish ripped through Maria's lips.

"No, Emilio. No!" She pushed herself harder, ignoring the burning in her lungs, the screaming of her muscles. The world around her closed in, tunneling to a single point.

Emilio's still form.

His eyes wide with shock.

A dark stain spread across his chest, his life bleeding out onto the cold concrete.

Maria fell beside him, her hands hovering over his chest —afraid to touch, afraid to make it real.

A bullet whizzed above. A strong arm clutched her waist, lifting her off the ground.

She thrashed and kicked. *"Suéltame. Tengo que ayudar-lo."* The words exploded from her in a desperate plea.

"Stop fighting, girl," a gruff voice commanded in American English. "I'm here to help."

Maria's heart shattered as the American grabbed Emilio's collar and drag his limp body across the asphalt. His eyes fluttered once, twice, then stilled.

"Lo siento, Emilio," she whispered, the fight draining out of her. "I'm sorry. I'm so sorry."

KARINA'S WORLD WAS TEETERING. She couldn't hear her screams. Eli moved toward Hector and his men, his weapon barking as he fired. He reloaded, aimed, and fired again.

Dakota sprinted past, scooping up the girl Emilio ran to. He clutched him by his collar, dragging his still body behind him—an endless nightmare she couldn't escape.

Karina flung open the Suburban's door. She helped Dakota ease her brother into the back seat, her heart fracturing with each passing second.

Emilio's face was ashen. His shirt a vivid crimson. His eyes fluttered. He struggled to breathe. Karina cradled his face, her tears mingling with the blood on his cheeks.

"Stay with me," she pleaded, her voice a broken whisper. "Please, Emilio, stay with me."

But with each shallow breath, Karina felt her brother slipping away. His pulse fluttered weakly beneath her fingers, life draining from him with each beat. Sofia's sobs filled the car as she clutched Emilio's hand.

Eli herded the rescued children into the Suburban, ordering them to stay down. The engine roared to life as Dakota sped away, the sound of gunfire fading behind them.

Karina held Emilio close, feeling the warmth leaving his body. His eyes blinked once, twice...then stilled...his final breath a soft sigh against Karina's bloodstained blouse.

In that moment, the world ceased to exist. All that remained was the weight of her brother's body in her arms, Sofia's muffled cries, and the crushing realization that nothing would ever be the same again.

"*Vaya con Dios, mi hermano,*" Karina whispered. "Go with God, my brother."

PART 4

FORTY-EIGHT

Wednesday, 7:02 PM, Juarez City

From the front passenger seat of the speeding Suburban, Eli fixed his focus on the passing shadows. The acrid stench of chemicals and smoke clung to his clothing, a constant reminder of the horrors they'd just escaped.

The fire. The destruction. The lives lost. The innocence that'd been shattered. His stomach churned at the sight of Emilio's lifeless body, cradled in Karina's arms as she wept.

Emilio's death hung heavy with every soul inside the cramped the Suburban. In the third row and cargo area, the eight boys they'd rescued from the fentanyl lab huddled in stunned silence. Sofia's sobbing cut deep into Eli's core. Dakota's eyes glistened with unshed tears as he turned the steering wheel.

Eli's heart ached with questions and doubts. Could he have done more to save Emilio? What would they do with these boys they'd rescued? What would they do to protect Karina and Sofia and their mother now that Emilio was gone?

In the suffocating silence, Eli nodded to himself. There would be no rest until Diablos was brought to its knees. No going home to Louisiana until Karina and her family could live in peace.

Outside, the streetlights broke through the darkness, and the distant glow of the burning complex became smaller and smaller.

"Now what?" Dakota said, his words cutting through the thick fog of grief and uncertainty.

The question bore into Eli, demanding an answer. He closed his eyes for a moment to consider their options—stay and fight Diablos against overwhelming odds with limited resources, or retreat to regroup. Staying was a tempting prospect. Taking the fight to the cartel to make them pay for Emilio was the emotional choice. But they were outnumbered and outgunned. Plus, would staying in Juarez put Karina and her family at greater risk?

Or they could return to El Paso, gather reinforcements with Blackwell's team, and return with a full force of manpower and weaponry. Retreating to El Paso was the logical choice, offering the best chance of ultimate success. But the thought of leaving Karina, her family, and the girls Emilio died protecting, even briefly, felt like a betrayal—a failure to those who needed them most.

He opened his eyes with a heavy sigh, his gaze meeting Dakota's once more. "We go back to El Paso." His voice was rough with emotion. "There, we can regroup with Blackwell, use our intel to plan, and come back with everything we've got." The words, a concession to the reality of their situation, were like chewing glass. But as much as it pained him, he knew it was the right call. They'd achieved their objective and had gathered the information they needed. It was time to use that knowledge to their advantage and bring the cartel down once and for all.

Dakota tucked his chin and tightened his jaw. "Go back? You can't be serious." He glanced over his shoulder at Karina caressing Emilio's pale forehead. "We've got to make the cartel pay for what they've done."

Eli couldn't argue with his friend's courage and determination. But their challenge required more than just nerve. He and Dakota would return to El Paso, and when the time was right, they'd bring the full force of their fury down on Diablos and Garza and all those responsible for the terror he'd witnessed over the past five days. They'd find justice for Emilio. No matter what.

KARINA GENTLY RAN her fingers through Emilio's tangled hair. Air left her chest slowly. Scalding, salty tears flowed across her lips. Dakota's face flushed as if he wanted vengeance. But as her heart demanded retribution against those responsible for her brother's death, Karina agreed with Colt's perspective.

She lifted her gaze from Emilio's face, meeting Dakota's eyes in the rearview mirror. "Dakota, Eli is right. You can't do this alone."

Dakota's expression fell. "I won't leave you and your family here to suffer alone. Colt can go back across the border. I'm staying."

Emilio's expression was serene. Peaceful. He was home now—home with his Jesus. "My brother deserves justice. Juarez deserves justice. But not at the cost of more innocent lives."

She glanced over at Sofia, her petite body shaking with

silent sobs. Karina's heart broke all over again, the sight of her sister's pain a reminder of all they'd lost.

"I have to think about my family. My mother and Sofia," she said. "If you stay to fight Diablos and Cesar alone, you'll only be putting us in more danger." She wiped away another tear. "Please, Dakota. I can't lose anyone else. Not like this."

The rage in Dakota's eyes softened. His shoulders slumped. He nodded slowly. "Okay." His voice was now soothing. "We'll go back to El Paso. But I'm coming back, I promise."

A fierce determination rose inside Karina. She brushed away the moisture beneath each eye. "I know." Her voice was steady. She must protect her family now.

Her phone buzzed.

Mamá.

How would Karina tell her mother that her son was dead?

ELI LEAPED from the Suburban before it fully stopped, as Dakota pulled up behind Karina's childhood home. The warmth from Eli's previous visit had vanished, replaced by a darkness that now enveloped the family.

As he approached the front door, it swung open. The tear-stained face of Karina's mother was pallor. "Where's my sweet boy?"

Eli stepped back to the Suburban to help Dakota carry Emilio's body into the house.

"*Mi hijo*," his mother sobbed, reaching for Emilio with shaky hands. "My boy, my precious boy."

Karina stepped forward, her own tears flowing freely as

she embraced her mother. "*Lo siento, Mamá,*" she said, her voice choked with emotion. "I'm so sorry."

As Eli and Dakota crossed the threshold, the weight of the neighbors' stares, curiosity, and concern radiated from nearby houses.

Eli tensed. Someone was approaching in a hurry from down the street. Diablos had eyes everywhere. He hurried Emilio to a bedroom, then reached for his gun.

But as he listened to the crowd that gathered outside, the anger and frustration that simmered in their conversations, he realized these people were not there to harm. They, too, were victims, victims who'd suffered under the cartel's reign of terror for far too long.

One man shouted, "*Ya es suficiente!*" His voice was raw with rage. "They murdered *El Santo de las Calles.* We must fight back."

Other voices rose in a defiant chorus. "*Es hora de que retomemos nuestra ciudad.*"

A flame ignited in Eli's chest. The people wanted to take back their city. Maybe there's hope for Juarez after all.

Suddenly, a commotion arose from the street. A gaunt man with weathered skin and calloused hands burst through the crowd, his faded blue-collared shirt damp with sweat. "Maria! Where's my Maria?" he cried, his eyes wild with desperation.

Maria emerged from the bedroom, tears streaming down her face. "Papa!" They embraced fiercely, the man's shoulders shaking. He looked up, his gaze falling on Emilio's still form. "Gracias," he whispered, crossing himself. "Your son saved my daughter." He glanced up at Maria's mother. "We will never forget his sacrifice."

But the moment was shattered by the buzzing of Karina's phone. She pulled it from her pocket. The color drained from her cheeks as she studied the screen. "It's Cesar. He wants me to meet him at the hotel."

The room fell eerily silent, as if all the air had been sucked out. Eli's thoughts tumbled over each other. *Does Garza know something?*

Karina's mother stepped forward, her face set in hard lines. "*Si vas.*" Her voice steady despite the tears. "Sofia and I will go with you. You'll face him with your family. Not alone."

A young man who'd eavesdropped at the open door relayed the woman's message. The neighbors erupted in harmonious support. "*Estamos contigo,*" they cried, "We'll go too."

Eli's heart swelled for the courage of these brave people. A revolt within Juarez against Diablos could accelerate Blackwell's assault against the cartel.

Karina motioned to Eli and Dakota. Her features were still clouded, but there was fire in her eyes. "Look, return to El Paso. Regroup, yeah? But don't take too long. And when you come back..." She paused, her eyes pleading. "Remember your promise. Take us to America. This city... there's nothing for us."

Eli glanced at Dakota as Karina's words settled between them. The task she'd asked was not small. Between immigration and the political fervor in the United States, they couldn't make such—

"We promise," Dakota said with little hesitation. "I swear to you, Karina, I'll come back for you and your family. And you won't have to wait long."

WITH THE SETTING sun came an eerie calm, broken only by the faint rumble of distant thunder. A cold sweat moistened Karina's palms as she lowered her mobile phone, Garza's icy demand still ringing in her ears.

Karina's gaze drifted to a wide-eyed Sofia. How could she shield her baby sister from Cesar's horrors at his hotel? But then again, how could she protect her from Diablos at her mother's home?

She swallowed the lump in her throat that threatened to choke her. It was Emilio's death that gave her neighbors courage. They were willing to fight against evil. "Okay," she said to her mother. "But understand that Cesar is danger-ous. You leave him to me."

Mamá responded with a halfhearted nod. "We know the risks, *mija*. But your brother's killers must be destroyed." She glanced at Emilio's body. Her shoulders sagged. "Look what they did to my boy."

Colors faded to gray. A relentless ache settled in Kari-na's bones. She closed her eyes, then opened them again, but the same pain reflected in her mother's eyes. "I'm sorry. I never meant for this to happen. If I'd known what Garza was capable of, I would never have been involved with him."

Mamá took Karina's hand. "God forgives you, *mija*. And so do I. And now we have the chance to make a differ-ence. To honor Emilio by standing up to those who took him from us."

Her mother's words reinforced Karina's sense of purpose. Facing Cesar at the hotel would be difficult, but her family and neighbors made her stronger than she'd ever been before.

Dakota stepped closer. "When we return, where will you be?"

Karina took a deep breath. "At Hotel Celebracion. We should be safe there, at least for a few days."

"But where in the hotel?" Eli asked. "Things might get a bit dicey there when we return."

"Hopefully my suite," Karina said. "But if we need to hide, we'll go back to the rooftop. So far, that's worked pretty well."

"How will we know?"

Karina tapped her chin with a finger. "I'll put out a signal."

"A signal?" Dakota said.

"A red signal," Karina smiled. "Look for something red."

FORTY-NINE

Friday 10:30 *AM—El Paso, TX*

Juan Morales clasped his hands as he observed from behind the two-way mirror at FBI headquarters in El Paso. The pale white walls of the interview room seemed to encroach on the two men inside. The room contained only a metal table, bolted to the floor, and two chairs on opposite sides, emphasizing the power imbalance between interrogator and suspect.

Seated in one of the chairs was Cesar Garza's El Paso banker, Doug Whittaker—a portly man with a shiny face, a pressed blue suit straining against his ample frame, and thinning gray hair combed over in a futile attempt to conceal his hair loss. His pale blue eyes darted nervously around the room, never quite settling on anything. His pudgy fingers drummed an anxious rhythm on the tabletop.

Opposite Whittaker sat Special Agent Marcus Blackwell leaning back in his chair, the wrinkles in his off-the-rack suit deepening with each subtle shift. His tie hung askew, the knot pulled low enough to reveal the unbuttoned top of his rumpled shirt. Despite his long night, his eyes remained sharp, darting between the folder and the sleek electronic device on the table. His fingers drummed a quiet rhythm next to the gadget, a silent testament to the hours of wiretapped conversations and transcripts it held—the fruits of the FBI's meticulous surveillance of Whittaker's office.

The steady drone of the air conditioner was the only sound. Morales took a deep breath. The stale recycled air did little to calm his racing heart.

Morales exhaled and fogged the glass as Blackwell pressed a button on a small recorder. Static crackled for a moment before the smooth, commanding voice of Cesar Garza spilled out of the intercom.

"Doug, I need you to move the funds from the Cayman account to the one in Zurich," Garza's voice was smooth and commanding, with an accent that betrayed his Mexican roots.

"Of course, Mr. Garza," Whittaker replied, his tone oily with a touch of nervousness. "I'll make sure it's done by the end of the day."

"Good. And what about the shipment? Did it arrive as planned?" Garza's voice took on a harder edge.

"Yes, sir. The drugs and uh... the... the children... they arrived last night. The buyers are ready to make the exchange."

Morales' gut twisted in disgust.

"Excellent," Garza said with obvious delight. "Keep this up, Doug, and there'll be a substantial bonus at the end of the month."

"Thank you, Mr. Garza. I appreciate your generosity."

The recording ended with a click. Nausea hit Morales like a sharp jab to his gut, sending a sour taste rising in the back of his throat.

Blackwell's fingers laced together behind his head, forming a cradle of calm authority. His face settled into an inscrutable mask, a blank canvas except for his eyes—sharp, unwavering, boring into Whittaker with the intensity of a laser sight finding its target. "Mr. Whittaker, I believe you have some explaining to do. Why are you laundering money for a foreign interest involved in trafficking drugs and children?"

Whittaker's face paled, and he tugged at his collar as if it were suddenly too tight. Beads of sweat formed on the banker's forehead. His eyes shifted right and left, never quite meeting Blackwell's steady gaze.

But he said nothing.

Leaning forward, Blackwell rested his elbows on the table. "Come now, Mr. Whittaker. We have the recordings. We have the evidence. You're in deep. So deep, the only way out is for you to cooperate."

Clasping his hands together, Whittaker made a futile attempt to still their tremors. He opened his mouth as if to speak, then clenched his lips tight.

"You're looking at serious prison time, Doug," Blackwell continued, his voice firm and unyielding. "May I call you Doug?" Blackwell paused. "Laundering money for drugs is bad enough, but human trafficking puts you in Supermax for life."

Whittaker's face crumpled. He opened his mouth once again as if he might break down completely. But then, he seemed to gather himself, drawing in a deep, shuddering breath. "Where's my lawyer?" The words barely escaped his lips. "I called him an hour ago."

A sharp tap at the door behind him jolted Morales from his focus. He turned as an agent popped his head into the observation room.

"Mr. Whittaker's attorney has arrived," the agent informed him in a respectful yet urgent tone.

A sinking sensation hit the pit of Morales' stomach. He'd hoped, perhaps naively, that Whittaker would choose to cooperate without the interference of a defense attorney. But the banker's request for his lawyer was a clear indication that he intended to fight. Good luck with that.

Morales nodded his understanding. "What's the attorney's—"

The impeccably dressed Preston Somerset, the high-powered defense attorney from San Diego who'd effectively orchestrated Marco Domingo's avoiding prosecution, strode into the room. The hairs on the back of Morales' neck stood on end. This attorney represented the worst of the worst, criminals with deep pockets who thought themselves above the law. And now, he was here on behalf of Doug Whittaker; and surely, on behalf of Cesar Garza too.

What did Somerset's presence mean for the case against Garza? And how would Morales navigate this new speed bump?

"Mr. Morales, I wish I could say it's a pleasure to see you again but given the circumstances..." Somerset's voice was smooth and polished and condescending.

"Mr. Somerset." Morales kept his tone cool and measured. "I'm surprised to see you here. I wasn't aware that Mr. Whittaker was one of your clients."

The lawyer's chuckle sent a ripple of irritation through Morales. "Mr. Whittaker is a respected member of the El Paso business community, and he deserves the best legal representation available, which is why he called me."

"Your respected client was caught on tape admitting to laundering money for a drug and human-trafficking enterprise from across the border." Morales lifted his chin for effect. "For Cesar Garza, who I'll guess is another client of yours?"

Somerset's smile didn't falter. The glint in his eye made Morales uneasy. "If such wiretaps exist, and I don't doubt your word, I'm confident they were obtained illegally."

Blood warmed Morales' face. He'd rarely wanted to punch a man like he did now.

Somerset threw his head back and laughed, a deep, belly laugh that filled the small observation room. "Oh, Counselor." He wiped a tear of amusement from his eye. "You really have no idea who you're up against, do you?" He reached into his briefcase and pulled out a document, holding it out with a flourish. "This is a motion to suppress those wiretaps. I think you'll find that your case against my client is built on flimsy evidence."

Morales took the document, flipped through the pages, and read the legal jargon.

Somerset's smile was all teeth and no warmth. "Now, if you'll excuse me, I need to confer with my client." He brushed past Morales to enter the interview room. He pointed an accusing finger at Blackwell. "You. Out."

Following Somerset into the interview room, Morales braced himself for the planned confrontation. Blackwell remained seated, his expression calm and unruffled despite the tension Somerset tried to bring with him.

"Agent," Somerset said, his voice dripping with disdain. "I believe I made it clear that this interview is over. My client will not be answering any more questions."

Blackwell didn't move, his gaze steady as he met Somerset's glare. "Your client is under arrest, and so are you."

Somerset's face twisted. He leaned forward as if to

touch Blackwell's nose with his own. "How dare you? Do you have any idea who you're dealing with? I'll have your badge for this, and I'll sue you and your entire agency for harassment and wrongful arrest!"

Hot blood surged through Morales' veins at Somerset's arrogance. He wanted to lash out, to put the smug attorney in his place, but he held his tongue. This was Blackwell's show, and the agent remained unflappable in the face of Somerset's threats.

Blackwell's finger hovered over the device on the table. A heartbeat passed. Another. And another. He pressed play.

A voice filled the room. Familiar. Damning. Garza.

"Preston, I need you to make sure those kids from Honduras get through customs without any problems. I don't care how much it costs, just get it done."

"What are you worried about, Cesar? I'll take care of it. I always do."

It was Somerset's smooth and confident voice; the voice that showed no hint of hesitation or fear; a fear that now flared in the defense attorney's eyes.

A satisfied smile spread across Morales' face. They had him.

Blackwell lifted a pair of handcuffs and waved them. Its metal glinted under the LED lights. "Preston Somerset, you're under arrest for conspiracy to traffic children from Mexico. You have the right to remain silent..."

They'd done it. They'd not only taken down Whittaker, but they'd also ensnared Somerset, the Diablos fly in Morales' battle against child trafficking.

Now that they had in custody, Morales' next move was crucial. Using the two men to bait Garza would require careful planning. Garza was slippery, a mastermind who rarely made mistakes. Morales had to ensure the trap was tight enough to leave Garza no way to escape.

"Now, we reel in the big fish," Morales said to Blackwell. The fight was far from over. The real battle was about to begin.

FIFTY

Saturday, 9:14 AM—Hotel Celebracion, Juarez City

Karina's fingers froze over the door handle to Cesar's office. She took a deep breath to calm the turmoil inside her stomach, then forced her hand to turn the knob. The door swung open. Karina entered. Her heels sank into the carpet as she approached Cesar behind his massive desk. His focus was on scattered documents; his jaw set in a rigid line of impatience.

Isabella sat perched on the edge of the leather sofa, her eyes bright with excitement. She wore a tight-fitting yellow dress that hugged her curves, her long hair cascading over her bare shoulders in perfect waves. Had she told them about seeing Karina with Dakota and Colt?

Raul loomed by the window, his muscular arms crossed over a loud Hawaiian shirt, his fingers occasionally twirling the ends of his mustache. His dark eyes were set on the streets below. His broad frame was tense, as if ready to spring into action at any moment. He gave Karina a brief nod, then returned his attention to the view outside.

They know. The realization hit Karina like a punch in

the gut. She clasped her trembling hands behind her back, hoping to hide her uneasiness.

"Is everything alright, *mi amor?*" Cesar looked up from his documents. "You look pale."

Karina breathed out and met his gaze. "I'm fine." Her voice sounded unconvincing. "Just a little tired, that's all."

Cesar's chair groaned as he leaned back, his eyes narrowing to probing slits that seemed to dissect her every movement.

She breathed in through her nose and held it, willing her racing heart to slow..

"I'm leaving for El Paso immediately," Cesar said, lifting his frame from behind his desk. "Urgent business requires my attention." He gestured at Isabella, who practically vibrated with euphoria. "I'm taking Isabella across the border. She is meeting with her new employer, and then they're off to Washington, DC."

Isabella bounced up from the sofa. "Isn't it wonderful, Karina? I'm going to work in America." Her eyes sparkled. A wide grin spread across her face. "For an American senator."

Karina's face ached with the effort of her forced smile. "That's great, Isabella. I'm happy for you." The words felt like shards of glass in her mouth. She wanted to scream, to warn Isabella of the danger that awaited her, but Mamá and Sofia's presence in her room silenced her.

She glanced at Cesar, trying to gauge his reaction. He'd been watching her closely, his dark eyes unreadable.

Does he suspect something? Is that why he's sending Isabella away? Or is he testing me?

Raul shifted his weight, drawing Karina's attention. He leaned against the window frame, his gaze flicking between

Cesar and Isabella. *What secrets lurked behind those watchful eyes? How much did he really know?*

"You'll be in charge of the hotel while I'm gone, Karina." Cesar's voice snapped her back to the present. "I expect everything to run smoothly in my absence."

Karina's throat constricted, choking back the questions and accusations that threatened to spill out.

Isabella flitted around the office, a butterfly oblivious to the spider's web she was about to enter. Karina's hands itched to grab her, to shake sense into her naïve head. But she couldn't. Not with Mamá and Sofia so close, so vulnerable.

A commotion erupted outside, muffled shouts growing louder. The office door burst open, banging against the wall. Carlos Ramirez stormed in, his face contorted with rage. "There's a revolt going on out there," he boomed. "People are taking to the streets, demanding justice for this so-called *Santo de las Calles* death."

The air vanished from Karina's lungs. Emilio. *My brother is dead, and they don't know I know.* The room spun around her. Grief and panic threatening to overwhelm her carefully constructed facade.

She gripped the back of a chair to maintain her composure. *They can't know. They can't suspect. One wrong move and everything—everyone—I love is at risk.*

Ramirez, hands balled into fists at his sides, pacing the room like a caged animal. "We need to do something, Garza. We can't let these people get out of control."

Cesar leaned forward, his palms on his desk. "And what do you propose I do, Carlos?" His voice was calm, but Karina could hear an undercurrent of tension. "I can't start shooting citizens."

"If you won't, I will." Ramirez's eyes blazed with fury. "They need to know who's in charge."

Look what you've done, Emilio. Karina's heart swelled with a bittersweet mixture of pride and anguish. *Even in death, you're shaking the foundations of their corrupt empire.*

"What are you thinking, Karina?" Cesar's voice reverted to sympathetic charm. "Did you know about your brother? Does your mother know?"

She looked up, schooling her features into a mask of surprise and confusion. "No, I... I didn't," she stammered, her voice sounding small. "What happened? Where is he?"

Ramirez's lips curled in a sneer. "She can't be trusted. Not her, not her mother, not even that little *puta* sister of hers."

Heat blazed through Karina, rage and fear battling for dominance. But she swallowed it down, knowing that one wrong word could seal Mamá and Sofia's fates. Heat rose from Karina's neck to the crown of her head, but she said nothing. She couldn't. Not without exposing herself and her family.

Cesar glanced at his gold watch and knitted his brow. "I don't have time for this." He grabbed his briefcase from beside the desk. "Raul, handle the situation here. I'm running late for my appointment across the river."

Raul nodded without changing expressions. "S*i, Patron.*"

Cesar turned to Karina, his eyes softening for a moment. "Walk with me," he said, his voice low and almost tender. "I have something I need to discuss with you."

What game was he playing now? She glanced at Isabella, who still beamed with excitement about her upcoming trip, unaware of the tension in the room.

Cesar's hand closed around Karina's elbow, guiding her through the door with a firm but gentle grip. The corridor outside was dimly lit, casting long shadows. "I'm sorry about your brother. I just found out myself," he murmured, his tone unexpectedly sincere. "How is your mother? Your sister?" His concern seemed genuine, catching Karina off-guard. *Was this another manipulation, or a glimpse of real feeling?*

He reached inside his tailored jacket and pulled out his wallet, extracting a thick stack of American dollars. "Here. For the funeral," he said, pressing the money into her hand. The feel of the crisp bills against her skin was almost surreal. "I'll try to make it back in time," he added, his voice wavering slightly as if he were battling some internal conflict.

Isabella followed them, then disappeared with Cesar behind the elevator door.

Back in the office, Raul hadn't moved. Ramirez moved to the Cesar's desk, his fingers trailing along its glossy edges. He glanced at the scattered papers, his eyes narrowed as if searching for something specific.

Then, with a heavy sigh, he sank into Cesar's chair. The leather creaked beneath his weight as he leaned back and clasped his hands behind his head.

Karina's stomach heaved with a toxic mix of grief, fear, and determination. How long would it take for Eli and Dakota to return? And when they did, would there be anything left of her world to save?

FIFTY-ONE

Saturday, 5:33 AM—Southern Bank of the Rio Grande River Outside Juarez

Eli exited the passenger seat on the south bank of the Rio Grande, his boots sinking into the mud-laden bank as if the earth tried to keep him in Mexico. Cumulative dark clouds rumbled overhead like nearby artillery. The heavens unleashed an incessant downpour that washed long, blurry waves across the Suburban's windshield.

For three days, Aldama families, their anger over Emilio's murder passionate, had sheltered Eli and Dakota from Diablos' relentless pursuit. With cartel sicarios guarding the Bridge of the Americas, they'd have to swim seventy-five yards across the river's churning waters to the United States—a daunting distance in these conditions.

The frigid wet wind whipped against Eli, pressing the quickly dampening fabric of his shirt against his arms, chest, and back. He and Dakota had left Karina and her family to face Cesar Garza and Diablos alone, promising to return soon with reinforcements. Now, they needed to reach the FBI team waiting on the American side to plan their assault.

According to Maria's father, this surge of bad weather was common during the Juarez rainy season. No longer the tranquil flow Eli and Dakota crossed when they'd entered Juarez, the Rio Grande River had transformed into a rush of untamed energy.

"You ready for an evening swim?" Dakota's voice pierced through the tumult. His face was a mask of determination, but Eli caught a glimmer of concern in his eyes.

"Not really!" Eli shouted. "You being part fish, do you have any advice for a land lover?"

"Yeah. Take off your boots and keep moving once you start crossing. Pace yourself but try to keep up with me."

Pace yourself but keep up? Right.

Dakota clapped Eli on the shoulder and dove into the rough waters, arms churning and legs kicking.

Eli yanked off his boots and chucked them on the bank. He sucked in a deep, steadying breath, tasting the bittersweet rain on his lips, and rushed in. The icy water stole his breath. His feet searched for purchase on the riverbed, but the shifting sediment offered no stability.

He started to swim. Had he made it ten feet? Ten yards? No way to determine. He couldn't see land. Only the enveloping water around him. The current, far stronger than he anticipated, pulled at his legs and threatened to sweep him under. He gasped. Water flooded his nose and mouth. Grimy silt and slimy mud coated his tongue. The icy chill of the water seeped into his bones, numbing his fingers and toes, making each movement a battle against the river's relentless grip.

Raindrops battered his face like tiny artillery. He blinked to clear his vision and keep sight of Dakota. But the torrent from above and below, obscured everything, reducing his world to a haze of gray and brown.

His clothing, now heavy, clung to his body like a second skin. Each of his clumsy strokes required effort. His adrenaline raged with his impaired vision. He searched for any sign of movement ahead, any sign of Dakota. But it was as if the river had swallowed him, with no intention of letting go.

A cold knot of panic danced in his gut. He opened his mouth to call out but the river flooded in. Rushing water filled his ears. The river's violence isolated him in a world of uncertainty.

Where was he? Which direction was he swimming? His muscles burned with each stroke, with each kick. He fought to stay afloat, not to swim in any particular direction.

Eli knew he must keep moving, to find Dakota, to reach the other side, but the river's grasp was unrelenting, and his strength was fading fast.

A glimmer of hope appeared on the horizon—the opposite bank. So close, so—

A searing pain exploded behind his eyes. The world around him flickered. The river and rain faded, replaced by the cold, sterile walls of an autopsy room. The stench of formaldehyde. The coppery tang of blood. The gleam of the metal table. The body of young Zoe Prevost, her lifeless eyes staring at him.

Eli's limbs froze as the coroner's voice echoed in his mind—a monotonous recital of horror—multiple lacerations... prolonged abuse... cause of death—asphyxiation.

The vice tightened around his head, past and present colliding in a nauseating swirl. Eli's vision swam. The girl's face morphed into Emilio's, his head cradled in Karina's lap. Like the river, an unforgiving guilt washed over him. A paralysis crept through his body, a slow, inexorable march that threatened to drag him down into the depths of despair.

But somewhere in his nightmare, a still, small voice

spoke softly, cutting through the chaos. It urged him to fight. To remember his purpose. To remember Karina and her family and the promise he'd made to protect them. To remember the boys who slaved in the fentanyl lab—lives that hung in the balance. Lives that depended on his mission.

With a herculean effort, Eli wrenched himself back to the present, focusing on the cold water against his skin and the burning in his muscles. His movements became mechanical, his direction led by some internal compass that refused to let him give up.

The migraine faded, his memories now fuel rather than burden. He clung to his singular purpose as he battled the river's might. The ghosts of his past would never leave him, but in that moment, all that mattered was the next stroke, the next breath, the next step towards fulfilling his God-given task.

A firm hand gripped his arm, pulling him forward. Eli's head broke through the water. Dakota's face came into focus. "We're almost there!" he shouted over the river's roar. "Just a little further."

Eli followed Dakota's gaze, his heart surging with hope. The rain seemed to part, revealing the American riverbank only a few yards away. The sight of solid ground, of safety, chased away the lingering tendrils of his PTSD.

Renewed energy flooded Eli's leaden limbs. His strokes grew stronger, longer, more purposeful. Dakota swam beside him, a reassuring presence as the river's grip loosened, its fury abating as if recognizing its defeat. Eli's feet touched soft silt, and he stumbled forward, his legs shaky from exertion and the weight of his waterlogged pants.

Dakota stayed steady, guiding him by the arm up the slippery embankment. They clambered onto the bank, their chests heaving, their bodies shuddering with fatigue and relief.

The clouds separated and a sliver of moonlight broke through—a symbolic victory over the dark river that had tried to claim Eli's life and sanity.

A familiar figure emerged from the shadows, her arms outstretched, her face etched with worry and love. Lindsey, his fiancée, his anchor in some of the worst days of his life. Eli stumbled to her embrace, his body sagging against hers.

"You made it," Lindsey whispered, her voice thick with emotion. "I was so worried."

Eli managed a weak smile. "It'll take more than a river to keep me from you."

Nearby stood Special Agent Marcus Blackwell. Eli met his gaze. They'd arranged this rendezvous point before Eli and Dakota left Juarez. Blackwell and his team had been waiting, hidden in the darkness, ready to extract them as soon as they crossed.

"We need to talk," Blackwell said, his tone urgent. "Things have escalated in Juarez."

Eli's exhaustion evaporated, replaced by a surge of adrenaline. "What's happened?"

"Not here," Blackwell replied, glancing around. "Let's get you two dried off and debriefed. We don't have much time."

Eli nodded, his mind already racing. They needed to have a conversation about going back to Juarez, and soon. Karina and her family and the lives of many depended on it. But as he looked at the churning waters behind him, he knew that crossing back wouldn't be as simple as swimming across. The real battle was just beginning.

FIFTY-TWO

Saturday, 10:30–Bridge of the Americas (US / Mexican Border)

Juan Morales sat tense behind the wheel of the SUV, his eyes fixed on the Bridge of the Americas. This was it—the moment they might bring down Cesar Garza, the suspected kingpin of the Diablos cartel. The SUV's air conditioning did nothing to stop the sweat from forming on Juan Morales' forehead as his fingernails scraped against the rigid plastic of his binoculars.

Through the lenses, concrete and steel connected two worlds. On the surface, the bridge was just another border crossing. But today, it stood as more than mere infrastructure—it was the frontline for justice, where those who trafficked the innocent would finally face their reckoning.

CBP (Customs and Border Protection) agents, their dark uniforms crisp and authoritative, stood at the ready, some in plain sight, others blending in the throng of pedestrians and vehicles.

But where was Cesar Garza, the suspected kingpin of

the Diablos cartel? Would he cross like he told Somerset over the recorded line, to handle his banking problem, to deliver his human merchandise for sale to a senator in Washington DC? Morales and Blackwell's planning was a delicate dance of intelligence gathering and legal maneuvering. But would Garza show? Or had he been tipped off by some federal underling faithful to the senator, or worse, the cartel?

Morales bit his bottom lip. The countless lives shattered by Garza's empire of greed and cruelty—the lives ruined, like his neighbor Daniel Ortega, who'd been kidnapped in El Paso. They'd found his body in Juarez only a week ago, the memory still fresh and raw. Innocent lives caught in the crossfire. And his own family, his wife and children exiled to Dallas for their own protection because Morales had been picked to prosecute one of Diablos' own.

The air was thick with exhaust fumes. He knew that the next few minutes would be crucial. If Garza slipped through their grasp, if the laid trap failed to spring, the consequences would be devastating. But if they succeeded, if they could bring this billionaire monster to justice, it could be a victory for the soul of two cities—a chance to stem the tide of corruption and violence that had plagued the border for far too long.

Morales focused his binoculars once more. "Defend the weak and the fatherless," he whispered, the Psalm he'd learned as a child. "Uphold the cause of the poor and the oppressed. Rescue the weak and the needy. Deliver them from the hand of the wicked."

His heart stuttered as a sleek black Mercedes slowly crested the bridge, inching toward the border in the heavy traffic. Impatience surged through Morales, his fingers twitching with the urge to act. The vehicle crawled to where the CBP agents waited, poised to make their arrest.

The Mercedes ,now motionless, glimmered amid the battered vehicles around it, a reminder of the chasm between Garza's opulent world and the struggles of those he exploited.

Finally, the traffic moved. Morales leaned forward. The Mercedes approached the border. Thirty seconds to the American checkpoint. A minute or so before they cleared customs, then Garza was his.

Suddenly, from Mexican customs, a green-clad official burst from his station and hurried to Garza's vehicle. A cold trickle of unease slithered down Morales's spine. The official, with swift and purposeful gestures, waved the Mercedes through. Perhaps this was a formality, a show of deference to the powerful by expediting the process,

But the Mercedes pulled into a parking bay, coming to an abrupt halt before the point of entry. Morales' heart thrummed in disbelief as the customs agent hustled Garza out of the car and into the Mexican station.

A sickening sense of dread hit Morales. A cold sweat spread across his skin. This wasn't right. Something had gone wrong. Had Garza been tipped off? Had some corrupt agent, bought and paid for by the cartel, betrayed them?

"No, no, no," Morales muttered as he slapped the dash. He couldn't let this happen. He couldn't let Garza slip through. The carefully laid plans, the countless hours of preparation—all of it seemed to be crumbling like a sand-castle before an encroaching tide.

Suddenly, the door to the Mexican border station swung open. Garza emerged; his expression a mask of irritation, his cell phone pressed to his cheek. The Mexican agent scurried behind him like a dutiful servant, opening the back of the Mercedes with a deferential bow.

"Come on, come on," Morales urged under his breath, his heart pounding so hard he could feel it in his temples. Perhaps all was not lost. Perhaps Garza's detour had been nothing more than a momentary inconvenience, a minor hiccup in their carefully laid plans.

The Mercedes glided forward. The Mexican agent waved it through. Morales held his breath, his eyes fixed on the black car as it crossed the invisible line that separated Garza's power from Morales' jurisdiction.

And then, in a heartbeat, the Mercedes crossed.

The CBP agents swarmed the car like wolves on a wounded deer. Morales felt a surge of relief, a dizzying rush of euphoria that left him lightheaded and almost giddy.

The agents pulled Garza from the Mercedes, with firm and unyielding hands. And then, they extracted a young woman, her beauty so striking that it seemed almost otherworldly in the harsh desert light.

"Dear God," Morales breathed, recognizing her from the case files. Isabella, one of Garza's latest victims. The sight of her, so young and vulnerable, reignited the fire in Morales's belly. This was why he fought, why he risked everything.

A dizzying whirlwind of relief, triumph, and something else—something he couldn't quite name—swept over Morales. He'd done it. Against all odds and every setback and with God's help, he'd brought Cesar Garza to El Paso to answer for his crimes.

Yet even as he savored this victory, Morales knew it was just the beginning. Garza was merely one head of the hydra, his network of wealth and corruption stretching across borders and continents. Taking him down was a crucial battle won, but the war was far from over.

With hands that trembled slightly from the adrenaline crash, Morales lowered his binoculars. He watched as the agents led Garza and Isabella away, their figures growing smaller in the distance. The road ahead would be long and treacherous; there would be more setbacks and challenges to come. But he had the support of Customs and Border Protection, of Blackwell, and the unwavering strength of his faith to guide him against this evil plaguing the southern border.

For now, in this moment of triumph and justice, Morales allowed himself a small measure of peace, a brief respite in the eye of the storm. But even as he caught his breath, he knew the real fight against Diablos was only beginning.

"I'm your servant, Lord." Morales bowed his head. "Give me discernment that I may understand your laws and your judgment. Because you give wisdom, from your mouth comes knowledge and understanding. Give me this wisdom to fight for your cause."

His family couldn't come back yet—not until they ensured the cartel's power was fully dismantled. After shooting a final glance at the Mexican landscape, a land both familiar and foreign, Morales turned his gaze to the road back to El Paso. He'd arrested Cesar Garza, a victory that seemed impossible only hours ago. Now it was Blackwell's turn to destroy the cartel.

FIFTY-THREE

Saturday, 1:14 PM—Hotel Celebracion, Juarez City

Karina slipped inside Cesar's office to check his messages and hopefully learn what was happening in El Paso. But Cesar's center of power now had an intruder. Carlos Ramirez lounged behind the massive desk, one arm draped lazily over the armrest, the other inside Cesar's prized cigar box, its polished cedar glinting in the soft light.

Raul stood by the window, gazing down at the streets, just as he had during Karina's last visit. A flush crept up his neck threatening to crack his stoic exterior. His hands flexed at his sides, whitening his knuckles.

With deliberate slowness, Ramirez glared at Karina as he selected a cigar, rolled it between his fingers, and brought it to his upturned lips. The rasp of the match striking was harsh in the silence, the flame casting a sinister glow across Ramirez's features as he lit the cigar. He leaned back in the chair, and a thin trail of smoke spiraled upward from the cigar's glowing amber.

Ramirez took a deep pull of the cigar, then exhaled its

rich smoke slowly. He propped his feet up on the desk; his snakeskin boots thudded against the polished wood. The disrespect was unmistakable. His challenge to Karina's authority hung heavy in the air. His phone chirped and shattered the tense silence. He snatched it from his pocket and studied the screen. "What is it, Hector?" he barked into the receiver.

Hector's voice on the other end was muffled. Ramirez's face darkened; his hand with the cigar clenched.

"They think they can challenge us?" Ramirez growled like distant thunder. "They have no idea who they're dealing with."

Karina shifted her weight at the mention of a challenge. What's going on out there?

"Listen to me carefully, Hector," Ramirez commanded. "Gather the captains and lieutenants. Bring them to Hotel Celebracion. I'm making it our new headquarters."

Karina's body went cold. The hotel? Diablos is coming here? She glanced at Raul, but his expression was unreadable, his gaze fixed on Ramirez.

"We'll crush this uprising before it even begins." Ramirez's voice rose with each word. "We'll teach them what happens if they dare to defy us."

A vein throbbed in Raul's temple. Unspoken anger radiated from him in waves.

"I don't care how you do it, just get it done," Ramirez snapped. "And Hector? Make our response in the streets brutal. Use the young ones looking to advance through the ranks." He tossed the phone onto the desk with a clatter and leaned back.

A smirk played on his lips. "It appears we have a city in turmoil," he drawled, his gaze sliding to Raul. "But don't worry, we'll make sure they get what they deserve." His attention turned to Karina. "Like your brother. Yes?"

Emilio's name cut through Karina's chest. Grief and anger warred within her. She swallowed the fear that threatened to choke her. "Raul, I'll be in my suite with my mother and sister if you need me."

Raul gave a short, sharp nod; his expression still unreadable.

Ramirez mocked Karina with laughter. "Leaving so soon, *mi bonita?*" He pressed his elbows on the desk. "I thought you'd want to stay and see how we handle this little... situation."

"I have no interest in what you do," Karina said.

He smiled, a slow, cruel curve of his lips. "Ah, but you should, Karina. After all, your fate is tied to me now." He stood abruptly. "But by all means, go to your suite. Lock yourself away with your mother and that pretty little sister of yours." Ramirez ambled from around the desk. "Just remember, Karina. If you or your family leave your suite, I can't be held responsible for what might happen to you... or to your sister." He came within a step and leaned into her. His voice dropped to a whisper, his breath hot against her ear. "There are men coming to this hotel who wouldn't hesitate to take what they want if given the chance."

Karina's blood turned to ice. She wanted to scream, to scratch out his eyes. But she dropped her chin and pressed her nails into her palms.

Ramirez chuckled, stepping back. "So, for your and your sister's sake, stay locked away in your suite. And don't reach out to your American friends and make me regret my generosity."

Karina's muscles seized. *He knows.* She nodded, a jerky

motion, a submissive motion, but submission was the last thing on her mind. She turned on her heel and took long steps to the door.

As the door closed behind her, she leaned against the wall. *Go check on Mamá and Sofia in the suite now. Then go get something red.*

FIFTY-FOUR

Sunday 6:04 PM—FBI Observation Facility, Near Mexican Border

Beneath a black Texas sky, Eli's grip tightened on the steering wheel of the rented Tahoe as he guided it along the remote road. The FBI compound loomed ahead, a fortress of light against the dark desert. Lindsey shifted beside him in the passenger seat, her face illuminated by the dashboard glow. In the rearview mirror, Dakota's jaw clenched; a statue of determination.

Eli parked the Tahoe beside the building. The renewed faith he'd found swimming the Rio Grande tagged along as he, Lindsey, and Dakota passed two men standing guard at the entrance. Eli recognized the men from the Study Butte operation near Terlingua, Texas. The former agents nodded their recognition.

Inside the building was a high-tech staging area. Marcus Blackwell stood against a tactical display that dominated the room. "Welcome to Operation Jericho."

A taut energy thrummed through Eli like charged electricity as he introduced Lindsey to Blackwell.

"Psychologist, huh?" Blackwell said. "Well, maybe you can help us evaluate our little problem here."

Lindsey nodded.

Elis made a show of scanning the compound. "How'd you arrange the FBI letting you use this place now that you're ready to pull the pin."

"They've extended my service temporarily," Blackwell said. "Seems like we might have an international incident brewing that could put Americans in Juarez at risk. I convinced them I was their best bet to avoid it." He motioned to an isolated monitor. "Check this out. It's a live feed of Hotel Celebracion's perimeter from our drone overhead." He tapped a keyboard. "It appears a large segment of Diablos has infiltrated the hotel." The night-vision feed zoomed in to reveal a mass of humanity around the building. "This crowd encircling the building has been growing steadily for hours." Blackwell's tone carried a hint of confusion. "There are Americans staying in that hotel and part of my mission is to get those who are trapped inside out safely."

Eli squinted his eyes to analyze the footage. The crowd milled about with an odd mixture of aimlessness and purpose. "It's civvies," he said. "Dakota and I witnessed a coup forming in Emilio's neighborhood. Not against the government, but against the cartel."

Lindsey craned her head toward the monitor. "From what Eli has told me, Emilio Castillo was a beloved figure throughout the city. His death could have triggered enough sympathy to explain what you're seeing."

"Karina's neighbors were pretty worked up over Emilio's murder," Dakota said. "If I were a betting man, I'd say you're witnessing a grassroots revolt against Diablos."

"Maybe." Blackwell set his shoulders and placed his

hands behind his back. "But Mexican civilians are not my concern. Americans are. You still hell-bent on getting Emilio's family back to El Paso?"

Eli nodded his affirmation. "Like I said on the phone, we owe him." Eli cleared his throat to change the subject. "How do you want to play it?"

Blackwell turned his attention back to the large monitor. "I'll keep eyes on the crowd from here," he said with crisp directive. "You and Dakota will enter with blackout protocols to get Emilio's family out safely. My team will be charged with rescuing Americans. I'll adjust ingress routes on the fly if practical. We'll keep our exit strategy in place, and if necessary, we abort on my command." His gaze hardened. "Everyone gets back safe."

Blackwell turned his attention to a cluttered table and pointed to a collection of prints. "These are the hotel's plans you've requested, floor by floor. Not the best building for tactical navigation." Blackwell's finger landed on the service entrance. "Here's where you'll make entry."

"We're looking for a signal from Emilio's sister to show us where she is. Something red," Dakota said with blatant concern. "You see anything?"

Blackwell gave Dakota a side-eyed glance. "A signal?"

"To let us know where she and her family are in the hotel," Dakota said.

Eli felt his neck muscles tense. He glanced at Blackwell, noting the creases on his brow.

Blackwell shook his head as if he didn't need another thing to worry about. He shifted his attention to a whiteboard with several headshot photos assembled in a hierarchy triangle. "These are the faces of our primary targets." He extended a metal pointer at the picture on top. "This is Carlos Ramirez, aka *La Serpiente*. He's the linchpin."

Beneath Ramirez's photo, Hector, his brother and Marco Domingo stared back. Other enforcers, with youthful brutality etched into each face, followed down the triangular montage. Blackwell continued. "These are his closest lieutenants." He tapped his pointer to strike each photo on the nose. "Know these men. They're dangerous and would die for *La Serpiente*."

Dakota's eyes darted from one photo to another. "Any pressure points?"

Blackwell leaned back on the edge of a desk. "You probably won't find many who'll surrender, if that's what you're asking. Our friends at the CIA tell me the men in these photos are brutal cusses."

Eli narrowed his eyes at the photo. "Then we'll match their brutality with shock and awe. It's been our experience that the rank and file of this gang has only been successful at bullying a scared population." He stepped back to the hotel prints. "We know firsthand, when confronted by a fight, they tend to run."

Blackwell raked a hand along his jaw. "That should make things easier for you."

Eli rubbed his brow. "But there's no telling what could happen once we're inside the hotel if we run into superior numbers. It could delay us getting Emilio's family out."

Blackwell nodded. "Well, maybe his sister will flash this signal before we launch our major assault."

Eli glanced from the print to Blackwell. "And if we don't get her signal?" Eli said. The question hung in the air like ozone after a lightning strike.

Blackwell hesitated, then massaged his neck. "I guess you'll have to rely on your ranger intuition and vast combat experience."

Dakota drew in a deep breath. "She'll signal soon

enough. I guarantee it." He broke away from the group to approach a nearby display of tactical equipment and weapons. A table arrayed with cutting-edge weaponry that seemed to overlap the lines between present-day armament and those from a sci-fi thriller.

Blackwell followed with contained excitement. "These beauties are the latest in military-grade engagement. Carbon-fiber blades, EMP grenades, and more goodies that the tech heads have dreamed up. Quiet as the grave and deadly as sin." He picked up a vest with padded shoulder straps and a mesh lining. "This may interest you, Dakota, given what happened in your firefight with the cartel. This adaptive vest system is body armor that will stop high projectile rounds."

"Looks constrictive," Dakota said shaking his head. "I'd rather have full mobility."

Blackwell shrugged and picked up a sleek, matte device. "You'll be using silent comms. Vibrations and bone conduction tech—you'll hear through your skull. No chance of eavesdropping or intercepts. Just us, giving you good vibrations."

Eli lifted his brow slightly. A smirk flickered and died on his lips. "Talk about a modern-day miracle.".

"Cool," Dakota said with appreciation. "We'll be as quiet as a monastery's detention hall."

The air swarmed with determination from the three-dozen operators in the compound. Each face Eli met reflected the mission, reminding him of similar moments before other ops he'd conducted.

Blackwell's gaze met Eli's. A mutual acknowledgment of what was to come, and the faith they placed in one another from the Study Butte operation.

As the briefing room cleared, a few whispered prayers filled the air.

Dakota shifted the weight of his rigid frame. "How tight is security inside the hotel?"

"Like a fortress," Blackwell said. "Seems like every Diablo in Juarez has taken residence in that hotel or is patrolling outside it."

"And our window when they get wind of our assault?" Eli asked.

"Tighter than we're comfortable with," Blackwell said.

Eli stood with his arms folded. The mission had the same feel as Afghanistan and New Orleans—against an evil that proved to be everywhere.

They needed that red signal—a crimson thread between life and death inside the Hotel Celebracion.

FIFTY-FIVE

Monday, 6:13 AM—Bridge of the Americas (US/Mexican Border)

Eli clutched the wheel of the Chevy Suburban as he maneuvered through the light traffic on the Bridge of the Americas. Dakota sat beside him, with determined eyes locked on a convoy of SUVs ahead.

The vehicles in front of them were filled with thirty-six FBI and Border Patrol personnel assigned to Blackwell. Although Eli knew only a handful of the men personally, it didn't matter. The bond forged in the face of danger was one he recognized from his days with the 3rd Battalion of the 75th Ranger Regiment in Afghanistan.

As they neared the checkpoint, Eli forced himself to take deep, measured breaths as his mind played out the mission. *In and out, quick. Get Karina and her family to safety before the hotel and everyone in it was destroyed.*

The weight of past missions pressed on him – Afghanistan, the yacht *Leviathan*, the recent firefight in that Juarez alley. Each one a reminder of how quickly things could go sideways. But with every inhale, Eli reaffirmed his faith. *God is covering the mission. Trust the team. Trust Him.*

MONDAY, *6:59 AM—Hotel Celebracion, Juarez City*

Karina stood on her hotel suite balcony, scanning the bustling streets below. Outside the hotel, Juarez men, women, and children, many of them her childhood neighbors protesting the murder of Emilio, had surrounded the hotel. The cacophony of angry voices rose like a tide, punctuated by the occasional honk of a car horn. Inside, Mamá and Sofia wept for their son and brother.

Poor Emilio. The ache in Karina's chest intensified as she remembered their reconciliation just two weeks ago. She'd seen him stronger, and more courageous since he'd conquered his addiction and helped with the hardships that afflicted her entire family. "Oh God," she whispered, "why did you have to take Emilio and leave us alone?" Now, with Dakota and Eli back in the United States, who's left to protect us?

Her world had shifted on its axis since she'd met Eli and Dakota. Emilio had disappeared, then Sofia, and then her brother had been needlessly murdered on Cesar's property. Also, since Emilio's death, there'd been a change within the Juarez community. Its people were now in open revolt against Diablos. But a nagging voice in her head warned her —if *La Serpiente* is threatened, he'll strike back like a cornered rattler. He'd rather see Juarez burn than surrender his power.

Karina studied her balcony railing. It was time to put out the signal.

"Why are you out here by yourself, Karina?" Mamá's voice caught Karina off guard.

A leaden weight settled in the pit of her stomach. She turned, forcing a smile. "Trying to figure out what to do next. How to protect you and Sofia."

"Are you taking Emilio's place as head of this family?" Mamá asked, her tone a mixture of curiosity and concern.

"No," Karina choked out, her words thick with emotion. "I'm just a *puta*, remember?" The words tasted bitter on her tongue, a reminder of past wounds.

Mamá's face tightened. Her eyes flashed with a mix of pain and indignation. She reached out and grasped Karina's arm, her grip firm but not unkind. "No, *mi hija*," she said, her voice low and intense. "I should have never called you that, and I'll never do it again." She paused, her gaze softening as she looked into Karina's eyes. "We have all made mistakes, and mine was judging you too harshly. That word... it does not define you. It never did."

Mamá joined Karina at the railing, the warmth of her hand on Karina's arm settled her as if to anchor her daughter to this moment of a renewed relationship between them. Mamá gazed at the massing crowd on the street, her hand still resting on Karina's arm. "Emilio was a drug addict for many years. Now, these people are assembling and risking their safety to honor his memory. Something very powerful got a hold of that boy."

"God?" Karina asked, her voice barely above a whisper.

"Yes. God." Mamá pointed to the crowd below. "Who else could transform a weak drug addict into a preacher who gained so much respect from the people?"

The crowd seemed to have doubled since Karina came out on the balcony, their voices rising in a crescendo of anger and determination. "I wish I could be that strong," Karina murmured, her words nearly lost in the din.

"Oh, but you can, Karina, you can. With God's help, you can do anything."

"Can I?" Karina's voice faltered as she waved a hand to punctuate the opulence of her home. "I abandoned you and Sofia for a life of luxury as Cesar's mistress. I wear expensive clothes; drive an expensive car. Emilio sacrificed his life for others. What have I done but take the easy way out?"

"Don't think Emilio didn't have the same conversation with himself about his addiction as you're having with me now," Mamá said. "He conquered drugs by calling on Jesus. And now, *mi hija*, it's your turn to find that strength within yourself."

"He told you this?"

"Yes. When he returned from San Diego, he asked me to forgive him like Christ did."

Karina scanned the crowd again as more people assembled, their collective voice a roar of defiance against Diablos. The ache in her heart grew, but alongside it, a spark of determination flickered to life. "I need to go to the rooftop."

"Why?" Mamá's brow furrowed in concern.

"There's something there I need to get for a signal."

"A signal?" Mamá asked, her eyes widening in understanding. "For the Americans?"

Karina nodded. "They'll be coming soon. It's our only chance."

"How big is this signal?"

Karina rubbed her chin with her thumb and forefinger. "Fifty feet, maybe?"

Mamá's eyes widened in alarm. "You can't possibly carry that by yourself. How will you get it here?"

"I'll figure that out when I get up there."

COLT EASED on his brake as the FBI convoy slowed to bumper-to-bumper traffic. On the sidewalks and spilling into the streets, boisterous and irate pedestrians brandished signs bearing Emilio's picture and Spanish inscriptions. Their voices rose in a chorus of desperate anger. The streets were like a powder keg on the verge of an explosion.

Dakota raked a hand through his sun-bleached hair, his eyes darting nervously. "Looks like the good citizens of Juarez aren't too happy with Los Diablos right now. Karina should have never gone back to the hotel. She and her family would be safer out here."

Eli nodded, his gaze sweeping the crowd, searching for any signs of cartel members lurking in the chaos. The mayhem made it difficult for him to stay close to the convoy, each honk and shout fraying his nerves. "I hope this crowd doesn't place us in the wrong place at the wrong time like the last time we were here." He glanced at Dakota, whose worried expression betrayed his anxiety. Maybe it was because of the high risk of the mission, but more likely because he was concerned for Karina, caught in the crossfire of their dangerous world.

Eli tapped the wireless push-to-talk button in the side pocket of his parachute pants. "Eagle this is Blue Jay. We've lost sight of the flock." He tried to remain unflustered but his voice revealed impatience. "Please advise?"

Blackwell's calm voice from El Paso vibrated through Eli's ear pod. "Copy that Blue Jay. The team will assemble near the hotel and mix with the crowd. Move to your objective if practical. Keep me advised."

"Roger, Eagle." Eli tapped off the comm.

Dakota sat straighter. "Looks like it's showtime."

It took twenty minutes for Eli to circle the hotel twice. Meanwhile, Dakota searched the building's exterior for Karina's crimson signal. "I've got nothing."

Eli found a parking spot on the south side of the hotel and exited the Suburban, clenching the Glock 9 beneath his jacket. "Let's make our way to the service entrance and keep an eye out for Karina's signal."

Dakota's eyes darted up and down the building. "Roger that."

The crowd was ten deep from the hotel's perimeter and streamed slowly in a clockwise direction around the building. Eli glanced up at windows and balconies as he and Dakota rode the moving current of men and women. Still no signal.

"How many times do you want to circle until we enter?" Dakota said.

"Let's give it half an hour," Eli said.

Twenty minutes later, beneath the warming sun, Eli and Dakota flowed with seething protesters whose grief-stricken voices demanded justice. Suddenly, a series of shots rang out from several hotel balconies, cutting through the crowd. Panic rippled through the people, transforming the streets into a chaotic battleground.

"Take cover!" Eli's hand gripped his weapon. He pulled Dakota to the exterior wall, out of the line of fire.

As the crowd scattered, bodies weaved through parked cars and traffic.

"We can't let this stop us," Dakota protested.

Adrenaline pumped through Eli's heart. "I agree." He activated the comm. "Eagle, the crowd is taking fire. You have a bird in the air."

"Roger, Blue Jay. Up and running." Blackwell's voice crackled through Eli's earpiece. "All other units are taking defensive positions but are under strict order not to return fire."

Where was that signal Karina had promised?

KARINA'S LEGS wobbled like jelly as she stepped through the hallway to the elevator. If only she could avoid the young thugs who'd taken over the hotel. As she rounded the corner, however, brawny figures donned in white shirts and blue bandanas lounged against the elegant wallpaper that Cesar had chosen last spring. Panic sizzled in her veins.

A Diablo soldier leered past her. Maybe he knew she was Cesar's mistress. Or maybe they thought she'd be easy prey.

Her phone buzzed a shrill clamor in the corridor. Her breathing stopped as she reached for the phone in her back pocket to silence the call.

Too late. Heads turned. Eyes narrowed. The chance of reaching the stairway unnoticed, now shattered.

"Mamá" appeared on the screen.

A Diablo pushed off the wall.

The memory of Emilio's lifeless eyes fueled Karina's desperation. Would any of these boys be bold enough to take her life as well? With a steadiness she didn't feel, she straightened her shoulders and hurried, forcing her lips into the ghost of a smile. She could almost feel their eyes follow her as she quickened her pace to the stairwell.

Karina's breaths came in short spasms as she hurried up the stairs. Her stylish stilettos clattered through the confined space to highlight her vulnerability.

She prayed, trying to muster the same level of faith that Emilio had displayed when he died. But if faith could not save Emilio, how could it save her now? She struggled to breathe, not just from the exertion of four flights of stairs but from the burden of the need to think, the need to act, the need to be strong. The need to shield her family from the suffocating grasp of *La Serpiente's* wrath.

As she reached another floor, her thoughts churned—a sense of disgust for her life as Garza's mistress. She yearned for divine intervention—to believe what Emilio believed. To have his courage.

Freedom. Was that possible now? She'd never felt free in her lifetime—not even when Cesar was at his best. How could she seize it, to climb out of life's trappings as she climbed up these stairs? How could she find the same happiness that seemed to dominate Emilio before Hector Ramirez killed him?

The sun was rising over the horizon as Karina stepped onto the roof. Sweat slicked her palms as she clicked the code to open the storage room door. A soft beep and the lock clicked open with a creak that seemed too loud.

Her eyes flicked to the corner of the dim room where a lifeless Dakota had once lain. On a discarded end table, she found a utility knife with a retractable blade. She could cut the rug into a smaller section, light enough to carry down, but long enough to get the American's attention.

The door to the room swung open.

Her breath, despite the cool air, felt hot in her chest.

"I was told someone was up here."

Karina recognized that voice. She'd been hearing it since Cesar left for El Paso.

Carlos Ramirez—*La Serpiente.*

FIFTY-SIX

Monday, 6:37 PM, Outside Hotel Celebracion, Juarez City

Eli couldn't wait any longer. Too many lives outside and inside the hotel were at stake. "We're going in." Eli's voice was firm, but his insides stirred like a blender on high speed.

Dakota's eyes burned with hardened resolve. "Let's do it. We can get into position while we wait for the drone's intel."

The crowd drifted behind wide pillars, planters, and parked vehicles. Eli and Dakota navigated the chaos, reaching the loading area near the hotel's service entrance in mere moments.

A half-dozen cartel soldiers stood guard with grim determination. The metallic gleam of their fully automatic Stechkin pistols caught the harsh sunlight. Eli's palms grew slick with sweat as he gripped his weapon tighter, he and Dakota taking cover behind a series of rust-pitted dumpsters.

Without warning, Dakota darted to the opening. His Glock 9 split the air, downing two Diablos, hitting one in the throat, the other in the chest. Blood sprayed in a crimson mist as the bodies crumpled. The remaining sentries unleashed a deafening salvo of rounds that closely whizzed by. Eli let loose an unbridled counterattack. From behind the dumpsters, his own shots found the torsos of two cartel soldiers. The last two guards succumbed to Dakota's accuracy, their bodies folding like collapsed lawn chairs.

Advancing into the hotel, Dakota arched his weapon in a steady sweep. Eli trailed, hyper-aware of every shadow, every sound.

A cacophony of gunfire erupted beyond the threshold, reverberating off the walls and assaulting Eli's ears. Having fought battles together, from the deck of *Leviathan* to the Study Butte compound to the alley in Almada, Eli and Dakota moved in practiced synchronicity.

Adrenaline surged through Eli's veins as they breached the hotel's defenses, his heart pounding a frantic war drum. But beneath the rush of combat, a knot of worry tightened in his chest. He had no idea where to find Karina and her family.

As the attack subsided, Eli's chest heaved from exertion. He exchanged confused glances with Dakota. The fight to rescue Karina was ongoing, but where was she? Eli's fingers trembled slightly as he tapped his comm. "Eagle, we're in. Any sign of the signal?"

Silence greeted him, broken only by his labored breathing.

Eli tapped his comm again, "Eagle?" But Blackwell didn't respond. "Diablos must be jamming communications inside the hotel," he called out to Dakota.

"That means they're expecting more trouble than from the good citizens of Juarez," Dakota's voice was tight and tense. "So, what's the call, Ranger?" His eyes scanned the corridor for movement.

Eli weighed the options and potential risks of initiating a search for Karina and her family. "I say we search the most obvious areas—her suite or the roof. You choose."

Dakota's brow squinted in concentration. After a moment, he nodded decisively. "Rooftop. It's defensible. And if they're planning to signal for help, that's where they'd do it."

"Agreed," Eli nodded. "Let's move. And Dakota..." he paused, clasping his friend's shoulder, "Let's keep the heroics to a minimum."

With a thumbs up, Dakota ventured deeper into the hotel, the echoes of distant gunfire reminding them that their enemy was alive and well. And as of now, Karina and her family's rescue—and the takedown of Diablos—rested squarely on his and Dakota's shoulders.

KARINA CLUTCHED her chest as her heart quivered. Her terror had taken a physical form.

Ramirez entered the storage room, each step deliberate and slow, almost leisurely. His eyes shone with a wolfish delight as they lingered on Karina. A cruel smirk played on his face, making it clear he was savoring the moment.

Her fingers tightened around the edge of the heavy red carpet as desperation clawed at her insides.

"Well, if it isn't Garza's plaything." His words dripped with menace and condescension. "Didn't I warn you to stay in your room?"

His face seethed with unquenchable lust, his eyes dark and predatory. "What do you plan to do with that rug? Maybe we can do something together."

A fleeting gasp escaped Karina's lips, her mind racing

for an escape. "I need to get this red carpet to the lobby for Cesar's birthday party next week," she lied, trembling slightly.

Ramirez laughed with a sinister savor. "Haven't you heard? Your Cesar has been arrested in El Paso." He cornered her against the carpet, his breath hot and suffocating. "Now, everything that was his is mine."

Karina's mind spiraled. Her heart pounded with such violence that she feared it would burst from her chest.

Ramirez pressed his lips against her cheek. "Such fire in your eyes, begging to be gratified." The air grew heavy with his advances.

His touch sent chills across Karina's neck and arms. "I must get downstairs and back to my room," she said. "My Mamá is waiting for me."

Ramirez brushed his hand against her thigh with deliberate slowness. She froze, the warmth of the room turning to ice as her world shrank to the distance between them.

His fingers traced her shoulders, a violation that sent ripples of dread beneath her skin. Adrenaline pumped through her, but her anger couldn't overpower her sense of helplessness.

"Now, now. Don't resist. You'll need protection now that Cesar is gone." His words flowed in a twisted melody. "And protection can be found in the most unexpected places."

Sweat broke out along her spine. She must get to her room. Display the signal. She struggled with her composure, trembling as she faced his relentless advance.

"Don't resist me," Ramirez spoke as a snake hisses. "Think of the comfort I can provide for you and your family."

Karina knitted her brow with defiance. "I'd rather die."

Ramirez laughed, a haunting echo. "Perhaps later. But not right now."

"You won't have me." Her voice faltered, but her spirit remained firm. "You'll never have me."

Ramirez's gaze darkened. "Your resistance is useless, *puta*. I get what I want when I want it."

Karina's mind whirled. She couldn't shake her fear of being raped. She clutched the utility knife in her back pocket. "I can't." She clenched her jaw tightly. "I won't."

"You will!" he screamed.

Karina inched the utility knife from her back pocket. She'd cut his cheek first, the most vulnerable spot. Then when he clutched the wound, she'd open his throat.

Her body trembled. Her heart hammered like a tambura in a cantina.

Ramirez ripped her blouse.

A guttural scream from deep in Karina's core bubbled through her. The coppery taste of terror filled her mouth. "Get away from me!" her voice bellowed as she shrank away from him.

Ramirez's growing impatience rippled with waves of fury. "You have no choice, pretty *chica*," he shrieked. "With Garza gone, you belong to me."

Karina's face grew hot with anger. "You'll never have me. Not what's inside."

"No." *La Serpiente* raised his head like a serpent ready to strike. "When I finish with you, I'll have your sister. Sofia, is it? Maybe she'll succumb to my irresistible charms."

For a fleeting second, the world seemed to pause. Fury scorched through Karina's veins like molten lava. She released her breath as she extracted the utility knife from her pocket.

But before she could strike the worn door of the storage

room exploded inward. In the doorway, silhouetted by the dim light of the rooftop's floodlights, stood the broad-shouldered Dakota with his pistol drawn.

Ramirez's sneer faltered briefly, but he quickly regained his composure. "Decided to join the fun, have you? What a shame."

A charged silence followed as Ramirez raised his hands. But the quiet was shattered by a sleek hum from above that grew louder and louder—a mechanical whirring ringing through the metal walls.

Karina's eyes shot upward. Dust rained down from the ceiling. Something was happening outside.

FIFTY-SEVEN

Monday, 7:07 PM--Hotel Celebracion Rooftop, Juarez City

Crouched on the hotel's rooftop, his Glock drawn, Eli gazed skyward at the familiar buzz. Dakota crouched over the storeroom threshold, his weapon trained on their number one target—Carlos Ramirez.

One of Blackwell's drones hovered overhead. Shots continued to ring out from the lower floors. A stray bullet punched through the drone's lower shell, sending it bucking and spinning, with a shard of metal shearing off. Smoke belched from the stricken device, coiling skyward like a dark omen.

The drone listed to the side, teetering ever closer to the edge of the high-rise before smashing into the storeroom's metal wall. It crumpled in on itself, settling into a smoldering heap wedged in the hole it had created.

Ramirez clutched Karina, yanking her against him as a shield and unleashing a salvo of gunfire over her shoulder.

Dakota dove for cover behind a barricade of discarded tables, his movements fluid and practiced.

Eli ducked low, circling past Ramirez's position, and

took up position behind a cluster of stainless-steel shelving and metal cabinets.

Every fiber of Eli's being raged against the restraint he and Dakota were forced to show. His core ached to destroy *La Serpiente*—yet reality kept him tethered, unable to unleash justice for fear of killing Karina.

The concussive blasts from Ramirez's weapon mingled with the dying purr of the drone's engine, still stuck in the wall.

A hail of gunfire pinged off the metal and steel surrounding Eli. Suddenly, Ramirez's aim focused on Dakota—there was a pause before a single shot; deafening.

In his peripheral vision, Eli saw Dakota double over, his mouth agape as if stunned into silence. Eli's heart constricted in horror as his comrade crumbled.

Karina let out a terrified scream.

"No!" Eli bellowed, his faith unraveling.

"Your partner is hurt, gringo," *La Serpiente*'s voice slithered like venom. "Maybe now I kill the girl."

"Dakota...hang on." Desperation glistened in Eli's voice.

"S-sorry," Dakota choked out through clenched teeth.

"Stop, you devil!" Karina cried out in a damning tone.

An earsplitting crash erupted a half-dozen feet from Ramirez and Karina. The drone that had been lodged in the ceiling had fallen, its spinning rotors bent and fractured, severed wires protruding from exposed components. It crashed into a stack of old refrigerators and freezers, sending sparks flying from its damaged circuitry.

Through a veil of dust and smoke, Eli glimpsed Karina seizing the momentary distraction. With cat-like agility, she wrenched herself free from *La Serpiente*'s viselike grip and sprinted to Dakota.

La Serpiente whirled towards Karina's fleeing form and raised his pistol.

Eli's muscle memory, honed over countless battles, guided his Glock in a fluid motion. He exhaled and squeezed the trigger. A sharp crack boomed through the heavy air.

La Serpiente let out a pained grunt and clutched his shoulder as a flood of dark blood seeped between his fingers.

Karina scrambled to Dakota's side.

As the dust from the mangled drone settled, an ominous stillness descended upon the room. Ramirez had vanished behind a cluster of storage bins. Eli hurried to Dakota, who lay grimacing against an overturned end table, his shirt sporting a ragged tear.

Karina sat with Dakota's head in her lap, her face contorted with concern.

"You okay, partner?" Eli's voice was taut yet gentle. "How bad are you hit?"

Dakota winced. "Hurts like hell, but I'll live."

Eli grabbed a sheet from the stored linens and started tearing it into bandages. He bent beside Dakota to rip open the hole in his shirt to stop the bleeding, but found no blood.

Karina's eyes glistened. "I'm so sorry. This is all my fault—"

Dakota lifted a hand. "No, it ain't. You didn't pull the trigger. Besides—" He ripped open his shirt to reveal the textured webbing of an AVS body armor vest.

Eli's knees nearly gave way as his adrenaline ebbed. A chuckle escaped him. "Thought that would slow you down, huh?"

Dakota managed a pained expression. "It still hurts when you're shot." He paused to glance around the rooftop. "Where'd the nut job go?"

Eli clenched his jaw. "I'm on him."

Stepping into the open, Eli strained to hear any sound that would reveal Ramirez's location. The stinging smell of gunpowder lingered. Sirens wailed in the distance. He knew he could end it all now by killing Ramirez.

Eli narrowed his eyes, alert for any movement, and ambled to where Ramirez had disappeared. The shuffle of debris beneath his boots shattered the heavy stillness.

A footfall echoed against concrete from a shadowy alcove of boxes. Eli swept his pistol in a steady arc, his muscles tensed and ready to fire.

A shadow flickered to his left.

Eli's finger tightened on the trigger as a sheet of metal from the damaged wall swung freely.

Then he heard it, unmistakable this time—hurried footsteps receding to the doorway. Eli broke into a run to cut Ramirez off, arriving just in time to see him slip through the storeroom's open door.

Eli's weapon snapped up, his finger curling around the trigger. But before he could squeeze off a shot, a deafening crack shattered the air. Heat seared past his ear as a bullet carved through the space where his head had been a heartbeat earlier. In that fleeting moment, Ramirez vanished like a ghost into thin air.

He found Dakota standing but bent over, one arm clutching his chest. "May have busted a rib."

"Ramirez is gone." Eli's words came out razor sharp. "And from the sounds outside, something big is going down."

Fine lines creased Dakota's brow as he stood erect. He glanced at Karina. "Where are you with displaying that signal?"

Karina's eyes brimmed with emotion. "That's why I'm

up here." She ran to the mound of carpet that had served as Dakota's hospital bed.

"That's my girl." Dakota managed a pained smile.

Karina's face blanched. "But my family...what if El Diablo is headed to my suite?"

Eli gripped her shoulder. "Let's get that signal out. Then Blackwell can assault the building."

Karina searched Eli's eyes.

Eli shot her a wink. "Let's get to your suite and hang this rug outside your balcony. Then we can put this nightmare in our rearview mirror."

They moved to the exit, into the dim light of evening. Eli grimaced, knowing he'd had Ramirez in his sights, yet the cartel leader was still breathing.

FIFTY-EIGHT

Monday, 7:36 PM—Hotel Celebracion Rooftop Storehouse, Juarez City

Karina staggered under Dakota's weight, her shoulder braced beneath his arm. Eli led the way out of the storehouse, red carpet dragging behind him, pistol ready.

They inched down the stairway, celebration sounds drifting up from the nightclub. Karina's pulse quickened. Was Ramirez down there? Did he know where to find them?

The stairwell felt endless, each step a battle against exhaustion and fear. The sounds from below, once distant, grew clearer—laughter, the clink of glasses, snatches of drunken conversation. It was surreal, this bubble of normalcy existing just beneath their desperate flight. Karina's mind raced, imagining Ramirez among the revelers, plotting their demise over tequila and cigars. She shuddered, pushing the image away. Focus. One step at a time.

Her mother and sister. She had to reach them. Now.

Eli paused at the foyer, then gestured—two fingers at the elevator ten steps away.

Karina nodded. Her throat tightened.

They plunged forward. Her heel caught a bottle, sending it skittering across the floor. Four Diablos soldiers snapped their heads up, drinks forgotten.

"Move!" Eli barked.

Karina and Dakota bolted past him, Eli's pistol trained on the club. Snarls replaced laughter as they dove into the elevator.

"Floor?" Eli demanded, sliding in behind them.

"Nine," Karina gasped.

The doors whispered shut as a knife-wielding Diablo appeared. Footsteps faded as they descended.

The elevator hummed, a metallic cocoon insulating them from the chaos they'd left behind. Karina's heart thundered in her ears, drowning out the mechanical whir. She stole a glance at Dakota, noting the pallor of his skin, the tightness around his eyes. The vest had saved his life, but the blow took a toll.

Eli stood rigid, his focus unwavering, their guardian angel between them and whatever waited beyond those doors. The floor numbers ticked by, each illuminated digit bringing them closer to uncertainty. Karina's fingers curled into fists, nails biting into her palms. Whatever came next, she'd face it. She had to.

A chime. Eleventh floor. Two young cartel soldiers gaped, caught in the harsh light of the elevator carriage. Eli struck with a brutal flurry of his fist and pistol.

A third soldier emerged. Gunfire boomed. Smoke curled from Dakota's weapon.

Karina surveyed the fallen, satisfaction warring with an unwelcome pang of pity. "*Muéranse*," she hissed, banishing compassion.

The aftermath of violence lay at her feet, a tableau of

twisted limbs and spreading crimson. These were boys, really, not much older than the children she'd seen Diablos prey upon. In another life, they might have been students, sons, brothers. But here, now, they were the enemy. The thought should have comforted her, should have justified the carnage. Instead, it left a hollow ache in her chest. She pushed the feeling down, burying it beneath layers of rage and determination. There was no room for sympathy in this war.

Eli pulled a radio from one of the bodies. Karina helped Dakota clear the crumpled forms from the elevator opening. Tears stung her eyes. She blinked them away, furious at her weakness.

Dakota sagged against the wall. The display blinked—nine.

Eli's eyes softened. "Ready?"

She nodded, barely.

At her door, Karina's fingers trembled on the keypad. Two misses before the lock clicked open.

Eli shouldered in first, Dakota close behind.

"Mamá? Sofia?" Karina called, voice frantic with worry.

Her mother appeared, the lines in her forehead etched deep. Sofia peeked out, wide-eyed. "You're back."

"What happened?" Mamá asked Dakota, frowning at his haggard appearance.

"I got shot again," he said before collapsing onto the sofa.

The familiar confines of her suite felt alien now, tainted by the violence that had followed them. Karina's gaze darted from object to object—nothing there said home. Each item a reminder of the life she had lived to regret. The air felt thick, heavy with unspoken shame and the metallic tang of gunpowder that clung to their clothes.

Eli sliced the red rug from the roof into strips, fashioning a signal. "Marcus, we're ready," he called out, as if the American could hear him.

A faint thrum built outside. Karina stepped onto the balcony, scanning the darkening sky. The drone grew louder, an angry swarm unseen.

The air vibrated, then shrieked with mechanical fury. The city below fell silent, as if holding its breath.

"Away from the windows," Eli ordered. "It's about to get ugly."

They huddled in the center of the room. Sofia pointed, mouth open. "Look!"

Sleek shapes sliced the air. The American drones had arrived.

Mamá crossed herself as shouts erupted in the hallway.

"Diablos. A handful," Eli reported, peering through the peephole.

"Get them to the bedroom," Dakota said, struggling to his feet. "You too, Karina."

She ushered her family to safety but stayed, hefting a statuette. "I'm done hiding."

Eli barricaded the door, leaving a gap. "Funneling them," he explained, positioning himself with Dakota. Their bodies tensed, ready to spring.

Chaos erupted outside. A soldier burst through. Eli's blows were lightning, felling him instantly. Another charged in.

Dakota lunged, elbow crashing down on the man's neck.

A third rushed forward. Karina swung her makeshift weapon. It shattered against his skull. Eli's boot finished the job.

"How long before your friends come inside the hotel?" Karina asked, breathing hard.

Eli gathered the Diablos weapons. "When they're sure they can take it without heavy losses."

The phone's shrill ring cut through the mayhem.

Eli answered, face hardening as he listened. "Raul?" he said, offering Karina the receiver. "For you."

"Hola?" she said, wary of why Raul had called her.

"Karina, thank God." His voice shook. "Get out of the hotel. Now."

"Why?"

"Ramirez wired the hotel with explosives."

FIFTY-NINE

Monday, 7:53 AM—Hotel Celebracion, Juarez City

Eli's stomach clenched at the word, *explosives*. "What did he say?" he asked Karina.

Karina sank into a chair, her trembling fingers barely keeping hold of the phone. "That *La Serpiente* has filled the hotel with explosives."

Her words slammed into Eli's chest like a battering ram. The radio he had taken from the Diablo in the elevator cracked to life. Eli's nerve endings ignited as rapid-fire Spanish filled the room. *"Todos salgan del hotel. La Serpiente explotará en quince minutos. Todos salgan. El hotel soplará en quince minutos."*

"It's true," Karina's voice quavered, "The radio just confirmed it."

Dakota stood with his jaw set in a hard line. He rolled his shoulders, wincing slightly with the movement. "What now?" he asked, his tone deceptively casual, as if they were discussing lunch plans rather than a bomb threat.

Memories of IEDs in Afghanistan flashed through Eli's thoughts. He pushed them aside and nodded at Karina.

"Ask your friend if he knows where the detonator for the explosives is hidden."

After a brief burst of excited Spanish, she clutched the phone to her breast. "He says they're on the fifth floor. Room 502."

Eli peeked at his watch. "Okay, I'll need to get started."

I'd come with you," Dakota said with visible frustration. "But I'd only slow you down."

Eli felt for his M3 trench knife he'd kept from his Afghanistan deployments, opting for silence. As he moved to the door, his mind plotting the quickest route to the fifth floor, a new problem presented itself. He'd stick out like a sore thumb in the hallways crawling with Diablos. He needed a disguise.

VOICES RESOUNDED from the stairway entrance—Los Diablos guarding the back routes. An unassuming door labeled *"Mantenimiento"* appeared just before the corner. It was locked, but Eli made quick use of his pick set and slipped inside.

Among buckets and mops and cleaning solutions were uniforms, work boots, and tool belts stacked on shelves. Eli stripped off his clothing and donned a dark jumpsuit, opting for the largest size to better conceal his weapons. He smiled at the faded Hotel Celebracion logo on the breast pocket.

He tucked his hair under a matching cap, took a deep breath, and eased out of the storage room, closing the locked door behind him. He examined his reflection in a mirror across the hallway—no longer a battle-hardened ranger, only a humble laborer working for small wages. The image stirred a memory of his first undercover op in Afghanistan—

a loose-fitting kameez worn over baggy shalwar, topped with a pakol on his head. The stakes were just as high then as they were now.

Eli's pulse jumped a tick at the sight of the two cartel soldiers posted as sentinels at the stairway entrance. They laughed, their words punctuated by coarse jokes that didn't need translation. His grasp of Spanish was limited to a few phrases, but nothing that would carry him through a conversation.

From his borrowed tool belt, he clutched a heavy pipe wrench with purpose. He kept his head down as if he was intent on maintenance duties. Sweat slicked his palms. The wrench, cold and unyielding, threatened to slip from his tight grip.

The taller of the thugs had eyes that were hard and unforgiving. "*Hey, tú. ¿Qué haces aquí?*" No doubt he expected a response.

Pretending not to understand, Eli touched his ears and shook his head. Then he pointed at the stairwell door, miming a need to fix something urgently.

"*Estás sordo o qué?*" the other soldier challenged with a biting laugh.

Eli nodded but gestured with greater urgency.

The two thugs exchanged glances. The taller one dismissed Eli with a wave of his hand. "*Vaya, vaya.*"

Eli shuffled past without acknowledgment and raced down the first flight. They'd bought it. But would the next thug he encountered buy it too?

Easing the stairwell door open, Eli winced at its soft creak. The smell of cigarette smoke and cheap cologne wafted through as he stepped onto the fifth floor. He found himself face-to-face with Diablo built like a heavyweight boxer. The man's broad shoulders and tattooed arms strained against his too-tight T-shirt. A jagged scar ran from his left eyebrow to his cheekbone, etched into a face seemingly chiseled from granite. The thug's piercing gaze locked onto Colt, his eyes narrowing with suspicion.

Heart pounding, Eli managed to kept his expression passive. He clutched the wrench tighter, prepared for what came next. *Please God, if ever I needed you, I need you now. Please guide my hand.*

The thug stepped forward, blocking the narrow passage completely. "*Alto ahí! Quién eres?*"

Again, Eli feigned confusion and pointed to the wrench, then to the door. But the guy's eyes narrowed. He took a threatening step closer.

The thug reached to grab Eli's shirt.

Eli feigned a stumble.

The thug moved to correct his grasp.

Eli swung the wrench in an arc that landed on the thug's left temple with a sickening thud. The impact reverberated up Eli's arm, a familiar sensation from his combat training.

The brute staggered but his fall was the inevitable.

Eli closed the gap, unleashing jabs and punches honed in the unforgiving arenas of hand-to-hand combat. Each strike was precise, targeting vulnerable points—solar plexus, throat, kidneys. Eli's muscles burned with exertion, but a burst of adrenaline fueled his assault. The thug's imposing size was rendered useless. He fell to the concrete landing without a twitch or movement.

Eli stepped over the mound of muscle and flesh. He pressed through the door, unsure if the sounds from his battle had alerted reinforcements.

The hallway stretched before him—a carpeted fifty-foot path to traverse with speed and stealth. The

Burgundy carpet muffled his footsteps. He was close. Just around the corner was room 502. Get inside and figure out the explosives. But a low rumble of voices pierced Eli's confidence.

Diablos reinforcements, he guessed, and many.

A maintenance cart to his right, laden with linens and towels and cleaning supplies was a Godsend. Eli grasped the handle and eased it to the corner. Then he gave it a mighty shove in the direction opposite room 502. The cart rolled and careened down the hallway. Its contents clattered in a cacophony of confusion.

Voices shifted to alert murmurs. Frantic footfalls approached. With heavy steps pounding, the thugs were drawn to the commotion like moths to an inferno.

Eli slid into the nearest alcove and held his breath. He pressed tight against the rough vinyl wallpaper of burgundy and deep green, trying to make himself invisible in the sleek shadow.

The sounds of men running whizzed by. Angry screams followed.

Eli peeked for a visual.

One Diablo kicked the cart. The others laughed as his partner hopped on one leg. But they didn't return. Why was that? They just disappeared into a room where loud music spilled out when they opened the door.

Eli bolted to 502. Anticipation ran like wildfire in his veins. He tried the door handle locked. He knocked on the door with authority as if he were a shift change.

No response—no rustling, no curses—just oppressive silence.

No time for the lock pick. He stepped and readied his body to breach the door. With focused energy, Eli broke forward, driving his good shoulder near the frame that splintered and gave way. His heart raced as he drew his weapon to confront whoever stood guard.

But he found the room eerily empty, the expected rush of resistance absent. His eyes cut through the stillness. A lamp in the corner cast an eerie dull light across the room. A faint whimper from the bedroom reached his ears. He advanced inside the bedroom, Glock first. The whimper grew louder, more distinct. He ducked down and peered under the bed.

A shadowy figure quivered, matching its sobs.

Eli holstered his gun and lifted his hands—trying to appear as non-threatening as possible, trying to coax the scared woman out. "It's okay, I'm here to help."

Familiar green eyes peered up at him. He glanced down at the girl's name tag—Lucia, the clerk at the front desk. She reached out her small hand—

"You... you're the American," Lucia whispered, her voice trembling. "Please, help me."

As Eli grasped her hand, a wave of dizziness washed over him. His vision blurred, the room seeming to tilt on its axis. He blinked hard, trying to clear his head, but the disorientation intensified.

"Are you alright?" Lucia's concerned voice sounded distant, muffled.

Eli opened his mouth to respond, but no words came out. The last thing he saw was Lucia's frightened face before—darkness.

SIXTY

Monday, 8:39 AM—Hotel Celebracion, Juarez City

Eli blinked his eyes open. The world seemed distant—distorted. Everything blurred as if he were wearing thick glasses. Sound filtered through the fog—a panicked voice from the end of some long tunnel. He'd been hit in the head —again.

He managed to keep his eyes open but only by a tiny fraction. A furious face loomed over him. The man with the twisted mustache.

"You," Eli rasped through a dry throat.

The man narrowed his eyes. Then he lifted Eli's weapon and trained it on him. "*Eres el americano. Qué estás haciendo aquí?*" Eli's Glock shook between the man's unsteady fingers.

Eli raised his hands to show he meant no harm. "I'm here to help." He winced. "*Ayuda.*"

There was movement to Eli's left. "He asks why he should trust you?" said the girl with green eyes. Lucia.

An eerie silence followed for several seconds. Then,

Lucia's expression changed to one of concern. *"Esta... bueno? You good?"*

"Yes, good," Eli's gaze found the speaker. *"Si, bueno."*

"You're the American with Senorita Castillo." Lucia flashed a nervous smile. "I'm Lucia. This is Raul."

"No tenemos mucho tiempo," Raul said, twirling the end of his mustache.

The fog in Eli's brain was lifting. He steadied himself and pushed himself up with a grimace.

Raul studied him. His expression turned from suspicion to doubt. As if something warred inside him. A determination set in his jaw. *"Vale, Confiamos en ti. Ayúdanos."* His voice fell and he lowered Eli's gun.

Lucia nodded. "He says he trusts you."

The tight knot in Eli's chest unraveled. "Okay, then. Let's get out of here. *Vámonos.*"

Raul surrendered Eli's gun.

"Where are the explosives?" Eli asked.

Lucia walked into the living room. "Down the hall, a room three doors down."

Eli moved into the hallway with Lucia and Raul a step behind.

Angry male voices erupted nearby.

"They're mad about the invasion," Lucia whispered. "La Serpiente has put a price on any American head."

The thump of a door shutting announced the voices from a nearby room. Eli turned and guided Lucia and Raul to the wall.

Three men, each marked with tattoos and exuding confidence, smoked in the hallway outside a room. The tallest of the group paced the hall with undeniable swagger, his white shirt draping loosely over his shoulders, and a crisp blue bandana tied firmly around his forehead. Every step he took radiated authority. Leaning against the wall, another man dressed exactly like the leader from the knot behind his bandana to how his shirt tail hung out of his pants—looked much like a shorter, shadowy clone.

The third man guarding the room stood with blatant detachment. His posture was slouched and languid, his shirt wrinkled, his bandana dangling askew revealing the weakest of the three.

Eli, still suffering from a mild migraine from the blow he'd taken earlier, signaled with an open hand for Lucia and Raul to stop. Then he closed the distance in silence, striking the weak link with a vicious blow to the head.

The man's legs collapsed.

The other two pivoted, stunned by Eli's unexpected assault. The clone charged, but ran into a blur of Eli's lightning fists to the head and torso, and a low leg sweep that put him down. Eli's powerful crack to the temple had him go still on the carpet.

The leader with the swagger stood in stunned shock.

Eli aimed his Glock at the man's forehead.

The man turned and bolted for the stairway.

Eli considered shooting the fleeing target but glanced at the room's door instead. "Let's check it out."

Surprisingly, the door was unlocked. The dim room had but a single lamp casting a glow over a makeshift workstation. The desk was cluttered with wires, batteries, and various pieces of equipment.

Eli approached the station, locking his eyes on a military-grade detonation system, rigged with high-end C-4 explosives. A piercing chill shot straight through him.

He scanned the room for an immediate threat. The explosives were wired intricately to a digital countdown timer reading "00:30:00" but not counting down. On a table next to the explosives was a rectangular device with several antennas; the jammer blocking all communications in and out of the building.

"Pull that plug," he told Lucia.

She hesitated.

"Don't worry," Eli said. "It's not the explosives. It's a communication jammer."

She slowly lowered her hand to the wire, then jerked the plug from the outlet, shutting her eyes in the process. The device powered down with a faint hum. He replaced his ear pod and tapped his comm. "Eagle, this is Blue Jay, over. Eagle?"

The static cleared, and he heared Blackwell's urgent voice. "Where've you been?"

"Comms were jammed," Eli said as he exhaled. "But I've got a bigger problem."

"What's that?"

"Explosives. Military-grade C-4. Ramirez has the hotel set to blow." Eli waited for Blackwell's response.

"You have any EOD training?" Blackwell said with reassuring calm.

"Enough to know it's fixed for remote detonation," Eli replied. "You have anyone who can talk me through disarming it?"

"Hold tight," Blackwell said with little excitement. "We're combing the ranks now."

Four minutes later, the comm came back to life. "EOD Specialist Miller here. I hear you have a situation."

Eli described the setup as concisely and calmly as he could. "C-4 rigged to a digital timer that's not counting. Looks like a dual-trigger setup. Remote detonation a distinct possibility."

"Alright, stay calm," Miller instructed. "First, you need

to access the control panel on the side of the timer. There should be a panel with screws—can you see it?"

Eli spotted the panel and frantically searched the room. "I need a screwdriver."

"Here," Lucia pulled a multi-tool from her purse and dangled it between her fingers.

Eli raised his brow in disbelief. "You've got to be kidding?"

Lucia shrugged, a hint of a smile on her lips. "What? A girl can't be prepared?"

As he shook his head at his good fortune, Eli turned the panel screws loose. "Remind me to never underestimate to hotel staff again." He tapped the comm. "Okay, Miller, it's open."

"Okay, listen carefully," Miller said. "You need to locate the primary power source. It's usually a red wire connected to the battery."

"Got it," Eli murmured as he found the red wire beneath a tangle of other colored cables.

"Now, cut the red wire," Miller said, his voice a bit shaky. "But be ready to cap it off to prevent sparking."

"Lucia." Eli pointed to a roll of black electrical tape. "Tear me off a strip of that, will you?" Steadying his hands with a huge intake of air, Eli snipped the red wire, then capped it with the tape Lucia handed him. The timer started counting down.

"Done," Eli breathed out his held breath. "But the timer is activated."

Raul wiped the sweat from his forehead with his shirt sleeve as he muttered something in Spanish.

"No problem," Miller said. "Now check for a secondary trigger. Any pressure switches or mercury tilt sensors?"

Eli inspected the device quickly. "No pressure switches,

but there's a secondary circuit connected to another battery."

"Alright," Miller said, his voice growing more intense. "Cut that circuit. It should stabilize the system."

With another steady snip, Eli severed the secondary circuit. The timer froze.

Eli exhaled deeply, "Timer's stopped."

"Well done," Miller said, almost laughing. "Secure the area and keep the device safe until operatives can dismantle it fully."

"That's a good copy," Eli said and signed off. He picked up the detonator and handed it to Lucia. "Hold on to that, will you?"

Lucia's eyes widened.

"Don't worry, it's as harmless as a desk lamp now," Eli said. "Now, call Karina's suite. Tell her, I'm on my way back."

As Eli stepped into the hallway, the entire floor plunged into darkness.

SIXTY-ONE

Monday, 9:27 AM—Hotel Celebracion, Juarez City

The lights flickered once, then everything went dark. Karina reached for the nearby couch to keep her bearings. The suite, which moments ago had offered a fragile sense of security, now seemed like a dark, inescapable trap.

"*Madre de Dios.*" Her mother's voice cut through the darkness. "What's happening?"

Karina swallowed hard against her dry throat. She groped for the flashlight in the drawer of an end table, her fingers fumbling for the cool metal.

"Everyone, stay still," Dakota said. "Don't move until I check this out."

Sofia's soft whimper burst through. "Karina, I'm scared." Fear threaded her every word.

"I know, Sofia," Karina said soothingly, forcing her voice to be calmer than she felt. "It's going to be okay. We just lost electricity." Her fingers finally closed around the flashlight. Its narrow beam cut through the darkness to find Dakota coming to her.

"We need to barricade the door—now," he whispered.

With her legs driven by adrenaline, Karina moved behind the flashlight beam.

Her mother's breaths came fast and shallow. "Karina, what are you doing?"

"Mamá, it's okay," Karina said. "We're just securing the room." Her pulse almost drowned out the creak of the door as Dakota eased it open. The flashlight beam illuminated his jaw muscles, twitching as he peeked into the hallway.

After what felt like an eternity, Dakota turned back to her. "No movements. No sounds." His voice was barely more than a breath.

"What do you think happened?" Her voice trembled despite her best efforts to stay composed.

"I don't know," he said in a low rumble. "Could be a power outage. Could be deliberate."

"Do you think Diablos is responsible?" Karina whispered, hoping the answer would ease her worry.

His gaze softened, but the tension didn't leave his forehead. "I can't say. But let's barricade the door, just in case."

Karina nodded, moving quickly.

Her mother, still clutching Sofia, huddled closer, eyes darting in fear.

Karina decided to keep her busy. "Help me with this," she urged Mamá.

The clumping of furniture stacked against more furniture disrupted the quiet—magnified by the darkness pressing in. Karina kept her gaze on Dakota, drawing strength from his determination.

The barrier was barely in place when muffled footsteps sliced through the silence like a serrated blade. Karina held her breath to catch every sound but mostly caught the words of her mother's prayers that drifted across the room. A muffled rumble of voices outside the door followed.

Karina glanced at Dakota, who kept his gaze fixed on the door.

The footsteps paced slowly as though whoever was out there was searching, hunting. Karina's damp palms tightened around the flashlight. She leaned into the door to decipher the murmurs. Her ear touched its surface.

The creak of a door opening down the hallway sounded outside. A shrill scream followed and was abruptly cut off. Karina's knees weakened. She leaned against her door's molding for support.

Dakota's whisper broke the silence. "Get down," he said, a calm thread in his voice.

A fist closed around Karina's heart. "We need to move," she said. "Leave the hotel. If we stay here, they'll find us." Karina recounted Ramirez's comments about Sofia in the storage room. "I don't want my sister and mother exposed to that."

"If we leave this room, we're vulnerable," Dakota said, his face flushing slightly. "As far as we know, the only people who know we're in this suite are Eli and Blackwell. That red rug flapping outside your balcony protects us from Blackwell's assault. And with Eli in the hotel, trust me, Diablos doesn't know what they're up against."

Did Dakota say what he said to calm her? Or was Eli Colt that good?

ON THE FIFTH FLOOR, Eli tapped the comm in his pant pocket. "Blackwell, did you kill the power to the hotel?"

No answer.

The darkness pressed, thick and oppressive. Eli's fingertips trailed along the wall, guiding him through the fifth-floor corridor. Every sense was on high alert, straining to detect any threat in the pitch-black hallway.

Pulsing crimson lights suddenly flashed from the ceiling to transform the dark corridor into a blood-drenched passage. Two silhouettes stood guard at the intersection of two hallways. Eli tensed as he timed their inattentive glances, slipping into a service passage. The musty smell of cleaning supplies filled his nostrils as his mind mapped out the quickest route to the stairway.

His pulse had steadied. An island of calm compared to his disarming the explosives in room 502. He'd instructed Lucia and Raul to get under a bed somewhere and wait. Hopefully help would arrive soon.

He approached the stairwell, carefully placing his steps to minimize noise. The cool metal of the door handle shocked his senses as he eased the door open.

He paused. Voices echoed above. Seconds later, three Diablo enforcers, each with assault rifles, eased down the stairs.

Eli pressed himself against a shadowed alcove, the rough texture of the wall digging into his back. He held his breath, the scent of sweat from the passing men signaling how close they were.

Time seemed to stretch as he waited for the stairs to clear. His muscles coiled, ready to spring into action at any moment. When the silence settled, Eli bounded up the stairs, emergency lights still pulsing.

INSIDE HER SUITE, Karina crouched beside Dakota, the plush carpet digging into her knees. Her focus shifted between Eli, the couch with her mother and Sofia, and the commotion outside where muffled explosions punctuated bursts of gunfire. "How many do you think are out there?" she whispered.

"Too many," Dakota replied, glancing back at Mamá and Sofia. He moved, positioning himself between the door and Karina's family. "You still have that gun?"

She retrieved the pistol from her bag. Dakota's weapon was already in his grip.

Footsteps in the hallway. Voices grew louder. The handle jiggled. Karina raised her weapon, trying to mirror Dakota's calm.

"Mamá," Sofia whimpered.

"Shh, *mi amor*," Mamá soothed, fear edging her voice.

A thud in the hallway.

Karina steadied herself, and aimed. Sweat made the gun slick in her palm.

Then a knock at the door. Karina's heart raced. She knew what Diablos did to women.

A commanding voice barked orders outside.

"Karina." Dakota's eyes met hers. So much left unsaid.

"Our Father, who art in heaven," her mother began.

Another knock. More forceful. Karina's finger tightened around the trigger.

AS ELI CLIMBED up to the ninth floor in the stairway, bedlam erupted like a Kansas tornado.

A muffled boom shook the building. *Ramirez. Diablos— attacking?*

Another boom. The floor shook. A battle raged and called Eli's name.

A clammy chill crept across Eli's skin as he reached Karina's floor. Sweat drenched his temples. He dropped to one knee, steadying himself against the trembling floor.

Another explosion.

Eli's mind raced for tactical scenarios, but vertigo gripped him as he eased the door open. Dread coiled in his gut. *Could Dakota defend the suite alone?*

Panicked voices echoed down the hallway, curses in Spanish mixing with the sound of men running.

Eli peeked through the doorway. Bullet holes peppered the walls, and wisps of smoke drifted, carrying the smell of cordite. Debris littered the floor—splintered wood, shattered plaster, spent shell casings covering the carpet.

A half-dozen fallen Diablos soldiers lay scattered in the hallway. A half dozen more hovered at Karina's door. And standing behind them—Carlos Ramirez—*La Serpiente.*

Eli shook his head. *What is happening here?*

Ramirez's reptilian gaze swept the hallway. Eli ducked back, the rush of blood in his veins roaring like rushing water.

Suddenly, the frightening sound of wood splintering boomed through the hallway. Eli's body curled like a compressed spring. Every nerve rose to heightened his awareness.

He burst into the hallway. The remains of Karina's door lay sprawled on the carpet. Ramirez pulled his weapon and followed four Diablo soldiers inside. Two remained outside, one tall with streaked hair, another with a shaved tattooed head. They flinched at Eli's arrival and fumbled with their pistols tucked in their jeans. A staccato of gunfire exploded from inside. Each shot had Eli shutter as if each round had slammed into his sternum.

Karina's scream pierced through the gunfire, a sound that chilled Eli to his core. He had to get in there. Now.

The hallway became a collision course as Eli and the two Diablos rushed each other. With his enemy firing wildly in the narrow space, Eli closed in, hands free and ready. He opened his assault with twin-thumb eye gouges that blinded the streaked-hair soldier, then struck the man's throat with the hard groove between his thumb and forefinger, collapsing the trachea. Two elbow strikes to the cervical spine dropped the man hard.

Eli trapped the bald Diablo against the opposite wall as he tried to reload. Eli rammed his palm up into the man's nose, hitting him once and then again. His pupils went from two millimeters to nine in less than a breath. He fell to the carpet face first, blood bubbling from his nostrils.

As the hallway fight ended, the battle inside raged on. Eli lunged for the doorway. A bullet whizzed past. He dove, rolled, and came up ready—

The world tilted. Warped. Eli's vision tunneled, the corridor stretching into darkness. His lungs screamed for air, each shallow breath inadequate. A metallic taste flooded his mouth, mingling with the scent of gunpowder. A high-pitched ringing filled his ears, drowning out the madness around him. His hands shook violently, the tremors traveling up his arms.

"Not now," he muttered, his voice sounding distant and unfamiliar. He pressed his back against the wall, focusing on the rough texture, using it as an anchor to reality. His fingers tightened around his pistol, the cool metal a lifeline to the here and now.

Doubled over in the stairway, Afghan memories threatened to overwhelm Eli. The faces of fallen comrades flashed, their voices resounding in his brain. Eli squeezed his eyes shut, fighting against a flood of traumatic images.

One step at a time. Clear the room. Protect the innocents. Complete the mission.

He fought to regain control. He focused on the weight of his body against the wall, the solidity of the floor beneath his feet. Slowly, his vision began to clear, the trembling in his hands subsiding to a manageable level.

He approached Karina's breached opening, each step a battle against body and mind. Inside, he could hear muffled voices and a man's agonized groans.

Dakota?

Eli's body thrummed. He took a steadying breath, pushing away the last vestiges of his episode. Beyond that threshold, death awaited. But whose? His? Dakota's?

Tightening his grip on his Glock, Eli braced himself. Whatever happened next, he was ready.

But before he could step over the splintered remains of the door and into the suite, the menacing figure of Carlos Ramirez staggered into the hallway, blood blossoming across his chest, staining his shirt and chinos. Surprise flickered across *La Serpiente's* face as he locked eyes with Eli. Then, as if in slow motion, he crumpled to the floor, his unseeing gaze fixed on Eli.

The imposing figure of Marcus Blackwell emerged from the suite, his assault gear covered in dust and debris. Smoke curled from the muzzle of his pistol as he holstered it with practiced ease. His eyes swept over the scene, lingering on Eli for a moment before he pulled out a cigar.

"Colt," Blackwell nodded, his voice gruff. "Glad you made it. Things got a bit dicey there for a minute."

"How did you—" Eli started, his voice hoarse.

"Your friends in 502," Blackwell cut him off. "The man with the mustache said you might need some help."

The elevator chimed. Blackwell lit his cigar. "We've got company."

Eli spun, weapon raised, his finger tightening on the trigger. But a group of Aldama citizens poured out, brandishing weapons taken from Los Diablos. Up front leading the rebellion was Maria Perez's father.

"The city rose up," Blackwell explained, noting Eli's bewildered expression. "Our drones gave them the opening they needed. Most of Diablos either surrendered or fled."

Eli lowered his weapon slowly, his mind struggling to process the sudden shift in the situation. He stepped into the suite, his senses gradually unclenching from their battle-ready state.

Lowering his weapon, his mind reeled from the abrupt shift. As the gunshots faded, quiet spread through the hallway like ripples on a still pond. He stepped into the suite ready for a threat that no longer existed. Slowly, painfully, his battle-honed senses began to stand down.

Blackwell's men moved with efficiency in securing the area. On the couch, Karina's mother cradled Sofia, whispering soothing words in Spanish. Their eyes, wide with fading fear and dawning hope, met Eli's.

In the corner, Karina knelt beside Dakota, her fingers gently combing through his curls. She met Eli's gaze and nodded, a silent thank you passing between them. Dakota's face was etched with pain, but his eyes held a glimmer of triumph as they locked onto Eli.

Eli's gaze moved from face to face—Karina, her family, Dakota, Blackwell. Each had played a crucial role in this victory. With the grace of God, they'd struck a decisive blow against an evil that had terrorized this city for too long. They'd done it. They'd destroyed Los Diablos.

It was more than relief that flooded Eli at that moment. It was hope. Hope for Karina's family, hope for Juarez, and maybe, just maybe, hope for himself. But the cost... Eli's thoughts drifted to the fallen Emilio. The price of victory had been steep.

As the adrenaline began to ebb, exhaustion settled deep in Eli's bones. He leaned against the wall, letting out a long, shaky breath. There would be time later for debriefings, for planning next steps. But for now, he allowed himself to simply breathe, to feel the full weight of what they had accomplished.

"You okay?" Dakota's voice, strained but steady, cut through Eli's thoughts.

Eli met his partner's gaze and managed a slight nod. "Yeah," he said softly. "We did it."

A ghost of a smile crossed Dakota's face. "We did."

SIXTY-TWO

Monday, 2:45 PM, El Paso, TX

Eli's hands trembled slightly on the wheel of the rented Suburban as they crossed the border into America. The throbbing in his head intensified, a relentless reminder of the ordeal they'd survived. He blinked hard, willing the pain away as the familiar landscape of Texas came into view. Beside him, Dakota's chest rose and fell in a deep sigh of relief.

Eli glanced in the rearview mirror. Karina sat sandwiched between her mother and sister, her eyes wide and glassy as if taking in the reality of their newfound freedom. The weight of Juarez seemed to lift with each mile marker they passed.

As they pulled up to the FBI compound, Eli's stomach clenched. He'd spent so long focused on the mission, on survival, that the idea of *after* felt foreign, almost dangerous to contemplate.

Blackwell stepped out of the vehicle ahead of them, his cigar already lit. The aroma drifted through the air as Eli eased himself out of the driver's seat, his muscles protesting every movement.

A stream of blue smoke curled from Blackwell's lips. "Good to be back in the good ole' USA, ain't it, gentlemen?"

Before Eli could respond, the compound door swung open. Lindsey stepped into the harsh Texas sunlight, and Eli's heart leapt. The urge to hold her, to breathe her in, overwhelmed him. She rushed forward, slipping her arm around his waist and burying her cheek against his chest. Eli closed his eyes, drinking in her warmth, her familiar scent of lavender and home.

"I've got some news," Blackwell said, his gruff voice softening. "Miss Castillo and her family have been granted a temporary visa to stay in this country." He took a long pull on his cigar, then winked at Karina's mother. "That is, until a more permanent status can be granted. Seems your son had quite the reputation with our immigration department."

Sofia's gasp cut through the air. "Are we Americans now?" Her eyes shone with a hope that made Eli's chest tighten.

Blackwell chuckled, the sound warming his weathered features. "Pretty close, young lady. Pretty close."

Lindsey lifted her head from Eli's chest, her brow furrowed with concern as she studied his face. "Where do y'all plan to live?" she asked Karina, her voice gentle.

Karina rose on tiptoe and pressed her lips against Dakota's cheek. The kiss was brief, but charged with promise. "Wherever Dakota takes us," she said, her voice syrupy think.

Dakota's skin flushed pink from his neck to his forehead. His usual smirk softened into something more vulnerable, more real.

"Well, well," Lindsey whispered, her breath warm against Eli's ear. "When did this happen?"

"If I had to guess," Eli said. "The second they met."

Karina's mother murmured something in rapid Spanish, her face etched with worry. Karina nodded, then turned to Blackwell. "Excuse me, Agent. We've heard the American government has arrested Cesar Garza."

Blackwell tapped his cigar, ash drifting to the sun-baked ground. "You've heard right. He's been indicted on multiple felony charges, including drug trafficking and exploitation of children. The US Attorney in El Paso is handling the case." His voice dropped, heavy with certainty. "Expects a slam dunk conviction."

Karina's shoulders sagged, weeks of tension visibly draining from her body. Her mother let out a choked sob, quickly muffled by her hand.

Eli shifted his weight, breaking the momentary silence. "Any sign of Marco Domingo or *La Serpeinte's* brother, Hector?"

Blackwell's expression darkened. "Not among the bodies taken to the morgue or those arrested by Mexican officials." He sighed, smoke curling around his words. "Sorry, gents. Looks like a few got away. But the good news is, Los Diablos is done and dusted. They won't be bothering the good people of Juarez or El Paso again."

Eli pulled Lindsey closer, feeling the last of the adrenaline seep from his body. The pain in his head sharpened, and he knew he couldn't ignore it much longer. "Well, friends," he said, his voice rough with fatigue, "I've got to get back to Louisiana. My fiancée tells me I've got an appointment with a neurologist in a few days." He paused, the reality of their survival truly hitting him for the first time. "And then a wedding to plan. Oh, and you're all invited."

"To your MRI?" Dakota quipped, but his eyes were soft with concern.

Laughter rippled through the group, the sound a balm to their battered spirits.

"When's your wedding, Lindsey?" Karina asked, curiosity brightening her tired eyes.

Eli answered, his voice low and certain. "The date we set is three months from today." He turned to Lindsey, drinking in the sight of her. The Texas sun caught the auburn highlights in her hair, and despite the dark circles under her eyes, she'd never looked more beautiful. Eli kissed her forehead, his lips lingering against her skin. "But I'm not sure I can wait that long."

As Lindsey's arms tightened around him, Eli felt something settle in his chest. There would be challenges ahead – his health, the lingering trauma of Juarez, the shadows of those who escaped. But in this moment, surrounded by the people who'd fought beside him and the woman he loved, Eli knew that together, they'd face whatever came next.

The Texas sun beat down, harsh and unforgiving, but to Eli, it felt like the warmth of a new beginning.

SIXTY-THREE

One Week Later—Rio Grande Valley Five Miles Outside Juarez

The vast desert stretched to the horizon. Its barren expanse was broken only by the charred skeleton of Garza's plant. The area resembled a war-torn battlefield—debris scattered across the grounds, twisted metal glinting in the morning sun, and a haze of lingering smoke hanging in the air.

Adrian Badeau squinted against the sun as he leaned on the battered Dodge pickup's fender, the ruggedness of its exterior mirroring his own hardened past. In his mid-forties, his features had sharpened, gray hair peppered his temples, but his calculating gaze remained unchanged. He almost relished this chaos, sensing opportunity in the carnage.

Badeau almost enjoyed this type of chaos. It's where he thrived. He sensed opportunity in the ruins of Garza's abandoned plant. Besides, he was no stranger to destruction and despair. He assessed the scene without emotion as he plotted his next business venture. His past lingered like a shadow, especially his entanglement with Eli Colt, who, as the Mexicans informed him, was responsible for the scene he now beheld.

His nephew Freddy sat in the cab hunched over, his thin frame barely filling the seat. He fiddled with his lighter before lighting the bong that rested in his lap. Freddy was in his early twenties but looked older. Was it the drugs or the life they both led? His role as an accomplice in Adrian's crimes had instilled in Freddy a raw brutality, once shooting Eli Colt in the head. With the pleasure of Roatan Island still fresh in Freddy's mind, could he return to his former self?

The low buzz of an engine approached. A white Range Rover crested a nearby hill, kicking up dust that trailed the vehicle. His new partners? Maybe. Depends on how they responded to what Badeau would offer. Now that Garza and *La Serpiente* were out of the picture, did they really have a choice? Not these two. They were thugs and nothing more. Like Freddy, they could never be leaders.

The dust settled and the doors opened. Hector and Domingo stepped out. Each moved with a swagger that spoke more menace than authority. Hector was about the same age as Freddy, his muscular build making him look almost primal in the harsh landscape, except for those tattoos. Why all the tattoos?

And Domingo was no better. His hard expression was a carefully crafted mask that did little to hide his insecurity. And didn't he recently get arrested and released because Garza posted a five-million-dollar bond? Talk about over-head. Why did Hector even bring him? Birds of a feather?

Badeau's mind churned with the possibilities at play. As he studied these two figures, Adrian knew that the downfall of the Diablos cartel would be the end of these two if not for him. He'd have to convince them that it was now a new game where Badeau intended on having the winning hand.

He pushed off the truck as Hector and Marco approached.

Hector's jaw clenched as he scanned the charred remains of the plant. "Those wretched gringos," he spat, his voice a venomous growl. "The raid took everything from us. Diablos is in shambles."

Domingo's eyes narrowed. "And the *Policías*—those vultures—have seized almost all our property. Sinaloa is sure to come in and overrun our operation."

"The gringos think they're invincible," Hector's voice was thick with barely restrained fury, "retreating back to Texas after killing my brother."

Badeau said nothing, letting Hector's words settle. This was personal for Hector, and personal vendettas clouded judgment, which should work to Badeau's advantage.

"It was a slaughter," Domingo said, his voice breaking for the briefest moment. "Did you see the hotel?"

Sensing the timing, Badeau stepped closer, his voice low and measured. "It sounds like we have a common enemy. But emotion only gets you so far. You need a plan—a viable plan. And I have one."

Hector gazed at Badeau with skepticism. "You're a gringo, an outsider, operating from a different territory."

Badeau held Hector's gaze, unflinching. "No, I'm a Cajun. French heritage. European like your Latin blood. Plus, I've made a business out of grooming and trafficking. I know the market, the players, the routes. What you need is someone who can navigate beyond that border." Badeau nodded over his shoulder toward the Rio Grande. "And not just El Paso. I've proven that time and again."

Silence ensued.

Hector's eyes focused on a distant point and his mouth opened slightly.

"What do you think, Hector," Domingo said. "He's been efficient getting us product from Honduras so far."

"But this isn't Honduras," Hector said. "It's the Mexican border. We've been living here all our lives."

"But across that border is the United States." Badeau jerked a thumb toward the Rio Grande. "That you, Mexicans, have proven time and again, you know little about."

Hector bit the inside of his cheek. "So, what do you propose?"

"I move the product from Honduras to here. I also rebuild your infrastructure, which..." he pointed to the plant for effect, "is in shambles. You handle storage and getting the product across the river. For that, you'll never have to worry about money for the rest of your lives."

As the alliance solidified, Badeau panned a wide grin. This was the beginning of his new empire, and he planned to be at its helm for decades, from Honduras to Juarez to New Orleans—nothing would stand in his way. Not the Federales. Not the NOPD. And definitely not that smug ex-Mississippi detective, Eli Colt.

PLEASE LEAVE A REVIEW

If you have enjoyed this book, it would be a tremendous help if your could leave a review.

Reviews help me gain visibility and bring my books to the attention of other readers who may enjoy them. You can leave a review on My Amazon Book Page.

GET EXCLUSIVE WILL MARLER MATERIAL

Building a relationship with my readers is the best thing about writing. Join my Legacy Readers Club for more information on new books and deals plus:

A free copy of Eli Colt's adventure in Helmand Province, Afghanistan—"The Silver Star."

You can get your content for free by signing up on my website at www.willmarler.com.

ABOUT THE AUTHOR

Will Marler is an emerging author of Christian crime thrillers. He grew up in New Orleans, Louisiana and now lives on the Gulf Coast of Mississippi with his wife, Wendie, and their 100-pound Rottweiler, Bear.

For more information:
www.willmarler.com
will@willmarler.com

www.ingramcontent.com/pod-product-compliance
Lightning Source LLC
Chambersburg PA
CBHW030346120726
47901CB00007B/1935